Cosmic Background Radiation

THOMAS WALKER

MIDWESTERN BOOKS

POLK CITY, IOWA

ISBN 979-8-9857175-1-8 (Paperback Edition)

Cover design by: eBook Cover Designs

Published by Midwestern Books
801 W Washington Ave, Polk City, IA 50226

Contact: Info@midwesternbooks.com

For the young people who taught me so much.

Cosmic Background Radiation

Chapter 1

Welcome to Wheaton

I slumped in the passenger seat of the U-Haul truck. The October browns of the South Dakota countryside crawled by under sullen clouds that wouldn't even rain. Here and there a cadaverous field of corn stood waiting for a combine crew. Harvest was mostly finished and winter would be here soon. We'd been down this road to visit Gramps and Grandma Izzy many times. Normally on this final stretch Dad would laugh and say, "God's country, boys. Look at it. This is the way God intended his children to live on the land." I looked over at Dad clinging morosely to the mammoth steering wheel. He wasn't laughing now. To have a country, God needed to exist.

On the trip from Portland we stopped at Fleet Farm. Dad went into the store an Oregon banker and came out a South

Dakota farmer. His balding head and large nose were still pale, betraying a lack of outdoor work. But the determined set of his thin lips said he'd get that remedied soon enough.

"It looks like Mom has made it to Gramps' drive," Dad said, breaking a fifteen-mile silence.

The plume of dust we'd been following drifted away as a white Ford Expedition turned to wallow down the farmhouse lane. It was Dad's car, but Mom drove it all the way from Portland so Dad could drive the U-Haul, pulling my Honda on a dolly. The Honda belonged to both my brother Nathan and me, but it was mine now.

Dad steered the moving truck into the barnyard, pulling up beside a dark green 1956 Chevy short-bed pickup known as the Beast, and parked in the graveled area between the barn and the machine shed. Dad switched off the truck and sat, staring out through the big windshield. He looked stunned. Then he glanced up in an obvious attempt to gauge the weather before he sighed and shoved his door open. As he crawled out of the truck he said, "I'm going to unhook the dolly and leave the Honda here while we unload."

Gramps had his arm around Mom as they walked slowly across the yard toward the truck. Gramps' bushy eyebrows, visible at even this distance, were drawn together in a pained expression. Mom brushed back her chin-length light brown hair to reveal her broad face, splotchy red from crying. I'm not sure what Mom means when she says she's a plain woman. I think she's beautiful, especially when she smiles with her eyes sparkling. It'd been a long time since I'd seen that and I was beginning to wonder if I ever would.

I climbed down and walked around the front of the truck. My dad had finished detaching the Honda and walked toward Gramps and Mom. He loomed nearly a foot taller than either of them. Mom slipped away from Gramps and stood, arms at her side, staring up into my dad's face. There was a long moment as they looked at each other, then Dad reached out and pulled Mom to him. They didn't kiss, but Mom melted into him as Dad bent himself protectively around her. Gramps watched for a moment and then headed my way. He looked a lot younger than 72 years old, with his stocky build and broad features like Mom's. A nearly bald head hid under his Wheaton Co-op baseball cap, which was stained with hard use to match his Carhartt jacket.

"Hey, Josh. Good to see you." He reached out to shake my hand and then he pulled me into a man-hug. I was startled to realize that I was taller than he.

***

For the next six hours the rain held off as we carried the remains of our life in Portland into the little yellow farmhouse.

"We're not going to kick you out of your bedroom, Dad," my mom said in her I-mean-business voice.

"Rachel," Gramps responded patiently, "let's think this through. That old room where you grew up is half the size of my room. You and Ben will never fit in there, so please be reasonable about this."

"But Gramps, you and Gram were in that room for over forty years. We just couldn't feel right about it."

"You two are moving here to take over the farm. It's only right that you should have the master bedroom. I'll be just fine in the other one, really."

Mom looked at Dad and plaintively said, "Ben, what do you think?"

"I think Gramps is right. Nothing about this situation is completely comfortable. But that's a practical solution and I think we'll get used to it." That determined set to his mouth was back.

In the end we moved all of Gramps' stuff into the small downstairs bedroom and the bedroom set from Portland into the big one. Mom and Dad's fighting had gotten bad by Christmas and sometime last January Dad had started sleeping in Nathan's room. In April, Dad moved out of the house altogether. I'm not sure where he went, but Mom said it was a cheap hotel. But in August, just before school started, Dad moved back home, back into Nathan's room. They said Gramps had called and offered them the farm in South Dakota.

After we got everything moved in, Dad and Gramps headed for Sioux Falls to drop off stuff at Goodwill and to take the moving truck back. Mom started unpacking downstairs and I went up to the second floor. I surveyed my new sleeping quarters, which was one big room under the eaves. It had plenty of space to put my things.

Mom came upstairs carrying a plate with a sandwich and chips. "How is this going to work out for you, Josh?" Mom leaned on the stair rail at the corner of my room.

"I like it. Gramps' old desk will work great for homework. Thanks for letting me have the bigger TV for my Xbox."

"Looks like we need to get a lamp for your desk. That corner is a little dark," Mom said, looking around.

"Mom . . ."

"Yes, Josh?"

"Are you guys going to be okay? You and Dad?"

A haunted look crept into Mom's eyes, but with a courageous nod she said, "I hope so, Josh. I certainly hope so."

***

I woke up the next morning to the loud growling of an ancient starting motor followed by the rumbling purr of the Beast coming to life in the yard. I got to the window in time to see Gramps idling it up the drive. Pulling on my clothes, I went downstairs to the kitchen. Mom and Dad sat at the table together, silently sharing a pot of coffee. Mid-morning sunshine filled the room as Mom tapped at her laptop and Dad poked at his iPad.

"Good morning, honey," Mom said looking up from her computer.

"Hey Josh," Dad chimed in. "How did you sleep?"

"Pretty good," I said. "It's so quiet out here in the country.

I don't know whether that helps me sleep or not. I woke up a couple of times listening for noise that wasn't there."

Dad chuckled. "Yeah, I did too, but then I had your mom's snoring to keep me going."

Mom huffed indignantly. "Ben! I don't snore!" Then she turned to me. "Can I get you some breakfast, Josh? I think all we have is cereal, but there are some fresh strawberries in the fridge."

"Sounds good," I said as I sat down at the table. "Where did Gramps go in the Beast?"

"Oh, he always drives that old thing to church." Mom emerged from the pantry carrying a box of bran flakes.

"I think he wanted us to go with him," Dad said.

"I know he did," Mom said with her head buried in the refrigerator. "But we're just not ready yet."

"I have a feeling it won't be that long until we are." That determined set to Dad's lips was back.

"Don't push, Ben." Mom lowered her voice, but I could hear the argument starting like a thousand before.

Mom handed me the cereal bowl without comment. I scanned my parents' faces as the tension stretched across the silent seconds. Dad just looked down for a long moment and then scratched his chin. "Yeah. No rush, Rachel." His voice was level, as if all the emotion had been squeezed out. I caught him glancing in my direction.

Mom leaned against the counter near the sink, thinking hard. Then, with a large dollop of calmness stirred in, she said, "It's just that some of my old friends go to that church.

I need time to adjust to being back here. It's like half my life vanished when we drove down that lane with the U-Haul." She was looking at me as she spoke.

Another silence stretched between us, then Mom sighed and picked up the coffee pot to pour Dad and herself another cup. After sitting down and cradling her mug through a couple of sips, she said, "Josh, there's an email from Sandy Nicholson, the school counselor at Wheaton. She says that your records have arrived and that she'll be available first thing tomorrow to get you oriented. She wants you to be there by 7:30 so she has time to show you around before school begins."

"Okay." I took a quick bite of cereal to hide the swelling panic.

"It shouldn't take that long. Wheaton High is not a very big place," Dad said.

A look of annoyance crossed mom's face. "Yeah, but you need to know your schedule and where your locker is. I think an orientation is a good thing."

"I suppose," Dad said and then bowing his head he added, "Sorry, dear."

As silence returned, I looked down at the few soggy flakes floating in the last of my milk. All the strawberries were gone. That's how I felt—fruitless mush. My whole life had been about Nathan. Then Nathan was gone, our friends went to college, and Portland was way the heck down the Interstate. My eyes started to burn, but I fought the tears. Mom and Dad needed all the help they could get, even if tomorrow I'd be a stranger in a sea of kids who'd known each other since kindergarten.

***

After breakfast Dad pulled on his coat and handed Mom hers. "We should look this place over and take stock of what we need to do."

"Yeah, that's a good idea. But Ben, I should warn you, farming is more like hedged betting than keeping a banker's ledger. And it's going to be a lot of work. Physical work."

Dad chuckled. "Are you trying to scare me out of this, honey? It might be a little late for that."

"Yeah, I suppose it is." Mom reached up and patted Dad's cheek. "I know you can do about anything you put your mind to."

Dad took her hand and held it in both of his. "Rachel, we're going to make this work. I'm completely confident. Let's go take a look at what we're up against."

I watched them through the porch window as they crossed the yard and went through the fence out into the back pasture. On a whim I snatched my coat from the hook on the back porch and headed for the barn. I loved the smell of that place. The odd sweetness of hay permeated every inch, even into the dusty beams and the weather-worn siding. But it made me think of Nathan. We had played out here for hours on our annual visits. Hay forts, feeding the livestock, and long hours in imaginary worlds made those visits some of the best times of my life.

I grabbed the rungs of the worn ladder and bounded up into the loft. It was full of hay for the winter, but there was a narrow path that lead to the big loft door on the gable end. It creaked open at my push and I plopped down with my feet hanging out in the open air. It was twenty feet down to the hard packed earth in front of the barn. Not really far enough but it still called to me. Not like the 130 feet of the water tower in Portland. From up there, the ground was fatal, for sure.

I leaned my head against the door casing and closed my eyes. I remembered the giddy height from the top of the tower near our house last July. Nathan was dead. Dad was gone. Mom was barely functioning, dragging herself to work when she could and spending the day in bed when she couldn't. The ground 130 feet below had called out. Life had screwed me. All I had to do was let go and I'd screw it for good.

I had decided to ride it out. Now Dad was back and Mom got dressed every morning. The whole flurry of yard sales, sorting, and packing had been a mind-numbing relief in a strange way. I opened my eyes, realizing that now we were here in South Dakota . . . a long way from bad memories.

Chapter 2

Wheaton High

Monday morning I felt nauseous during the fifteen minute trip from the farm to school. As I drove through town, I tried to think positive thoughts, but they blew away like brown leaves from the oaks beside the road. A water tower stood sentinel as I approached the main part of town. It wasn't as tall as the one in Portland, but tall enough. The whole Wheaton business district would fit on the block where I'd lived in Portland. The fact that I wouldn't be getting lost brought little comfort. I turned left at the single red blinking traffic signal and was out in the country again almost immediately. I could see the school ahead, a quarter mile out of town.

I circled the school once, trying to figure out which was the main entrance. The building had a series of additions. Some looked like they dated from when Gramps was in school and other parts must have been built during my mom's time. A construction trailer, scaffolding, and power lift suggested that they weren't done tacking on new wings. The result was a bewildering set of entrances. I decided that the glass double door closest to the flagpole was a good bet. I was right and soon found myself in the school office area where I was directed into an inner office with a sign on the door that said "School Counselor – Sandy Nicholson."

"You must be Josh," Mrs. Nicholson said, holding out her hand as she came around her desk. "Today's a good day to start school at Wheaton High. It's the beginning of a new quarter, football is done, and basketball hasn't started yet."

She looked young, but she took charge, going over my schedule and showing me the textbook for each class from a stack she had waiting on the corner of her desk. Math, history, Spanish, and English were in the morning. I had P.E. after lunch, and then a study hall. My last class of the day was physics.

"My husband, Fred Nicholson, is the science teacher," Mrs. Nicholson said standing and picking up the books. "I think you'll enjoy getting to know him."

I stood up too. "I love science. It's my favorite subject." I hoped that Mr. Nicholson was as nice as his wife.

"Let me show you to your locker." Mrs. Nicholson led the way through a quirky labyrinth of hallways, caused by building additions. I relaxed when I realized they would only make navigation interesting, not challenging.

"Josh, I'm sorry. All the lockers for upperclassmen are already assigned. We lost several to the new construction.

You'll have a locker with the freshmen and sophomores," Mrs. Nicholson said.

I shrugged my acceptance. "Okay. I'll make that work."

I felt a flutter of confusion, unsure of what this development meant. In Portland everyone in the same grade was always together in classes, in the halls, and at lunch. In fact, it was a real pain to get to see my friends at school, who were Nathan's age. I looked around to see that the students starting to fill the halls were various ages.

Mrs. Nicholson handed me a slip of paper. "This is the combination to locker number 114." She pointed to one of the lockers we were facing. "See if you can get it open."

I worked the dial, getting the combination right on the first try. That seemed promising. As she handed me my books I said, "Thanks for getting me set up, Mrs. Nicholson."

"You're welcome, Josh," she said with a pleased smile. "Be sure to stop by my office if you have any questions. Oh hi, Eddie." A short wiry boy had come up beside us.

"Hey Mrs. Nicholson." Eddie smiled brightly as he began to work the combination on the locker next to mine.

"Josh, let me introduce Eddie Martinez. Eddie's mom is the School Office Administrator. This school couldn't function without her. Eddie, this is Josh Cooper. His family just moved here from Portland, Oregon to take over his grandfather's farm."

"Yeah, I heard about folks moving to the Neilson farm. Welcome to Wheaton."

"Word sure gets around fast."

"That's life in a small town," Eddie laughed.

I liked him immediately, crew cut, wispy mustache, and all. His dark eyes sparkled with friendly mischief.

"Say, Eddie," Mrs. Nicholson said. "Would you make sure Josh knows his way around, especially to Mrs. Arlington's classroom? He has math first period. I've got to get back to my office."

"Sure thing," Eddie laughed as he slammed his locker door shut. "Come on, Josh. Right this way."

I sorted through the stack of books Mrs. Nicholson had handed me, selecting the math book and pulling a notebook and pencil from my backpack.

"You're going to love it here." Eddie spoke enthusiastically. "This might just be the best class B school in the state. In fact, Wheaton is probably as good as most of the A and double A schools. And who would want to go to those monster schools in Sioux Falls? You'd never get to know folks." He hopped and slapped the top of the doorway as he led me through it. I could have touched it without jumping.

"Hi, Jerry! Hey, Bill," he said to a pair of students, one kneeling to tie his shoe, the other waiting.

"Hi Eddie," the waiting student said. "What are you up to?"

"Just showing Mr. Josh Cooper the ropes. You can ignore these peons, Josh. They're just lowly freshman," Eddie laughed.

"Like you aren't a freshman too, Martinez." Jerry called after us as we passed on down the hall.

Eddie laughed even harder. "We don't make much of the differences in grade levels here at Wheaton. We're together for things like sports and music, so we're all friends."

"Hey, Zoe! Andrea!" Eddie called to a couple of girls talking in a corner of the hall. "Looking good." He shook his hand like he'd touched something hot.

The girls giggled and then managed to get out "Hi Eddie" as we turned the corner to head up a set of stairs. At the top of the stairs we came to a hall with a long glass case on one side.

"And here is where we keep all our bragging rights." Eddie waved toward the shelves of trophies. "This is our most recent acquisition." He stopped and pointed to a golden football teed up on a circular walnut block.

I bent to read the brass plate on the stand. "You guys won the state class B football championship this year?"

"Yup," Eddie answered with obvious pride. "I was the best safety this state has ever seen. Too bad I had to do all my play from the bench." He doubled over laughing and I couldn't help joining him. "I thought they were going to have to send me in as quarterback since Marshal was having trouble getting his helmet back on that swelled head of his."

At the end of the hall we rounded another corner into an older, but well-maintained section of the building. A long hall was lined with lockers and a regular sequence of doors opening on both sides.

"This is where most of your classes will be." He waved grandly down the hall. "P.E. is back in the gym by the trophy cases we passed and science is up that ramp to the right." He pointed further down the hall. "Here's Mrs. Arlington's room where you have math this period. I'll probably see you at our lockers during the day if you have other questions."

"Thanks, Eddie. I think I'm good."

The first bell rang as Eddie, with a friendly wave, left me standing at the door to a room full of strangers. I pushed my way through a surge of anxiety and walked into my first class at Wheaton High School.

Chapter 3

Cosmic Background Radiation

"Class, I'd like you to meet Josh Cooper. His family just moved here from Portland, Oregon," Fred Nicholson said to the whole physics class. He pointed to an open place in the semi-circle of desks.

I smiled as I sat down and gave a wave of acknowledgment. I'd gone through this ritual every hour all day long as my teachers introduced me to each class. I was starting to get embarrassed.

Mr. Nicholson wasn't done. "Now I'd like to go around the class and have everyone introduce yourselves to Josh." This would have been impractical in other classes, but was easy with only seven students. Physics was the school's only advanced science course and it was optional except for college-bound juniors and seniors.

"I'll begin, Josh," Mr. Nicholson said as he perched on the

edge of his desk. His smile brought out the dimples on his fair face. He ran a hand through his full head of tousled dark hair. "My name is Fred Nicholson. I'm the science teacher here at Wheaton and the boy's JV basketball coach. I think you've already met my wife, Sandy. She and I have two little boys who go to school here too. Let's go to you next, Jean."

The eyes in the room turned to a tall girl with short blond hair smoothing her denim jumper. Looking directly at me, she smiled broadly, saying, "Hi, Josh. My name is Jean Wilkerson. I know your grandfather because he goes to our church. I'm glad you and your folks are moving here to help him with the farm."

Then came an athletic young man slumped indolently in his seat. He tossed his curly blond hair and smirked. "Well, a city boy, huh? My name's Marshal James, captain of the State Champion Wheaton Rockets football team. I'll be happy to help you get to know folks in our little town. Me and my friend Allen Osgaard here are experts at sorting out who's naughty and who's nice."

"I'm Allen," said a skinny boy with wild brown hair and wire-rimmed glasses seated next to Marshal.

A pretty girl with long brunette hair sitting on Marshal's other side came next. She dressed the way popular girls did back in Portland and her make-up was perfect. Politely she could be called petite, but putting it bluntly she was scrawny. "My name is Melanie Crawford. Welcome to Wheaton, Josh."

Sitting next to Melanie was an intense-looking girl with dark, shoulder-length hair. Her make-up was dark, almost goth, and her pug nose sported large eyeglasses. She straightened in her seat. "Hi," she said. "My name is Shelly Waters. I hope you're a good student. We're serious about science in this class."

There was a general nervous titter in response to Shelly. I liked something about her. Maybe it was how serious she seemed to be about science.

A girl with an oval face, aquiline nose, and a ponytail of long, jet black hair sat alone with empty seats on either side. She turned to regard me with startling intensity.

"My name is Sarah Dirk," she said.

We settled back into our seats as Mr. Nicholson resumed control of the class. He wrote the words "Cosmic Background Radiation" in bold black letters on the white board.

"Can anyone tell me what Cosmic Background Radiation is and why it's important?"

Our class met Mr. Nicholson's question with an extended silence. But that didn't seem to bother him. He stood quietly, like a farmer waiting for his inquiry to sprout into answers.

After a bit, Shelly Waters put her hand up.

"Yes, Shelly?"

"Well, isn't that the electromagnetic radiation that fills all space due to the Big Bang?"

"Yes, Google is correct on that one, Shelly."

I glanced over to see that Shelly Waters had her smart phone tipped so that she could see the answer to her search.

"Cosmic Background Radiation is the sound the universe made when it came into being. Can anyone tell me why that is important? Why was the discovery of Cosmic Background Radiation in 1964 by Arno Penzias and Robert Wilson important enough to win a Nobel Prize in physics?"

His question met with silence. But as I looked around I could see thoughtful looks on the other students' faces. Why was the sound of the universe coming into being so important?

"Let's suppose that you are blind and you go to a Wheaton High basketball game," Mr. Nicholson prompted us. "You are sitting with all the Rockets fans. Are you with me so far?"

There were some chuckles and most of us nodded our heads.

"Then you hear the ball bouncing down the court, and the crowd around you erupts in cheers. What do you know?"

"You know that I just made a basket," Marshal crowed.

After the laughter died down, Mr. Nicholson continued. "Well, we wouldn't know that you, in particular, made the basket, but we'd know that somebody made a basket. Why is that?"

Melanie spoke as she put up her hand, "You'd know because the sounds you heard told you so."

"That's right, Melanie. Even though we couldn't see anyone make the basket, we would infer from the sounds that somebody did make it. It's the same thing with Cosmic Background Radiation. Since 1927 when Georges Lemaître, a Roman Catholic priest and scientist, first formulated Hubble's Law about an expanding universe, scientists were split between two theories of the universe's origin. The first theory, called the Steady State Universe, was that the cosmos always existed. The second theory, supported by Hubble's Law, was called the Big Bang. The Big Bang Theory says the beginning of the universe, exploding from a single point, created all energy, matter, gravity, time, and space. Both ideas were just theories, however, the discovery of Cosmic Background Radiation is considered key evidence that the Big Bang Theory is the most likely explanation for the origin of the universe."

Mr. Nicholson looked around at us. Then he said, "So what questions should we ask to explore Big Bang cosmology?"

I tried to think about where Mr. Nicholson was going with this question, but even though I came up blank, I was feeling more intrigued than ever.

Shelly said, "If the universe had a beginning, then it must have an age. So, a good question would be how old is the universe?"

"Yes, that's exactly the kind of question the Big Bang permits, which the Steady State Theory did not. Since I'm pretty sure you already have the answer looked up on your phone, Shelly, how old does Google say the universe is?"

Shelly ducked her head and poked at her phone. "It says that the universe is about 13.8 billion years old."

"That's what science considers the universe's age."

"No way!" An angry voice called out.

"I was wondering when you might express an opinion about this, Jean. What would you like to say?" Mr. Nicholson said calmly.

"The universe is only 6,000 years old," Jean Wilkerson roared. "That's what the Bible teaches. You're a Christian, Mr. Nicholson. How can you teach against the Bible?"

Mr. Nicholson smiled patiently at Jean. "I can't debate Biblical theology here, Jean. You know that. But what I can say is that the Big Bang Theory is an improvement, from a believer's perspective, over the discredited Steady State Theory of the universe."

"But the Big Bang Theory proves that God doesn't exist," Shelly Waters said loudly.

"No scientific theory ever says anything about God. By its nature, science must ignore theological questions. Science would never get anywhere if the answer to every question was that God did it. But people who use science to draw theological conclusions have no more authority than people who try to use theological doctrine to dictate what scientific hypotheses mean."

Shelly growled, "You mean like when the Church burned Galileo at the stake for discovering that the earth was not the center of the universe?"

"Shelly," Mr. Nicholson said quietly, gazing steadily at her.

"It's stupid when the fundies start in about what the Bible says like it trumps scientific findings."

Jean Wilkerson was turning a deep shade of red. She looked ready to explode.

"Let it go, Jean!" Mr. Nicholson said. They had a staring match and then Jean seemed to wilt. She clamped her mouth shut and stared straight ahead.

Mr. Nicholson watched her for a little bit and then said, "Shelly, it is vital in this class to be respectful of everyone's perspective. Do you understand?"

"Yes, Mr. Nicholson," Shelly said in slightly more humble tones.

"Also, Shelly, if you are going to cite examples of how religion abuses science, Galileo's story is not a good choice."

Shelly stiffened.

"Galileo didn't discover that the sun was the center of the universe," Mr. Nicholson explained. "The ancient Greeks knew it, and by Galileo's time, Copernicus had proved it mathematically. Galileo merely added to the evidence because of the improvements he made to the telescope. Furthermore, Galileo died peacefully at home in his bed — he was not burned at the stake. He was under house arrest by the church when he died, but that was because of his arrogant handling of church politics. Many of the best minds in the church fully accepted his findings and were searching for ways to adjust church doctrine to the new perspectives. It was Galileo's impatience that got him in trouble."

"Whatever," Shelly mumbled, poking furiously at the screen of her phone. I guessed that she wanted Google to disprove Mr. Nicholson. He sure seemed to know what he was talking about.

Mr. Nicholson turned back to Jean, who sat glumly in her chair with her arms crossed. "Jean?"

She turned her head to look at him.

Mr. Nicholson continued, "Please understand, your

perspectives are always welcome. However, our task in this class is to look at the scientific evidence. In physics, we set aside Biblical theology. At another time and place, we can talk about how scientific findings can never harm true faith."

As Jean maintained eye contact, her complexion paled. She nodded curtly in acceptance of what he said, but the look on her face said she wasn't going to drop this.

Mr. Nicholson walked back to the table at the front of the classroom, paged through his textbook, and then said, "Everyone, turn to page 138 in your physics book."

As he began to write an equation on the board, I wondered who was right, Shelly or Jean. How could we leave this unresolved? I had trouble focusing throughout the rest of physics class and was startled when the day's final bell sounded.

As I was gathering my stuff, I felt someone touch my shoulder. When I turned, it was Sarah Dirk.

"Hi Josh." She paused to look around as the room quickly emptied. "I just wanted to tell you that we're neighbors. You know the old house across the meadow with the antique barn?"

"Oh yeah. I saw that," I said. "So that's where you live?"

"Yeah, that's me." Her almond eyes turned downward for a moment and then looked directly into mine. "You shouldn't believe everything you hear around here." She turned on her heel and quickly walked away.

I watched her until she disappeared out the classroom door. Her graceful movement was uncanny, and the sense of mystery about her deepened with each step.

Chapter 4

After School

I stood in front of my open locker thinking through my first day at Wheaton High. It was better than I had expected. I realized that sixth-hour study hall was going to work out pretty well. I'd gotten all my homework done except physics, which I could get done that night.

As I zipped up my back pack to head for home, Eddie appeared. "Hey Josh," he said. "How tall are you?"

I held back a laugh. Eddie couldn't have been more than five foot six "I think I'm right at six feet. Why do you ask?"

"Sean and I were wondering if you'd be interested in going out for basketball. It starts in a couple of weeks."

I noticed the skinny guy standing at the locker next to Eddie's. He was about my dad's height, six foot two with an unruly shock of flaming red hair and freckles covering his face.

The tall boy laughed as he said, "Hi, Josh. I'm Sean Johnson. My vertically-challenged buddy here has such a thing about tall people that he sometimes forgets his manners." He slapped Eddie on the back.

"What do you mean? I was polite!" Eddie chuckled.

"Yeah, but you could have let the guy finish one day of school before you started recruiting him for the team."

"Hey! The bell has rung. The day is done. I waited. Now Josh, do you want to play the best sport ever invented or not?"

"I don't have much experience. I played some pickup ball back in Portland, but I was never on a team." I'd spent a lot of time helping Nathan practice and he had been good. He had been a varsity starter as a junior. But I didn't feel like bringing that up.

"Just your height would help us out," Eddie said. "We could really use you on the team." He was so serious that it caught me off guard. Mom had mentioned that going out for a sport at a small school like Wheaton was different from trying to make the cut for a big school team.

"I'll consider it. It might be kind of fun."

"Hey! That's the spirit!" Eddie said enthusiastically. "I promise you won't regret it. Even if this giant red-headed goon here ends up blocking all your shots like he does mine." Eddie punched Sean in the shoulder.

"It would be great to get a new upperclassman on the team." Sean dropped his voice and checked over his shoulder. "We're kind of sick of Marshal trying to run everything."

"Like I said, I'll think about it," I said with a smile.

***

"Josh, time for dinner." Mom's call floated up the stairs just as I stuffed my physics book into my backpack. Homework was done and an evening of leisure had begun. I got to enjoy three bites of pork chop before the grilling began.

Mom started the interrogation. "Tell us about your day, Josh."

"It was a day," I said stuffing a large bite into my mouth.

Gramps' laugh turned into a snort as he tried to tamp it down.

Mom rolled her eyes the way she did just before her speech about laconic answers.

Dad's head swiveled like a battleship turret taking aim. "We're going to need more from you than that, Son. Your mother and I have been on pins and needles about your day."

I held up my hand in surrender, stalling until I could finish chewing. "Really, it was pretty good," I said. "I liked Mr. and Mrs. Nicholson. They sure are young. All the teachers in Portland were practically grandparents. No offense Gramps."

"None taken, Josh," Gramps chuckled. "Rural school districts tend to hire younger staff."

"Did you meet any friends?" Mom asked.

"Yeah, one at least. His name is Eddie. He has the locker next to me. He wants me to go out for basketball."

"Really?" Dad shifted in his seat. "What did you tell him?"

"I told him I'd think about it."

"You should do that, Josh. I think you'd like playing on a team. It'd be a good way to get to know other students." Dad reached for the butter.

"Yeah, I'll probably do it." I'd already decided I would.

"How were your classes?" Mom's curiosity was still cresting.

"Pretty routine. I'm a little ahead in math, but I'll have to work to catch up in history. Everything else is about the same, except physics." I shouldn't have let that slip.

Eating sounds stopped and three sets of eyes swiveled in my direction.

"What about physics?" Mom maintained a casual tone.

"Well, nothing bad," I said quickly. "There was an argument in class today."

"Oh?"

"Mr. Nicholson was talking about Cosmic Background Radiation. Do you know what that is?"

"Yeah. It's a barely detectable electromagnetic field that is spread throughout the known universe. It's thought to be evidence in support of the Big Bang Theory," Gramps said.

We all turned to look at Gramps in surprise.

"What?" he said, "I read. So what happened in physics class?"

"One girl thought that the Big Bang Theory proved that God didn't exist and another girl was all upset that Mr. Nicholson was teaching against the Bible."

"Was he teaching against the Bible, Son?" Dad's voice had an edge to it.

"Now Ben, don't start that." Mom's voice moved up a pitch or two.

"Rachel, first school prayer and then anti-Christian

curriculum in our schools . . . I thought we were getting away from some of that when we moved here."

"We're talking about Josh's day, not social norms."

The tension stretched out a few tortured seconds.

Dad slumped back into his seat and ran a hand across his face. "Yeah, you're right, Rachel. Josh, tell us more about what happened."

It took me a minute to recover from the near miss. After a short pause I said, "Mr. Nicholson said there are two theories of how the universe came into being. I can't remember exactly what he called them."

"The Steady State Universe and the Big Bang Theory," Gramps said.

"Yeah, that's it. He said that Cosmic Background Radiation supported the Big Bang Theory. Then one girl said that meant the universe was really old, like billions of years, but another girl, I think she's from your church, Gramps, said that the Bible taught that the Earth was only 6,000 years old."

"I'm sorry that was uncomfortable for you, dear," Mom said.

"It was interesting. Mr. Nicholson was totally cool. He wanted us to understand how science worked."

"Did you feel like he was teaching atheism?" Dad asked.

That drew a sharp look from Mom, but she didn't say anything.

"He was just as critical of the girl who said she was an atheist as he was with the girl from Gramps' church. It kinda sounded like the Big Bang Theory had something to help believers, but he didn't say what."

"Really?" Mom sat back in her chair looking at me and then Dad.

"Sounds as if you like Mr. Nicholson," Dad said.

"He knows a lot about science."

"Fred Nicholson is a fine young man and a faithful member of my church. He is also one of the youth leaders," Gramps asserted.

"Is that so?" Dad asked with sudden interest. "Harlan, you know your Bible and it seems like you are up on the Big Bang Theory. Can you believe in the Bible and the Big Bang?"

"I do," Gramps said. "The Big Bang Theory establishes that the universe had a beginning. That's exactly what the Bible teaches. Amazingly, scientists have mapped every step of what happened in the Big Bang back to the very split second before it happened, but that's all the further they dare to go. If you want to know what happened just before the bang itself, I think you have to turn to the Bible. It teaches us that the universe was created when God said, 'Let there be light.' I've often wondered if Cosmic Background Radiation is God's word of creation still echoing around the universe today."

Chapter 5

An Accident

A couple of weeks after that first day at Wheaton High, I was starting to remember people's names. They all knew my name the second day I came, so it was a little embarrassing. Eddie and Sean were cool about helping me figure out who was who without making me feel like an idiot.

The Monday of my third week at Wheaton, basketball practice started. The boys and girls teams had to share the school's one gym, one team practicing before school and the other, after. Since the before-school practice had to start so early they alternated weeks for which team had early practice. The boys had early practice the first week of the season.

My eyes burned with fatigue from the early morning rise after a restless night. I gritted my teeth to fight back a yawn as I stared out into the darkness lit by my Honda's low beams piercing the flurries of snow. 6:30 a.m. What kind of time was that for my first basketball practice? I guess I was anxious about how I would do, but tiredness on top of nervous nausea was a terrible feeling.

My mood darkened further when my scratchy blinks didn't help much to see through the terrible weather. In Portland it would still be warm for weeks. I guess the weatherman had tried to warn us about this. Just as he forecast, it had rained all day Sunday then turned to snow overnight. The resulting slush became ice by morning.

I felt the car slide sideways. I backed off the accelerator and straightened out quickly. I loved that Honda. But the stupid car always reminded me of Nathan because we had shared it. My eyes burned with more than fatigue and I wondered if I would ever stop crying about his death.

A curve came up faster than I anticipated. Instinctively I downshifted, but instantly realized my mistake. The Honda lost traction on the icy surface, skidding to the left. I corrected, trying to stay on the road. In my panic I touched the brakes and the slide accelerated out of control.

"God, help me!" I called out as I headed inevitably off the road. It was a surreal moment. I felt like I was watching the crash in the third person. It wasn't that spectacular—the car just bumped up over the edge of the road and flopped down into the ditch. But the left front bumper dug in, and momentum carried the vehicle over onto its top. I felt a sharp strain against my seat belt, and as the airbag exploded in my face everything went dark.

***

Slowly, I fought my way back to consciousness. I didn't open my eyes because my face felt numb. I noticed a flickering light through my closed eyelids. It seemed warm and pleasant. I panicked. Was the car on fire?

My eyes popped open and I tried to focus on a red glow just a few feet away. That sure looked like some kind of fire. I struggled to get my seatbelt undone, but there was no seat belt. There wasn't a car either. My confusion grew when I noticed that I was on a low stone shelf, coming right out of the wall. I was lying on a coarse linen bag, filled with what smelled like straw and there was a thick woolen blanket draped over me that itched almost as much as the mattress.

Curiosity rose to the top of my stew of emotions and I pushed the blanket aside to sit on the edge of the bed. I was in an earthy-smelling chamber of crude stone. Focusing, I identified a low iron stand in the middle of the room as the source of the red glow. I think it was something called a brazier. The tiny flames dancing at the edge of the charcoal in the brazier provided a dim light.

Beyond the brazier, in the far wall, was a low archway, getting steadily more distinct. A light was growing brighter just beyond the doorway. A figure dressed in a long tunic and carrying a candle came into the room and said in a familiar voice, "Joshua, Joshua! I heard you calling out. Are you alright?"

An electric jolt ran through me as I recognized the figure holding the candle—Nathan. The sick feeling in my stomach intensified. I was about to faint. I tried to hold onto the sight of my brother alive and well, but my vision narrowed quickly as the walls seemed to close in. "Nathan!" I croaked as consciousness fled.

***

I still had that awful feeling in my stomach the next time I opened my eyes. I was back inside the Honda, hanging upside down by the seatbelt. I fumbled at the release and fell to the roof of the car. My head hurt. The airbag must have hit me hard. I stayed there on hands and knees for a few minutes trying to clear my mind. I started to panic as I tried to figure out what to do next. I felt in my pocket to make sure my phone was there. It was. I tried the driver's side door. It opened, tumbling me out into the cold, wet snow.

The Honda was upside down in the ditch with the wheels in the air. There was no way to drive out. The impact point where the car dug in had smashed the whole front fender. As I got back up on the road, I was relieved to feel the solid surface beneath my feet. I dug out my phone, trying to decide whether to call Mom or Dad, knowing the shock would be difficult. Mom was the emotional powerhouse in our family, but Dad was always calm in emergencies. I touched the link for his phone number. I needed calm at that moment.

"Dad," I said when the connection clicked through. "I've been in a car accident."

"Are you okay, Josh?" Dad's voice filled with calm concern.

"Yeah, I think so. Nothing hurts too much. I crunched the car up pretty badly, and it's upside down."

"Don't worry about the car, Josh. It's not important." I heard the back porch door bang shut through the phone. Then, I could tell from the sound of his dad's voice that he was outside. "Where are you, Son?"

"I'm down on the big curve by Benton Slough," I said. My voice was a little shaky. I heard my Dad's Expedition roar to life through the phone, muffling his response.

". . . that is. I'll be there in about five minutes. Will you be okay until I get there?"

"Sure, Dad. I'm fine. I'm not going anywhere." The weight of it all settled in and I felt exhausted. I looked for a place to sit down, but the early winter slop covered everything, so I decided to stand even though I was starting to feel dizzy. I rubbed my face, trying to get my head clear, and then regretted it as a throbbing pain flared up.

"Are you still there, Joshua?" my dad's voice came through the phone.

"Yeah, Dad," I said. It caught me off guard because I'd forgotten my dad was still on the phone.

"Hang on, Son. I'll be there very soon."

I heard the Expedition before I saw it approaching. Even in the urgency of his concern, Dad drove carefully through the icy weather. I heard the phone connection click off as the big white Expedition pulled up on the side of the road.

Dad emerged from the vehicle and strode quickly toward

me. Even in the dim light I could see the pinched look on his face, but it was concern, not anger. I relaxed a little.

"Let me look at you," Dad said, using his phone light to enhance the wintry dawn.

"I'm okay, Dad."

"There's a bruise on your right cheek and jaw. You must have turned your head when the airbag went off. Did you stay conscious the whole time?" Dad asked. His voice was anxious.

I remembered Nathan's face lit by a flickering candle. "No, Dad. I think I blacked out for a minute. But I feel fine now."

"Let's go sit in the car, Josh. You look unsteady on your feet. I want to keep you warm."

I crawled into the passenger seat of the big white SUV. Dad was poking at the screen of his phone as I shut the door. He said, "I'm going to call the Cenex gas station in town. I think they have a tow truck. They should be able to get the Honda out of there."

I reclined my seat and stretched my legs toward the welcome blast of warm air from beneath the dashboard.

Dad spoke crisply on the phone, explaining the accident and telling them where we were. "We'll wait here until you come. Okay. Bye."

Dad slipped the phone back into his pocket and we sat in silence for a while.

"Dad," I said.

"Yes, Josh?"

"I'm sorry about wrecking the car."

"Don't worry about that," Dad said, smiling a little. The

smile faded as he continued, "I can see how bad the road conditions are. I guess we haven't adapted to South Dakota driving yet." He paused a moment. "You're the same age Nathan was when he died. It's all I could think about. I'm so relieved you're okay. "

I turned my face to the window and shut my eyes. "Did you tell Mom?"

"No. I left too fast. Mom and Gramps were out feeding the cows. I just wanted to get here to see if you were okay."

There was another silence. I turned to stare out the windshield down the road. "Looks like I'm going to miss my first basketball practice."

"If I know your mother, you'll probably miss a whole day of school," Dad said, gazing evenly at me. "She'll insist on taking you into Sioux Falls to be checked out in the ER."

I said, "I'm fine. I don't want to miss school today." But the look on Dad's face convinced me that further discussion would be fruitless.

During the next tense silence, I tried to think of something safe to say. "Did you ever think you'd be a South Dakota farmer, Dad?"

"No, Son," Dad said, shaking his head. "I never imagined that would happen."

Before I could think, I asked, "What happened to you and Mom? Why did you move out? I was afraid you guys were going to get a divorce."

"That's hard to explain, Josh," Dad said, a quiet tension coming into his voice that scared me a little. "Your Mom and I agreed to be honest with you. After Nathan's death, we were both so sad that we lost each other in our grief and the fighting started. I just wanted the hurting to stop, so I left." Dad leaned his head on the steering wheel, then after a time he went on. "I suppose you're right. Your mom and I went a long way down the path toward divorce. That's how everyone solves their marriage problems."

"But are you guys going to get a divorce?" I held my breath for the answer.

"I don't think so," Dad said. "We're trying hard to make our marriage work. That's why we're in South Dakota."

"Don't you miss Portland and the bank?"

"Well, not yet. But it's only been a couple of months. In the flurry of selling the house, packing up, and moving out here, I haven't had much time to think about it." Dad looked thoughtful, staring out into the slowly brightening day.

I could tell that he had more to say. After a short silence he continued. "In the middle of all that sadness, camped out in that hotel room, all I could see was an endless series of days alone in my office. Then Gramps called to ask your mom and me if we wanted to take over the farm. It was like a bolt out of the blue, Josh. I knew what I wanted. I wanted to get away from the sadness in Portland . . . to start over with our marriage . . . to spend my life working with your mother, not separated from her. And Josh, I've never been happier than when I found out she wanted the same thing."

That had the ring of truth to it. I didn't say anything, but I think Dad knew that I liked his answer.

"Here he comes," Dad said, pointing to the wrecker coming down the road toward us. "Stay in the car, Son. I'll talk to him."

I watched as Dad got out of the car and walked over to the truck driver. The two men looked at the Honda and talked for about five minutes before shaking hands. The guy with the wrecker took out his cell phone to make a call while Dad walked back to the SUV.

"He thinks he's going to need some help getting the car turned over before he tows it out of the ditch," Dad said as he shifted the car into reverse. "After that, they'll look it over in town and let us know how bad it is before I call the insurance agent. I'm pretty sure it's gone."

"But the Honda was for Nathan and me," I said.

Dad didn't say anything.

That car had kept me tied to Nathan.

"I suppose I was pretty lucky."

"You have no idea, Josh!" Dad said. "We were all lucky. Now we need to get back home and fill your mother in on what happened."

I wasn't looking forward to that. "You could call her," I suggested.

"No. I want you standing in front of her when we tell her about this. I'm still shaking from the shock of your call, Josh. How do you think your mother would handle us telling her over the phone?"

"Yeah," I said. "You're right." He was right. It hurt every time I noticed Mom crying about Nathan. This was going to bring everything back—all the pain and all the sadness, at least for a little while.

I remembered the vision of Nathan's face. "Dad, where do you think Nathan is now?"

"My faith tells me that he's with the Lord," Dad said after a short pause. "I've no idea what that means. But I'm confident that we will see him again. And Josh, I think it would be a good idea not to mention Nathan when we talk to your mother. She's going to be thinking of him anyway, so let's not make it worse."

"Okay, Dad." The morning's events had left me with an eerie feeling that was hard to shake. I was sure it had been Nathan carrying the candle. It was his voice. It was even his smell.

Chapter 6

Emergency Room

The cold glass felt good on my aching face as I pressed my cheek against the window. When I opened my eyes I saw the countryside whizzing by at eighty miles an hour, and I wondered if going slower would be safer. We were on Interstate 90 then, well past the slushy snow on the side roads, with only wet pavement. Mom knew there was no emergency, but she was determined to get me to "quality medical facilities" as soon as possible even if they were 50 miles away.

When I straightened and glanced over at Mom in the luxurious bucket seat on the other side of the Ford F-250, she was slightly hunched behind the steering wheel, staring intently through the windshield with her typically lovely expression hidden behind cloudy concern. Mom had always driven a BMW, but that car had been sold before leaving Portland. She seemed equally at home in this monstrous pickup my parents had purchased for the farm. Mom took the news about my accident pretty well. I thought she'd get hysterical, but she just grabbed me in a hug and then examined every inch of me. I guess tearing off for Sioux Falls was a little emotional, but still, it was better than I expected.

"How are you feeling now, Josh?" Mom said, breaking my thoughts.

"I'm fine, Mom."

"Well, that's what we are going to check out. I'm just happy to have you alive. But we want to make sure you're okay."

After another period of silence I said, "Mom . . ."

"Yes, Josh?"

"Dad thinks Nathan is with the Lord and that we will see him again."

"I agree with your Father."

I stared out at the bleak winter countryside. "If God wants us to be together, why did he let Nathan die?"

"I don't know, Josh. I don't understand either."

"Maybe there isn't a God."

Mom's face tightened just like I expected, but no angry words followed.

After a long moment Mom said, "I can understand why you might think that, Josh. Sometimes I was so angry with God that I wanted him just to go away and leave me alone. Some days I tried to be an atheist," she continued, "but it's hard. I had to be angry with God all the time. I had to keep doubting him out of existence. Now, after everything we've been through, feeling any hope about our family's future is a miracle. But I have days now when I feel that hope."

"I'm glad we're together," I said, "But that doesn't mean there's a god. And if there is one . . ."

Mom just smiled. "Here's our exit."

At the hospital, Mom turned into the parking lot marked with a big red "Emergency" sign. There was a short wait before we went back to an examination room. The whole ER was buzzing with activity, and the nurse warned us that it'd be a while before the doctor would be in. Mom sat on a chair in the little room with many cabinets and gleaming instruments. I sat on the examination table. After the nurse took my blood pressure and checked my temperature, I felt tired and decided to lie down.

***

"Joshua, wake up! It's time for the evening meal." Nathan shook my shoulder roughly. "You've slept away the whole afternoon. If you don't wake, you'll miss dinner too."

Groggily, I climbed back toward consciousness. Something was very odd. My eyes snapped open. "Nathan!"

"Joshua!" Nathan parroted the tone with a laugh.

"Nathan, you're alive!"

"Well, what did you expect? Sometimes you say the strangest things, Joshua."

I was back in the little chamber. The brazier was out, but a pair of lamps sitting in wall niches lit the room. Nathan was older than I remembered, with much longer hair and a light beard. I tamped down the scream that started in the pit of my stomach.

"Come on, Joshua," Nathan said, raising his voice a notch. "You have to come. Mother's getting ready to call out the palace guard."

I stood up mutely and stared at my brother.

"Well, that's a step in the proper direction. Let's go. It's dinnertime!"

"I'll follow you," I managed to croak out.

Nathan looked at me with a puzzled expression on his face. As he picked up one of the lamps to lead the way out through a twisting passage, he said, "Okay, but that must have been some dream you were having."

I wasn't sure what was a dream anymore. Panic started to well up inside me as we made our way through the dark hallway.

"Nathan?" I said.

"Yes, Joshua." I could hear the amusement in his voice. It was achingly familiar.

"Where are we?"

The light ahead of me stopped. I saw Nathan's face on the other side of the light as he turned to face me. "What do you mean?" he said.

"I mean where on earth are we?"

"We're in our home in Jerusalem. "Are you playing one of your jokes on me?" Nathan's voice was still amused, but an edge of annoyance crept into it.

"Uh . . ." was all I could muster in the way of a response.

"I thought so," Nathan said with a barking laugh. "You're not going to get me to fall for it this time." He turned and continued down the passageway.

Soon we emerged into a paved courtyard open to the sky. A large canopy hung over rich carpets, brightly colored cushions, and a low table. Ceramic dishes sat on the table. We stepped out into the heat of the late afternoon sun. The rich smell of grilled meat and seasoned vegetables wafted from a cooking brazier set up just beyond the covered area.

"Ah, Joshua! You've returned to the land of the living," a tall man reclining on one of the floor cushions said to me. "We are so pleased you've decided to join us."

I stopped dead in my tracks and stared. The man was my father in a long robe and sandals. He was still bald, but he had a flowing beard.

"You may not be awake, even yet," the man said with a laugh.

"Go easy on the boy, Benjamin. He just got up. He may not be feeling well. Look how pale he is," my mother's voice spoke.

I heard the swish of long skirts as a woman stepped up beside me. I felt her soft hand touch my forehead. Involuntarily I turned to look into her face. There was my mother's face, but darker. Her hair was chocolate brown instead of the paler color I'd known all my life.

"I don't think he has a fever, Benjamin," my mother said. "But he's a little clammy."

"I never feel right for a while after a long nap, Rachel. Give the boy a chance to wake up."

I allowed my mother to lead me into the shade of the canopy and seat me on one of the cushions.

"Eli, would you please go get one of the water jars in the storeroom?" my mother said to a man standing at the braziers.

"Yes, ma'am," the man said with a slight bow, and left.

Nathan walked into the shade of the canopy and sat down on a cushion beside a young lady that I hadn't noticed until just then. He reached for a small ceramic bowl of nuts and dried fruit, and taking a handful, offered it her. As she took it, I recognized her jet-black hair, framing an oval face with an aquiline nose and dark almond-shaped eyes. The shock of seeing Sarah Dirk in this setting made my mind feel like tattered sheets snapping in the wind.

"Sarah, would you help me with this?" my mom said as she gestured to the large ceramic jar Eli was carrying.

She rose with her usual athletic grace and crossed quickly to take the clay vessel. Mother picked up a ceramic cup from one of the tables and held it out for Sarah to fill. Mother brought me the cup, putting her hand on my cheek in a familiar, affectionate gesture. "Drink this. It will help you to wake up."

"I think that most of the meat is ready," the man whom Mother called Eli said. "Would you like to eat now?"

"By all means," Father said enthusiastically.

Eli set a large platter laden with bits of roasted meat and

vegetables on the table. He came and sat down beside Sarah who'd returned to her place beside Nathan.

Mother set a large unlit candle on the table and lit it, and then sang a prayer in a rich contralto thanking God for this house, this food, and this family. Everyone respectfully listened until she finished, then began to eat from the dish Eli set on the tables, dipping the meat and vegetables in a spicy brown sauce.

It felt like everyone was looking at me. I played along. I picked up an unfamiliar looking tuber, softened from roasting and blackened at its tip. I dipped it in the brown sauce. The root was bland, but the sauce sent a "zing" up my nose and my eyes watered.

"Eli, have you heard anything from your family in Egypt? Do you think the Egyptians will help against the Assyrians?" Father asked.

I tried dipping some meat in the sauce this time.

"I haven't heard anything encouraging from my Egyptian relatives," Eli said. "I think the Pharaoh has his hands full. Judah's problems are of little consequence to him. But I've heard rumors that he may face the Assyrians in battle whether he wants to or not."

"I worry about the threats Assyria has made to Egypt."

I thought maybe I had heard of Assyria before, but I concentrated on the food because it made more sense than anything else in the dream.

"Well, if anyone would know, sir, it would be you," Eli said, bowing from a seated position. "Since you are the head of all Judah's spies."

"My spies have given me the same information," Father said. "And I do not believe King Hezekiah's ambassadors will be successful in gaining a peaceful solution. King Sennacherib demands that we replace the tribute King Hezekiah stopped paying when Sennacherib came to the throne five years ago. That money went into restoring the temple, but even if he strips the temple now to pay the tribute I doubt Sennacherib will turn away from attacking us."

"Do you really think it's that bad, Benjamin?" Mother asked.

"Yes. It looks more and more like Sennacherib will finish what his father started. He seeks to destroy Judah as his father destroyed Israel. If he makes good on his threats against Egypt, we will have no ally to call on."

"See," Sarah exclaimed, jumping up and turned to face Eli. "Father, let me train with the archers. I'll be better off defending the walls when the Assyrians come than tending a hearth. I'd rather die on the walls than be caught by Assyrian soldiers."

"We shall see, daughter," Eli said quietly. "But when I lost your mother, I lost half my soul. I don't know what would happen if I lost you."

"Joshua! Are you alright?" Mother said with sudden concern.

As I turned to look at her I realized that I felt like I was going to faint.

"Here, Eli. Help me get him back to his bed," I heard Mother saying as the edges of my vision began to darken.

I vaguely felt my mother and Eli carrying me back to my bedchamber. The last thing I remember was Mother holding my hand and stroking my forehead as I lay down on the straw mattress.

***

"Joshua! Are you alright?" I heard Mom say with concern.

When I finally forced my eyes open, I thought I could smell straw, but then I recognized the odor of hospital disinfectants. Mom was holding my hand and stroking my forehead.

"Josh, try to wake up, honey!" Mom said with increasing urgency. "The doctor is here."

"I'm okay, Mom," I said, letting her help me sit up. Then I noticed the doctor, standing beside her.

"Your symptoms indicate that you may have a concussion, so we want to get you in for a CT scan," the doctor said.

***

"But Mom, it was only a slight concussion," I said in the truck on the way home from the hospital.

"The doctor also said we have to be careful. I'm going to write an email to your basketball coach. You should only be doing light exercise for the next couple of days."

"Aw, Mom! Do you have to? I'm just getting started with

the team. I don't want to get the reputation of being a wimp before I even get a chance."

"Be reasonable, Josh," Mom said. "I'm letting you go to practice, but I want a promise that you won't overdo it, and I need the coach's help to make sure. Besides, it's better that I ask."

"Why?" I asked sullenly.

"Because then you'll get a reputation for having an over-protective mother, not for being a wimp."

"I suppose," I said.

I looked out my window at a billboard on the side of the road. It had a large image of a chariot charging straight at me. Underneath it big red letters said "The Assyrians Are Coming!"

I closed my eyes and shook my head. When I opened my eyes again, I saw that the billboard was really about internet broadband. It had a picture of a service truck on it and said nothing about Assyrians. I wondered if I had imagined that whole thing—the dream, the Assyrians, and the billboard.

I continued to stare at the sign as Mom drove by. I dared it to change back but it didn't.

Chapter 7

Basket Ball Practice

"Bzzzt! Bzzzt! Bzzzt!"

My first thought on waking was to call out to Nathan. But the chill in the air and the hefty pile of blankets anchored me firmly in South Dakota. I'd had this feeling before back in Portland shortly after Nathan died, but that was a long time ago. It must have been that weird dream. I didn't know whether to laugh or cry.

"Bzzzt! Bzzzt! Bzzzt!"

I reached to shut off the alarm clock. It said 5:30 a.m. I wanted to turn over and go back to sleep but I had to go to basketball practice. I had missed the first practice yesterday because of the accident. Would the coach cut me for not showing up even if my mom sent him an excuse? Would being cut be such a bad thing? Going out for the team seemed like a great idea two weeks ago, but I suck at basketball. It was Nathan who'd been the basketball star. Not only did he rise above the competition to make the team, but he was on the starting squad. It had looked like he was going to be a star before he'd been killed.

Frustrated, I jerked back the covers and braced myself for the shock of stepping out on the ice-cold hardwood floor. The old heating system didn't work so well up here in my room. Still, cold feet in the morning was a small price to pay for the luxury of all this space. My room was only dimly lit by the yard light coming in through the dormer windows. I fumbled around until I found the light switch. I pulled on my clothes, grabbed my gym bag, and headed downstairs toward some enticing breakfast aromas.

"Morning Josh!" my grandfather called over the sound of sizzling bacon.

"Hey, Gramps."

"Over easy?"

"That'd be great, and can I have three pieces of bacon? I'll need energy for practice this morning."

"Sure. There's plenty here. You can have all you want," Gramps said, pushing the bacon to the side of the pan to make room for frying eggs.

"Where are Mom and Dad?" I asked, pouring myself a large glass of orange juice.

"They're out feeding the livestock. They told me my job was to feed you. Fine by me," Gramps chuckled to himself.

I stood for a while sipping my juice and watching my grandfather work at the stove. Then I said, "Do you think they'll cut me from the team because I missed the first practice, Gramps?"

"Nope. I don't think Wheaton ever cut anyone from a team.
A small school like ours struggles just to get enough players for
each sport. You're fine. Besides, when I saw Coach at the Cenex
yesterday he was worried about you and relieved to hear that
you'd be practicing today." Gramps shoveled the bacon and
three big farm-fresh eggs out of his frying pan onto my plate.

Suddenly my morning hunger hit me full force and I dug
into breakfast with abandon. After a time I asked, "Gramps,
have you ever heard of King Hezekiah?"

"Yes, Josh. He was one of the good kings of Judah. You
can read about him in Second Kings and somewhere in
Chronicles, I think."

"Did he have anything to do with Assyrians?"

Gramps paused, looking at me for a long moment. "Yep,"
he said. "The Assyrians were the enemy that attacked God's
people at the time of Hezekiah. Why are you interested?"

"Oh, it's kind of random," I said. "Gramps, how come you
know so much about the Bible?"

"I read it every day. It's a good practice for anyone who
wants to figure out how life works. You should try it."

"It seems so old and hard to understand."

"That's true. But understanding comes as you become
familiar with more of the stories and teachings. The Bible has
a way of helping your comprehension as you read it regularly.
You could say it interprets itself."

"Really?" I said. I wasn't sure that made sense. I changed

the subject. "How am I going to get to school today? Can somebody drive me?"

"How would you like to use the Beast for your vehicle until we figure out what we're going to do about your Honda?"

I was stunned. "Wow! Are you sure, Gramps?" I finally managed to squeak out. I had fantasized about driving that old green pickup for years.

"Yup. It's the only rig we have available right now, and with all the farm work, we need you to get yourself to school."

"But Gramps, you love that truck," I said. My voice shook slightly with excitement.

"Yes I do," Gramps chuckled. "And you're going to take very good care of it, including learning about its maintenance."

"Of course I will," I said breathlessly. "I mean, I'll drive very carefully and learn how to take care of it."

Gramps grinned broadly as he fished a tarnished bronze key on a steel ring out of his pocket and handed it to me. "I put some sandbags in the back to help with traction, but you should take it easy. It's still slick out there even though this snow is likely to melt off by the end of the day."

"Thanks, Gramps," I said. "Thanks so very much."

In a matter of minutes I was starting the Beast and trying to believe my good fortune. I was going to miss the Honda, but driving this pickup was a dream come true.

***

It was still dark when I pulled into the school parking lot. I grabbed my gym bag and headed inside. The boys' locker room was empty when I sat down on a bench to pull on my basketball gear. I could hear bouncing basketballs out in the gym so I knew people were there. Worried, I checked my phone to make sure I wasn't late.

"Morning, Josh," Fred Nicholson called out as I came into the gym. He and Robert MacAllister were the entire boys' coaching staff for Wheaton High.

"Hey, Cooper. How are you feeling?" Coach MacAllister said, coming over to where I was selecting a ball off a rack.

"I'm fine, Coach."

"Your mom said you had a mild concussion. That's more serious than people think. We're going to keep an eye on you today."

"Yeah, that's okay. The doctor gave me instructions that if I feel faint or nauseous, I'm supposed to stop right away."

"Good deal!" Coach said. "Welcome to Rocket basketball, Josh. I know you've not played on a high school team before. Still, I'm sure you've had enough experience to make a meaningful contribution. And anyway, this sport is about having fun and doing our best at holding up the honor of good old Wheaton High." He chuckled warmly.

I found my way to the side of the court where Eddie and Sean were shooting baskets.

"Hey Coop," Eddie called out. "So you finally decided to get yourself to practice." He laughed good-naturedly.

"Eddie, don't be a jerk," Sean said. "I got a look at his

Honda behind the Cenex. That accident was no joke. Are you okay, Josh?"

"Yeah," I said. "Just got a mild concussion is all."

After about ten minutes Coach blew the whistle to gather everyone at the center of the court. By that time there were sixteen boys on the court.

"Where's Marshal James?" Coach MacAllister said as he took stock of the boys gathered around him.

"He's coming, Coach," Allen Osgaard said. "He's still in the locker room."

Marshal strutted onto the court.

"Glad you could join us, James." Marshal and Coach MacAllister stared each other down. When Marshal looked away, Coach began walking toward one end of the court saying, "We'll start with some drills today. Varsity, this way."

"JV with me!" Fred Nicholson called out as he headed to the other basket.

I stood on the center line, unsure of what to do.

When Coach MacAllister noticed he said, "Josh, you come with the varsity for now. We'll have you playing JV games at the start of the season to get you more experience, but today I want to keep an eye on you."

Coach took us through a series of drills for layups, field goals, and free throws. Then he said to me, "Looking good, Josh. We'll have to work on your shot, but your hustle is great. You need to sit out this next drill because I promised your mom I'd limit your chances of physical contact for the next couple of days."

As I took my seat in the bleachers, a figure in baggy sweats with a hood came through the far side door. Coach also noticed the newcomer and blew his whistle. "Okay. We're going to move to a full-court scrimmage now. Fred, would you please organize your team? I've asked Sarah to join us so you'll have a little extra muscle." He gestured to the figure in the baggy sweat suit that was trotting across the floor.

Sarah Dirk pulled off her hood as she came up to the JV team. Suddenly I saw her as the mysterious young lady sitting beside my brother Nathan in that strange dream, but the odd sensation passed quickly.

Mesmerized as she doffed her sweats and stretched to warm up, I was slow to pick up on the disgruntled murmurs coming from the varsity team.

"What's she doing here?" Marshal James said.

"Take it out on the court," Coach said. "You better watch it, James, or she'll clean your clock. Andrew and Thomas, you guys play with the JV for now. Cooper, you stay where you are. Concussions are nothing to fool with." Then he turned to talk to the remaining varsity players.

Sarah walked over to where Fred Nicholson was organizing the JV. The other players seemed glad to see her, but no one went out of their way to be friendly.

Both squads took the court. Coach threw the ball to Marshal James. "Varsity, you're on offense. Marshal, bring it up."

"JV, three-two zone defense," Mr. Nicholson called out. Sarah and the JV team members arranged themselves around the painted area under the basket with their arms raised, stances balanced.

Marshal dribbled over the half-court line, moving slowly and looking for an opportunity to pass in. Allen broke up from the baseline out toward the wing. Marshal made a pass to him. But before the ball reached Allen's hands, Sarah was there intercepting it. In a smooth movement so fast it was hard to follow, she dribbled four times, flashed the length of the court, and floated in the layup. The JV erupted in a cheer. The varsity glared at Marshal.

"Don't telegraph your passes, James," Coach called out, as Sarah saucily flipped the ball back to him on her way back to defense.

After that the scrimmage tightened up. The varsity had the upper hand, but Sarah continuously broke up plays on defense and made plays on offense. Her mid-range jump shot was flawless — if they left her any leeway at all, it was through the hoop. She moved like a wolf with her cubs, and the JV made an excellent showing for themselves.

Near the end of practice Sarah took a good pass from the wing, faked out her coverage, and drove toward the basket. Marshal saw the score coming but was in no position to stop it. Still, he moved like lighting and executed a hockey-style body check just as she finished the layup. Sarah went flying, but she managed to tuck and roll as she hit the floor. She was up in a flash and had her face in Marshal's with vengeance written boldly in her eyes. Marshal took a step back. As she walked away, Sarah's anger faded to a tight smile.

Coach blew the whistle loudly. "James! What was that?"

Marshal stood still, blatantly not answering.

"Twenty laps, James. We don't go in for unsportsmanlike behavior. Do you hear me?"

"Yes, Coach," Marshal said as he trotted toward the sideline to start his laps.

"Everyone else hit the showers. Practice is over for today. I expect to see all of you tomorrow morning at 6:15 sharp."

"Yes, Coach!" we chorused, as we trotted toward the locker room.

***

When I entered the dressing area there was none of the usual banter. As I came out of the showers, Marshal entered the locker room, sweat dripping in his eyes and darkening his shirt.

"Why'd you tackle Dirk, Marshal?" said Carl Bolstad, the varsity center. "Did you just need a hug?"

"Better not let Melanie find you out you were snuggling up with Sarah," Eddie taunted, drawing a sharp look from Sean.

"I'm not worried about Melanie," Marshal shot back. "She's way too into me. Besides, she knows I don't want leftovers."

"I don't know," Allen Osgaard said. "I enjoyed my ride on the town bicycle." Allen thrust his hips to make his point.

"Besides everyone knows she wants you Marshal. You should give it a try."

Marshal pointed at me. "Hey, Cooper, bet you didn't know you lived next to the Wheaton whorehouse."

I decided not to say anything in response.

"She'll do just about anyone," said Allen, "or anything. Right guys?"

The senior and junior guys laughed uncomfortably, but no one denied Allen's claim.

"Yeah," Allen said. "She's running out of guys her age. She'll have to go after peons soon. Ready for your turn, Eddie?"

Eddie looked as uncomfortable as I felt.

The locker room cleared out quickly after Marshal went in to take his shower. I threw my towel into the bin and headed out the locker room door, unsure what to think. I didn't know much about Sarah, but it was clear that both Marshal and Allen were jerks.

As I stopped in the hall to drink at the water fountain, I overheard Jean Wilkerson say, "Are you going to make practice today, Sarah?"

"No," came the resonant response. "Coach Arlington looked at the bruise on my leg and decided I should rest it for a day. I'll be there tomorrow."

"Was it Marshal?" Jean said.

"Yeah, he was his normal obnoxious self but everyone saw him back down. Maybe that'll slow him up next time."

"I wish I could believe that. Good for you anyway. After

all he and his friends have done to you it's good for people to see what an idiot he is."

Their conversation faded as they moved down the hall. I had to hurry to get to my first class.

***

The light was fading as I climbed into the Beast to drive home from school. I'd stayed late to make sure I understood all the homework I'd missed the day before. That made the trip home even darker than usual. As I came over the last hill before home, I noticed our neighbor's big barn door was open and the lights were on. I watched a slender, graceful figure execute a perfect jump shot.

I couldn't help myself. I slowed the Beast and pulled to the side of the road. Switching off the headlights, I watched through the open door as Sarah made a quick dribble and then another picture-perfect jumper. Suddenly I felt creepy, wondering if this were stalking. Just as I reached to turn on the headlights I noticed Sarah silhouetted in the barn door, staring straight at me. On impulse, I cranked the wheel around to guide the Beast onto the driveway. I hoped I could think of something to say.

As I pulled the pickup into the yard, a bright yard light came on, nearly blinding me. I shut off the pickup and climbed out. Sarah watched me from the barn door.

"I recognize that pickup. How'd you get old man Neilson to let you drive it?" Sarah said flatly.

The question unnerved me. It was the way she said it, like she was angry. I tried to match her tone. "My car got wrecked yesterday."

"Yeah, I heard about that. Still doesn't explain why you're sneaking around in your grandpa's pride and joy. Why'd you stop in here?"

"Uuh . . ."

"Did you get lost on the way home?" Sarah said with a snort.

I wasn't sure, but Sarah seemed to be enjoying my discomfort. I said the first thing I could think of. "Well, uh, I noticed you were playing basketball."

"Yeah, that's something I do."

The silence stretched to an uncomfortable length as I struggled for something more to say. "I saw you playing this morning at the boys' practice."

"You saw that, huh?" Sarah said. "Oh yeah. You were in the bleachers. Why weren't you playing?"

"I got a mild concussion from the accident, so Coach made me sit out the scrimmage." I hoped for a little compassion, but no such luck.

"What are you doing here now?" Sarah said with evident suspicion.

Flustered, I blurted, "I just wanted to say that you're awesome. At basketball, I mean." I hoped the poor light would hide the blush I felt burning on my face.

"Well, that makes one fan. But you haven't been here very long. There's time to change your mind."

Her defiant tone was achingly familiar. I'd heard it in her speech about becoming an archer in my dream. It took me a moment to recover. Then I said, "No. You are good. I've watched a lot of basketball. My brother was a varsity starter for our high school team in Portland. I know when I see a talented player."

Sarah stared at me. Her voice had a gentler tone when she broke the silence. "Where's this brother of yours? We could use somebody decent on the boys' team."

"He's dead. A drunk driver killed him," I said tonelessly.

"Oh!" Sarah raised her hand involuntarily. "I'm sorry. I didn't know."

"Don't worry about it. That's kind of the reason we're out here in South Dakota. Portland was just epic sadness. We had to get out. Gramps gave us a place to come."

Sarah dropped her arm back to her side and took a step forward. "I know a little about sadness. South Dakota is a good place to come."

Her voice had a softness that touched me. I looked at her quietly for a while. Her face was darkly outlined against the light inside the barn. I couldn't see her expression, but her words warmed something inside me.

My words came tumbling out on their own. "I'm not very good at basketball, nothing like my brother. Can you help me play better?"

Abruptly, Sarah's guarded manner was back. "Aren't you afraid I'll sully your reputation?"

"Huh?" I was caught off guard.

"I'm sure Marshal filled you in. He always does." Now she sounded bitter.

"Oh, that. No. I don't pay attention to rumors."

"That makes you unique in Wheaton," Sarah said with a harsh laugh. "There's still time to come to your senses."

"Will you help me?" I was on the edge of panic, hoping she'd agree. How had I come up with this idea?

Sarah stood in the doorway, staring at me for a long time. I froze and waited, not daring to push any harder. Finally, she smoothed her ponytail back over her shoulder and threw me the basketball she had been holding. "Let's see what you've got." As she turned to walk back into the barn, I could see a tight little smile spreading across her guarded face.

***

I made it home in time for supper, but my parents wanted to know what took me so long. I told them about seeing Sarah at basketball practice that morning, and made stopping to ask for help sound like something I'd planned.

Gramps said, "Sarah Dirk is one of the best basketball players in the state of South Dakota."

"That's not surprising," Mom said. "I remember her father, Paul, in high school. He made the South Dakota All-Star Basketball Team for three years in a row."

"I'd guess I'd feel better if it were Paul helping rather than Sarah," Dad said.

"Paul's not around very much, Ben. He drives a truck for a living," Gramps explained.

"That's not helping me feel better about this." Dad looked worried.

"Come on, Ben. We can trust Josh," Mom said. "We can't forbid him to be alone with a girl at his age."

"Okay, okay. But be careful, Josh. Remember, I raised you to be a gentleman," Dad warned.

I wondered what he thought I'd do that he needed to remind me to be a gentleman. Even if she was like everyone said, I wasn't about to do that. Without further comment I asked to be excused and headed upstairs to do my homework.

It took a while to finish all the homework. As I switched off my desk lamp and stood to stretch, fatigue rushed over me. I was barely able to pull off my clothes and flop into bed before unconsciousness swept me away.

Chapter 8

Water Tunnel

I woke in total darkness, which was odd because the yard light always came through my windows at night. Then I noticed how heavy my covers had become. I had lots of blankets because my bedroom was cold, but this was ridiculous—the weight was hurting me. Something sharp was poking me in the back and I couldn't move my arms to clear whatever was covering my face. It was hard to breathe.

Then I heard voices.

"Move that rock."

"Dig carefully there. Use your hands. A shovel might cut him. I don't think he's down much deeper."

"There's his foot, so his face must be about here."

Then I heard what was unmistakably Nathan's voice say, "Joshua! Joshua! Can you hear me?"

Whatever was covering my face shifted and I blinked furiously trying to get dust out of my eyes. Finally, I could see several flickering lights that looked like campfires on poles. It was another crazy dream, but why did it have to hurt so much?

"Joshua!" Nathan said, with his face inches from mine. "Are you alright?" His voice was tight with concern.

I tried to respond, but all that came out was a moan. My mouth was filled with dust and gravel.

"He's alive!" Nathan exclaimed.

I felt someone lift me into a sitting position. My back rested against a rough rock wall. I saw well enough to make out Nathan's figure in the flickering light of the torches.

"Here. Use this to wash out your mouth."

Nathan pushed what felt like a very thick water balloon into my hands. I had no idea what it was. When I tried to ask, all that came out was another gravelly moan. Nathan helped guide a nozzle-like protrusion to shoot warm water into my mouth. It tasted terrible. I couldn't tell whether the taste was the water or the dust in my mouth. I pushed the water bag away and spat. Then I gagged. But my head was starting to clear and absolute terror was starting to kick in. I had been buried alive.

"Nathan," I managed to croak.

"Here. Take some more water," Nathan insisted, as he squeezed more water from the leather bag into my mouth.

It was the water that tasted bad. I managed to take a couple of swallows without gagging, and then tried to speak again.

"Nathan, where are we? What happened?"

"We're in the Water Tunnel. But a cave in fell on you,"

Nathan said, adding confusion to my growing panic. I could see the faint outline of the narrow, low-arched passageway with roughly-cut stone walls.

"You were pretty lucky," said a voice behind Nathan, near one of the torches. "My dad got killed in a cave in."

"Asher, now is not the time to talk about that," another voice further back in the tunnel said.

"I suppose you're right," Asher said, bringing his torch a little closer so that I could start to feel its heat. "Nathan, is Joshua going to be okay?"

"Yes, I think so." Nathan was examining every inch of my body. "He's not bleeding anywhere. Do you think you can stand up, Joshua?"

"I'll try," I said, "but I might have a concussion."

"A what?"

"You know . . . when your brain gets a little bruised from being hit too hard."

"His words make no sense," Asher said.

Nathan helped me to my feet. "I'm going get him home. He needs rest."

I decided not to say anything. Talking only seemed to make things worse.

"Will you guys be okay? Our shift is almost over."

"Sure, Nathan," Asher said. "We have time to clean up this rockfall before we quit."

"Thanks," Nathan said as he pulled my arm over his shoulder to help me walk.

We made our way along the narrow tunnel. Guttering

torches provided little pools of light. In many places it was too tight to squeeze through side-by-side, so I leaned on the walls for support as Nathan guided me through from behind. Claustrophobia added to my panic, but Nathan's calm voice was soothing and the joy of being with him, alive again, was intoxicating.

The journey down the tunnel seemed endless, but it wasn't long before I saw a pinpoint of bright light far ahead, which turned out to be the exit. Soon we emerged into the bright sunshine, leaving the panicky terror in the darkness behind us.

Nathan said, "Sit here for a minute while I go get our clothes."

As I sat down on a large stone block, I noticed for the first time that I was nearly naked. I was only wearing a strip of cloth wound around my groin. But as I looked around, I saw that most of the men working nearby were undressed in the same way. Evidently this was what you wore to work in ancient Jerusalem. I began to wonder what they were trying to accomplish. Some were digging in the ground filling baskets with dirt and carrying them away. Some were shaping stones with chisels for building a circular wall.

"This new water pool is coming along quickly," Nathan observed as he came back carrying a couple of long robes and two sets of sandals. "I think it will be ready long before we break through to the Gihon Spring and the water starts to flow." Nathan handed me one of the robes and a set of sandals.

I looked at him blankly and said, "What?"

"Are you alright? Let me help you get into that." He nodded toward the clothes I was holding.

"No, I can do it." I pulled the long tunic-like robe over my head. It was like a T-shirt that hung to my calves. But the sandals confused me. I had to watch Nathan to see how to lace them around my ankles.

"Let's head home. I think you should lie down," Nathan said as he started across the construction area.

I followed him, trying not to gawk too obviously at the ancient city.

***

The trip from the tunnel entrance was a blur of images in the bright midday sun. Eli followed us through the house with a lamp, gathering a bundle of linen cloth and a bowl of water as we went. Soon we were in my now-familiar bedchamber where Eli put the light on a wall shelf. He handed the cloths and bowl to Nathan before leaving the room. Nathan watched as I sponged myself down, then I pulled on the fresh tunic Nathan handed me and lay down on the bed.

"Are you feeling any better?" Nathan said.

"Yeah, I think so," I responded.

Nathan lit a couple of lamps and the room brightened considerably.

"Joshua, you don't seem to be very upset for being buried alive," Nathan said.

"Well, it only took a matter of seconds for you to dig me out."

Nathan paused, staring intently at me. "You were down there for a long time. It took us nearly an hour to dig you out. Don't you remember? I thought for sure you were going to be dead when we found you."

Now it was my turn to stare. "Uh, I don't remember that. What were we doing in that tunnel anyway?"

"The cave in must have muddled your wits," Nathan said, as he sat down on the foot of the bed.

"Maybe I'll remember if you tell me what was going on. Pretend that I don't know." I propped myself up on an elbow.

Nathan sighed. "Tell me what you remember."

"I remember the meal where Father told us that King Hezekiah sent ambassadors to that Assyrian king. What was his name?"

"Sennacherib."

"Yeah, that's him."

"Joshua, that's most of two weeks past. The ambassadors have already returned. That's where Father is right now. He's down at the treasury, helping to pack up the ridiculous tribute Sennacherib demanded we send. We stripped most of the gold out of the temple to meet his conditions. Even Mother is there, trying to help."

"So what were we doing in that tunnel?" I asked.

"You don't remember?"

"Nope."

"King Hezekiah plans to block off the Gihon spring and

channel the water into Jerusalem down that tunnel we're digging. It will provide water if Jerusalem goes under siege, and blocking the spring takes away an invader's best source of water. You and I volunteered to help. We've been working for about ten hours a day ever since. Truly, you don't remember?"

"I don't remember anything. It seems like a big project to finish in a hurry."

Nathan stood up and began to pace around the room. "King Hezekiah has worked on the idea in secret for several years, although I'm sure Father knew. There are only a couple hundred feet of tunnel to go. Father supported our decision to volunteer. Mother threw a fit."

"I don't suppose my encounter with the rockfall is going to help calm Mother either."

"No, it won't. And neither will your loss of memory. That's even got me worried."

Just then, Sarah entered the room carrying a tray with a small pitcher and two clay cups on it. She set it down on the stone shelf that jutted beyond the head of the straw pallet. "How are you feeling, Joshua?"

Her voice was so familiar that I had to struggle to hold onto reality. "Uh . . . Fine. I think."

"Joshua is having some memory problems because of the accident, Sarah," Nathan said.

"Oh." Sarah stood up and crossed the room. She took a stopper out of a bottle that she carried slung over her shoulder on a rope. "How so?"

"He doesn't seem to remember anything from the last couple of weeks."

Sarah went up on her tiptoes and poured oil into the lamp by the door. "He doesn't remember anything?" She crossed the room to fill another.

We grew silent, watching her elegant motions. When she turned to look at us, Nathan said, "Do you remember anything at all, Joshua?"

Still staring at Sarah, my brain glitched and I asked, "Sarah, do you play basketball here in Jerusalem?"

"What?" Nathan asked.

Sarah walked over and sat down beside the tray she'd brought. She picked up the pitcher and poured a cupful. I sat up as she handed it to me. "You know well that I make lots of baskets. Weaving them is one of my regular household chores. But I'm not sure what that has to do with a ball."

I gulped, realizing what a mess I was making of this. I looked into Nathan's widened eyes for a moment and then turned back to Sarah. "Uh . . . yeah, I know that," was all I could get out.

Nathan stood up and motioned to Sarah. She followed him to the door of my room. Nathan glanced at me uneasily and spoke to Sarah in a voice that I'm sure he didn't think I could hear. "He's not well."

Sarah put a calming hand on his forearm. "Let him sleep. He'll feel better."

Nathan looked at me. His face was grim. He looked older not only than Nathan would be if he were alive in reality, but older than boys his age looked in my time. He looked like a man.

"He's just tired." Sarah said.

I felt like someone was turning down the volume on Nathan and Sarah's conversation. I rubbed my eyes and then yawned convulsively. Sarah and Nathan were suddenly there, helping me to lie down and pulling up the wool coverlet. Through increasingly heavy eyelids I saw them each pick up one of the two lamps and, without another word, silently leave the room. In the darkness, a more profound sleep came quickly.

Chapter 9

Saturday

I woke Wednesday morning with a start, unsure of my surroundings. I realized I was in South Dakota. The yard light shone through my windows. I reached over to check the time and the alarm went off as I picked up my phone. There was no chance to get back to sleep. With a shudder I remembered being pinned under the rockfall and decided that I'd rather get up anyway.

The shock of my bare feet touching the ice cold floor boards brought me back to reality. It all had to be an elaborate dream.

The rest of that day was normal. Coach still wouldn't let me go full bore. I fumbled the ball badly in the three-on-two drill and missed all of my shots. Sarah was going to have her hands full getting any decent play out of me. School itself was routine and the night passed without any disturbing trips to Jerusalem.

Thursday was normal. Friday morning, as I walked down the hall toward my locker after practice, everyone seemed to be staring at me. Some were whispering and sharing pictures on their phones. As I worked the combination on my locker, Eddie handed me his phone and said, "Sorry, man. Welcome to Wheaton."

Eddie's phone displayed an image of a woman dressed like a hooker with Sarah's school picture photoshopped in. The caption read "Seen on the streets of Portland with Josh Cooper".

"Who did that?" I asked angrily.

"We don't know," Eddie answered. "It's a bogus account. Probably Melanie Crawford. She's Marshal James' girlfriend. There's been trouble brewing ever since basketball practice on Tuesday."

"That's messed up."

"It's about average for stuff around here," Eddie said. "We may be out in the sticks compared to Portland, but we can do cyberbullying like the big time."

"Who's seen it?"

"Everybody in Wheaton High. Did you get it?"

I checked my snapchat. It was still full of snaps from Portland. "Nope. Nothing."

"Are you following Wheaton's geotag?"

I shook my head.

"That's where it was posted." Eddie patted me on the back. "Like I said, sorry, man. We're not all like that."

"I wondered why everyone was looking at me weird. Now I know."

I decided not to tell my parents about the incident. I had arranged to go over to Sarah's for a basketball lesson on Saturday and didn't want anything to get in the way.

***

I woke up before my alarm on Saturday and I was surprised to see that it was only 7:15. I guess I was so used to getting up early I couldn't even sleep-in. Mom had said I could sleep until 8:00 but then I had to help with a project she had planned for today. Before I could turn over to go back to sleep I heard the tractor rumbling in the barnyard and decided to get up.

I got dressed and joined everyone in the barn.

"We used to have horses here when I was growing up." Mom gestured to the tall wooden stalls filled with an odd assortment of items that Gramps had stored there.

"Are you sure this is a good idea, Rachel?" Dad asked. "Couldn't we just use a couple ATVs? We wouldn't have to feed them."

Storm clouds gathered on my mom's face. Dad got quiet and seemed to be holding his breath.

Mom looked away for a minute, then abruptly laughed. "Benny, you're such a city kid," she said.

"Well, I did grow up in Eden Prairie, Minnesota, honey. It wasn't cool to be a cowboy there."

"You'll like the horses when you get used to them, Ben. They really do make handling cattle easier," Gramps said. "Now, if I can just figure out where to put all this stuff."

Dad looked unconvinced but he didn't say anything more as we all pitched in under Mom's direction.

By noon, when we all went into the house for lunch, the two stalls were cleaned out and spruced up.

***

I knocked on Sarah's back door just after lunch for my first real basketball lesson.

"Hey, Sarah," I said when she came out.

"Hi, Josh." She led me out to the barn where she switched on the lights, bounced the ball twice, and levitated into a jump shot that swished perfectly through the hoop.

"So, what is it you want me to teach you?" she asked.

"I want to be able to make baskets like that," I said.

"There's a lot more to good basketball than shooting. Passing is more important. Here. Show me your chest pass."

Sarah had to explain to me what a chest pass was, and when I figured it out she laughed at my attempt. She spent the next hour teaching me about passing. I never realized there were so many ways to pass a basketball. There were chest passes, overhead passes, hook passes, bounce passes, and underhand passes. At first I had trouble catching her passes because they came so fast they bounced out of my grip. Sarah showed me how to relax my hands and give with the pass so that I could capture the ball and control it.

After a while she said, "Okay, let's spend a little time

working on your shot. Show me what you do." She threw me the ball.

I pumped deep and jumped into the shot with one leg splaying to the side. The ball hit the back of the rim and bounced wildly. I ran to retrieve the ball, and when I came back, Sarah was covering her mouth and trying not to laugh.

"Okay," I said, laughing, "I told you I needed help shooting."

Then she did laugh. "You might need more than help. Perhaps surgery?"

"Is it that bad?"

"Nothing we can't fix." Sarah's smile made all my embarrassment disappear.

We spent the next half hour on the mechanics of shooting. My shots repeatedly failed to go in,. If anything I missed more than ever. But I also started to feel how Sarah's suggestions made my shots more focused.

"You'll get this, Josh. You learn fast and are good at taking instructions. That makes you kind of unusual," Sarah said.

Her compliment was pure joy. "Thanks," I said as another shot only connected with the back wall.

***

"Let's take a break." Sarah sat down on what looked like a milking stool. She snagged her sweatshirt and motioned for me to sit on an old cane chair. "What did you think of Melanie's artwork yesterday?"

"Uh . . . you saw that?" I asked.

Sarah nodded gravely.

"Are you okay?"

Sarah looked directly at me for a second and then looked away. "I wasn't thinking about me. I'm used to it. I was asking about how you felt getting drawn into it?"

"People were always doing stupid stuff like that at my high school in Portland too. You just have to ignore it. Somehow it seems more personal here."

"It is personal."

"How so?" I asked, my curiosity piqued.

"I might tell you about that someday, but for now, let's just . . ."

There was an awkward silence.

"You seem to be friends with Jean Wilkerson," I said.

"Yeah, Jean and I have known each other for quite a while."

"What's with her, anyway? She really went after Mr. Nicholson on my first day here."

"Yeah, that's Jean alright." Sarah sounded relieved to change the subject. "She's a true believer. She's been working on me to become 'born again' for years."

"How's she doing with that?" I laughed.

"Not you too?" Sarah moaned.

"No! No way. My family went to church until Nathan died, and then we stopped for a while. I'm not really into it. I guess my family's going back to church tomorrow. We're going to my Grandfather's church, Wheaton Community Church. Know anything about it?"

"Yeah," Sarah said as she stood up and ushered me to the door. "It's the biggest church in town. You can say hello to Jean for me. The Wilkersons go to church there."

"I think I'll pass."

"She isn't bad. She's a lot more authentic than some of the fakers at Wheaton High," Sarah said as she turned off the lights and walked out into the yard.

Sarah was the least fake person I'd met. She probably knew what she was talking about. I crawled into the Beast and had a little trouble starting it. When it finally roared to life, I looked around, but Sarah was gone, so I headed for home.

Chapter 10

Sunday

"The school principal, Kathryn Longfeather, and her family are members," Gramps said as he drove us to church. "And the chairman of the Co-op Board, Chuck Wilkerson. The Wilkersons are nice folks. Susan's the assistant cook at school, and Jean's the captain of the girls' basketball team. You've probably met her at school, Josh. I think she's about your age."

"Yeah. She's a year older but she's in my physics class," I said.

"Oh, and like I said, the science teacher, Fredrick Nicholson, goes to our church too."

After we parked, Dad and Mom walked ahead holding hands.

The first person I saw as I entered was Jean Wilkerson. She was the towering shepherdess for a dozen tiny children in the church nursery. Smiling, she waved, and then went back to attaching name tags to her charges.

"Hi, Josh," a friendly voice called out as we made our way through the reception area. I looked around until I caught sight of Mr. Nicholson helping his sons into their jackets. "It's good to see you," he said coming up to us.

"This is Mr. Nicholson, my science teacher and one of my basketball coaches," I said.

"Ben Cooper, Mr. Nicholson. I'm pleased to meet you," Dad said, shaking his hand. "And this is my wife, Rachel."

"Call me Fred. Are you folks thinking of coming to church here?"

"These are my kids, Fred," Gramps said, reappearing with a cup of coffee.

"Oh of course, Harlan. I hadn't made the connection yet." Mr. Nicholson gestured to me and said, "Now I remember. Josh is your grandson."

"Yep! I couldn't be prouder to have another Rocket in the family."

"Well, we're sure glad he's here. Josh, I hope you'll consider joining the high school youth group," Mr. Nicholson said as he started to move his children toward the exit. "We meet on Wednesday nights after practice." I smiled and waved as Mr. Nicholson disappeared into the press of churchgoers.

"That sounds fun," Mom said.

"Yeah." I wasn't feeling enthusiastic.

"You should go," Dad said. "Make some more friends."

I shrugged and they didn't push it any farther.

"Hezekiah!" Pastor Andrew Cornelius Carter called out loudly, starting his sermon. I looked up from the program I'd been doodling on. All five foot seven inches of the prematurely bald, slightly overweight clergyman radiated energy. "Hezekiah was a good king." Pastor Andrew paced back and forth, carrying his Bible in one hand and gesturing with the other. "He called Judah back to the Lord. You see, the people of Judah had been practicing idolatry, even worshipping the bronze snake that Moses made. They had taken an instrument of God's grace and had treated it like it was a god itself."

I took out the pew Bible in front of me and opened it to the place in Kings that the bulletin said was the text for the day.

Mom smiled at me as I opened the Bible.

I read past the text. "He rebelled against the king of Assyria, and did not serve him."

My hands trembled, the leaves of the Bible shivering as I held it. I couldn't bring myself to read any further.

When worship ended Gramps took Mom by the arm and said, "Ben, Rachel, I want to introduce you to Chuck Wilkerson. You really should get to know the chairman of the Farmer's Co-op Board."

I watched as Gramps led my parents to a tall man with dark hair, graying at the temples, and a stout woman standing at his side. As my parents settled into a chatting mode, I sat down to wait. I considered opening one of the pew Bibles again. Had I heard about Hezekiah before?

In Sunday school? In church? I had a long time to wonder—Mom and Dad were deep in conversation with the Wilkersons.

***

"Josh, about Sarah . . ." Mom ventured as the big SUV turned off the blacktop onto the county gravel.

"Yeah?"

"Susan Wilkerson seems to think that Sarah may not be a very good influence."

"That's not true!"

"How do you know, Son?" Dad put in. "You haven't been here long enough to know."

"But I'm positive about Sarah," I dug in. "All you have to do is talk to her and you know she's not like that."

"I have to say that I'm with Josh on this," Gramps put in. "I knew her grandparents well. They were decent, upstanding folk. I know Paul has been through a tough time but isn't Josh a pretty good judge of character?"

"I suppose we shouldn't jump to conclusions based on town gossip," Mom conceded. "But it looks like you'll be spending a lot of time with Sarah, Josh. I think we should get to know her better." Looking at Gramps she said, "Dad, would you be willing to invite the Dirks for dinner tonight?"

"Yeah, I could do that. I promised Paul's father that I'd keep an eye on him."

***

"Thank you for inviting me for dinner," Sarah said after Gramps had taken her coat. "I'm sorry my dad couldn't make it, but he's out on the road. Still, it's fun to get a nice meal. We mostly just open cans at home."

Sarah looked great in boots, jeans, and a western blouse. Obviously she wanted to impress my folks. But I was afraid to meet Sarah's eyes as Mom led her into the dining room. The whole thing felt like a setup to me, and Sarah was the main dish at this meal.

Sarah seemed to know the common table prayer our family always used. She was graceful and friendly as the family passed the pot roast, potatoes, and gravy around the table. I caught her eyeing me when I stole a glance in her direction. I shrugged involuntarily and she smiled. Maybe she knew what was up.

"Where did you get your boots, Sarah?" my mom asked. "I'm thinking about getting a pair like that."

"Haegle's Western Wear in Sioux Falls," Sarah answered. "When we had horses, we used to go there a lot. They sell tack too. Now I only buy boots there." Her face saddened.

"Did Joshua tell you that we are planning to get a couple of horses to help us with the cattle?"

"No, but that sounds like a good idea." Her mood recovered quickly.

"You should come over and take them out for a ride," Gramps said. "Sarah used to be a good little rider when she was younger. Her grandpa and I watched her compete as a sub-junior in the rodeo at Huron. You did pretty well, Sarah."

Sarah nodded.

"Well, maybe she could teach us a thing or two about horses," Dad said. "For heaven's sake, I know I'm going to be lost trying to get on one of those four-legged monstrosities."

"What did you do before you came to Wheaton?" Sarah asked.

"I was a banker."

"Not just a banker," I added. "He was a vice president at the big bank downtown."

"That sounds important," Sarah said, impressed.

"It was a good living," Dad said with evident pride. "But we're determined to make a new life here in South Dakota. It's kind of like early retirement, except that I'm working harder than I ever did."

"What did you do in Portland, Mrs. Cooper?" Sarah asked.

"Call me Rachel, honey," my mom said. "I owned a marketing firm. We specialized in helping small businesses get started. It was a small company and there were only five of us on the team. The other four bought me out when I left."

"Do you miss it . . . Rachel?" You could tell that Sarah was uncomfortable calling Mom by her first name.

"Yeah, sometimes." Mom almost seemed surprised by her admission. "But I love coming home to this farm. I have it in my blood. Ben and I needed a break from Portland, and Dad needs our help here."

"That I do," Gramps said with a laugh.

"Tell us a little about yourself, Sarah," Dad said. "I hear you're a fine basketball player."

"Yeah, lots of people know that about me," Sarah grinned. "But I love the outdoors more than anything. I taught myself to bow hunt at twelve. The venison I get and the results of my fishing are our main source of meat. I also run a trap line in the winter to earn money for college."

"That's unusual for a young lady," Dad said.

Sarah laughed. "Yeah, I don't spend much time with Miss Manners or going to slumber parties with my girlfriends."

"Your grandma was like that. She always went hunting with Elias." Gramps said.

"That's about it for me," Sarah said, a steely glint in her eyes. "Basketball and hunting. I don't have a lot of friends and I don't drink, smoke, or do drugs. Or anything else you might have heard about."

There was shocked silence around the table. My parents blushed, obviously feeling ashamed. But Sarah smiled at us all without a trace of anger.

"Jean?" I asked.

"Yep," Sarah replied with a grin. "Jean called and let me know that her mom had been passing on the town gossip about me to you folks. I just thought I should set the record straight."

Gramps burst out laughing. When he finally regained control, he said, "Set the record straight!" Then he had another fit of laughter. "You're a chip off the old block."

"Oh, Sarah," Mom said, embarrassed. She reached over and laid her hand gently on Sarah's forearm. "Please forgive us for listening to gossip. Yes, we were kind of checking you out."

"Of course, Mrs. er, Rachel," Sarah said, putting her other hand over Mom's in a gentle gesture. "I understand how you folks feel." She looked straight at Dad, who was sitting stock-still. "I've found it's best to just come straight at it. That seems like the right way to make problems go away."

"You'll make a good business person someday," Dad finally said. "That kind of direct communication helps to get things done."

"I'll say!" Mom agreed. "Sarah, we're glad you're our neighbor and friend. I was feeling that way even before you told us . . ." she paused, ". . . told us what you told us."

Dinner finished with some small talk of little consequence. Dad pretty much thawed out and Mom's apple pie, along with a generous dollop of vanilla ice cream, made a delightful ending to the meal.

I got Sarah's coat and walked her to her truck.

"Say! This is a really cool truck," I said, running my hand over the rear fender of the 1972 Dodge D100 pickup Sarah had parked in our driveway. It still had its original orange paint with cream accents. "Don't you have trouble keeping this old bugger running?"

"I've spent many hours under the hood fixing stuff. But I think it's worth it. You probably understand, judging by that dinosaur I've seen you driving around."

"Yeah," I said. "My Gramps is the one who keeps that running. But he's teaching me some stuff. He says it's always good to know which end of the wrench to stick on the twisty thing."

We both laughed and as she drove away I decided that the ordeal had gone pretty well.

However when I got back inside, Dad was waiting for me at the door. He beckoned me into the living room, leaving Mom and Gramps clattering away, cleaning up after dinner.

I sat down on the couch and Dad slowly paced the length of the room.

"Josh," he said after a while, "I want to talk this through with you."

"Okay."

"I know you've had female friends before, but that was when you were running with Nathan's group."

"Yeah."

"This situation with the Dirk girl is different."

"How so?"

Dad paced the length of the room again before he answered. "She's a loner and has some odd proclivities for a girl. From what Mrs. Wilkerson said she isn't very popular." He held up a hand to forestall my outburst. "I know her reputation probably isn't deserved, but there might be a kernel of truth there, Son."

"Dad, she's not that way! Honest!"

Dad looked at me for a long moment. "I'm not telling you to stay away from her, Josh. I just want you to be careful, okay?"

I gritted my teeth. "Okay."

Chapter 11

Jerusalem

I woke to the smell of fresh straw and slightly smoky air. Evidently the brazier had gone out—it was cold. I wrapped the coarse wool coverlet around my shoulders and sat up on the edge of my bed. It was odd that something so foreign felt familiar. I was back in Jerusalem.

As my eyes adjusted, I could just make out the archway that led out of my bedchamber. I stood and carefully stepped across the rough stone floor, putting my hand out until I came to the opening, then I felt my way out into the hall. I'd never been here by myself before, but I thought Nathan's room was close to mine.

Working my way by touch, I proceeded down the hall. I came to another opening, much like the archway into my chamber. The brazier burning in the center of this chamber gave off just enough light for me to make out the dim outline of a bed on the far wall. In a tangle of bedding, I thought I saw a figure.

"Nathan," I called out softly. "Nathan, is that you?"

The figure on the bed stirred.

"Nathan, it's Joshua."

"Joshua?" It was Nathan's voice.

I crossed the room and sat down on the edge of the bed. I said, "Nathan, it's me, Joshua."

"Joshua," Nathan moaned. "What are you doing awake? It's the middle of the night. Go back to bed."

I sat there for a minute, thinking. "Nathan, how do you understand history?"

"Why are you tormenting me?" Nathan moaned.

"Just humor me, Nathan."

"History is about past events. Things that happened years ago. I'm an apprentice scribe. I've copied lots and lots of documents about past events, like things that happened in the time of King David."

I took a deep breath. "What if you could go back and live in the time of one of those documents? What if you could go back and experience life under King David?"

"You can't do that, Joshua. God has ordained time to only move forward."

"But what if somehow God wanted to send you back to the time of King David? Could he do it?" I asked.

"Everything bends to God's will, but why are we talking about this now? Let me go back to sleep."

I crossed my arms and took a deep breath. "Well, for some reason that I don't understand, I have come back in time."

Nathan barked a laugh. "You can't be serious!"

I said nothing.

"Are you serious?"

"Yes," I said firmly.

"But that can't be. You're Joshua. Joshua, my brother. You look like Joshua, sound like Joshua, and you are even annoying like Joshua. How can you be from the future?"

"I didn't say I understood," I said. "In the future I have a family just like your family here. My dad's name is Benjamin. My mother's name is Rachel. They look and act just like your parents. And I had a brother named Nathan . . ." Then I choked up, unable to continue, my eyes burning.

The silence stretched to where I thought Nathan had gone back to sleep.

"Joshua," Nathan growled, rolling up on his elbow. "That's not funny. Quit trying to trick me. Go back to bed!" Nathan twisted angrily and buried himself in his covers.

I sat there in silence wondering what to do.

After a few minutes Nathan emerged and said, "Are you still here?"

"Yeah."

"Come on, Joshua. Why won't you go back to bed?"

"Because I'm not sure I can find the way. What did you mean when you told me to quit trying to trick you?" I asked.

Nathan was silent again for nearly a whole minute. Then he said, "Okay, you got me. Light a lamp so we can talk."

"I don't know how to do that."

Nathan sighed. "At least you're consistent." Throwing back his covers, he got out of bed and walked to the brazier. Taking a set of tongs hanging on the side, he picked up a lump of coal and blew on it. Then he walked to a lamp set on a little shelf in the wall and lit it. He brought the light back, sitting down and placing it between us.

"You take pleasure in tormenting me," he said. "I'm up now. Are you happy?"

"The Nathan from my family in the future died two years ago," I said flatly.

"You're utterly crazy!" Nathan exclaimed, throwing his arms up into the air. "I'm right here. I'm alive, not dead. I probably saved your life a couple of weeks ago."

"I remember that. I woke up under a pile of rocks. I remember being dug out."

Nathan's face grew serious. "What did I tell you Dad was doing when we brought you back from the tunnel?"

"You told me that he was down at the treasury helping to pack up a tribute for what's-his-name."

"Sennacherib," Nathan answered. "And what did you ask Sarah when she came in to change the lamp oil?"

"Uh . . ." embarrassed all over again, I said, "I asked her if she played basketball."

Nathan was silent for a long time just staring at me. Finally he said slowly, "The morning after the cave in, we had a long talk, you and me, or my Joshua. This is confusing. Anyway, I asked about . . . basketball. The question you asked

Sarah. He didn't remember it and he didn't remember being dug out or coming home."

"I was here in Jerusalem during the cave in. And not again until now," I said.

"How do I know that you're not an evil spirit?" Nathan asked. He looked afraid.

I stopped to think. Was I an evil spirit?

"What are evil spirits like?" I asked.

"Normally people writhe on the floor and foam at the mouth."

We both stopped and waited. I did not fall on the floor and start foaming at the mouth. "I'm from a different time. We use light switches and electric lights, not these goofy oil lamps. I drive a car. I don't walk clear across the city." I examined the perplexed look on his face. "Oh, it's hopeless! You don't even understand the words I'm saying. I'm going back to bed. Maybe I can wake up again in my own time."

"Wait. Wait!" Nathan caught my wrist and pulled me back down beside him. He lifted the lamp to examine my face. "You are exactly like my Joshua down to that funny little fuzz you like to call a beard, but you're different too. Different in a way that is hard to describe."

"So do you believe that I'm Joshua from the future?" I asked.

"For now, I'm going along with it," Nathan said.

"That's something," I replied.

"If you're from the future, tell me about it. I want to know everything," Nathan said eagerly.

"Uh, I don't think I should do that. All the movies and books about time travel say that you can mess up the space-time continuum by sharing information from the future."

"Really? I have no idea what you just said, but it sounds bad."

"I don't know for sure. I've never traveled in time before. I'm not even sure this is time travel. I just go to sleep in South Dakota and wake up in Bible times," I said.

"Bible times? What are Bible times?" Nathan asked.

"Well, you know, the Holy Bible. The book that tells about God's people."

"I'm still not understanding, Joshua," Nathan said. "I know about God's people. That's who we are. Jerusalem is the capital of our nation, Judah. Back in King David's time there were the twelve tribes of Israel. But Assyria destroyed Israel about twenty years ago, just before I was born. Now there are only two tribes left. But I've never heard of a book called the Holy Bible."

"Well, the Bible tells all about King David. You must have books about him."

"We do. I was just copying a scroll yesterday about David's fight against a Philistine named Goliath. It's from a group of scrolls about Samuel the Prophet. They have many stories about David's life."

"So, you don't have a book called the Bible?" I asked.

"No, and I should know because I'm an apprentice scribe," Nathan said.

"You said that last time I was here. What does it mean to be an apprentice scribe?"

"It means I'm training to be a royal scribe as a member of the Royal Scriptorium. We record all of the king's business and do his correspondence with other nations."

"Wow! That sounds important," I said.

"I just had an odd thought. If what you say is true, then you don't know much about our family."

"Yeah, like nothing."

"For instance, Father is already a royal scribe. He works directly for the king managing Judah's spies. He gathers critical information about Assyria and other countries," Nathan said.

"Really? I heard Eli talking about his work but didn't realize how important it was."

"Yes, and you, I mean, my Joshua is trained in reading and writing. He'll probably be a scribe too."

"It sounds like it runs in your family," I observed.

"Yes, service to the temple and the king is the central work of the Levites. That's our tribe. We're Levites. Have you ever heard of Levites before?"

"Yes, in the Bible," I said.

"Hmmm, that Bible thing again. Maybe that's why you're not supposed to share stuff from the future. It's too confusing. We probably should go ahead and get ready for the day. I don't think we're going to get any more sleep."

Nathan taught me how to work the lamps, put on my clothes, and find my way around their apartment. We lived in a large building that housed the royal scribes, their families, and servants. Our apartment, with its private courtyard, was especially nice because our father had an essential position in the king's court.

"I don't think we should tell Mom and Dad about you being from the future," Nathan said as we headed for breakfast.

"You're probably right," I agreed.

***

Our breakfast was simple. Dried dates and nuts topped a small bowl of grain that had been softened by boiling. Eli had the food on the low table in the courtyard for us. While I was trying to figure out how to lie down to eat, Mother came out into the courtyard.

"Mother, where's Father?" Nathan asked.

"One of his scouts came back with important news. He's gone to the palace."

Just then, Sarah came into the courtyard. She kissed her father on the cheek as she sat down beside him. "Good morning, Sarah. Glad to see you could make it out of bed before noon," Nathan said in a teasing tone.

She gave him a haughty look and then said, "Whoever blesses his neighbor with a loud voice, rising early in the morning, will be counted as cursing."

"Okay, you got me with that one. How do you remember so many of King Solomon's proverbs? Sometimes I have to copy them for whole days straight, but I can never remember them well enough to use them like that."

"Father is a good teacher," Sarah said, her smile waking the beauty in her face.

Eli just grinned.

"Sarah, normally I would want you to help Eli and I with the laundry, but I need someone to go get our allotment from the temple," Mother said.

"Joshua and I could do that," Nathan said.

Mother eyed him carefully. "That would be good, but don't you have to work at the Scriptorium today?"

"Master Joah expects to receive a lot of correspondence tomorrow when the traders come into the city. He won't need me until then."

"All right, but bring your dirty clothes down to the storage room before you go."

***

"This will give me a chance to show you Jerusalem," Nathan said as we emerged from the apartment building onto the street. "I suppose you really haven't seen it yet,"

"Uh, no." I gawked as I slowly turned in a circle.

"Well, come on then! Let's take a look."

We walked under a stone archway out onto a flagstone terrace. The air felt dry and cool. I quickly understood why we had added robes over our tunics. I'd have been cold without a robe. There was a low stone wall around the edge of the terrace, broken only by access to a steep stairway leading down. It wasn't very light yet. I stopped just before descending the stairs and looked back at the building. It was two stories of dressed stone squared off to a flat top. As we reached the bottom of the steps, we followed a narrow pathway between the buildings out onto a street. Looking uphill, I was amazed at how steep the road was. We were about halfway down from the top of the residential area.

Noticing where I was staring, Nathan said, "That's the way to the upper city and mount Zion."

He turned to stride confidently over the stones that sometimes made the roadway surface unpredictable. The traffic increased as we went downhill, mostly women carrying water jars and laborers headed for work. Nathan explained that the farmers were long gone so they could start their work in the fields outside the city walls at dawn.

As we reached the bottom of the V-shaped valley we came to a pool of water where a lot of people were gathered. It took a minute to comprehend what they were doing. Some had come to get water and were filling their jars. But two groups of men were working on the stone walls.

"They're lining the sides and bottom of the pool with stones to keep the water clean," Nathan explained. Then he asked, "Don't you recognize it Joshua? This is the pool created by the water tunnel we were digging. Shortly after the cave in, the two teams that were working from opposites sides of the tunnel met up. It has been flowing ever since. Sarah says it's a lot easier to get water now. You still don't remember the cave in?"

"No," I said. "Not at all."

Nathan shook his head with concern.

Soon we came to a massive stone wall about twenty feet tall. We went through a gate that opened into a small court-yard. An even more enormous wall, rising to our right, looked newer. I could see workers on the top.

"What are they doing up there?" I asked.

"That's the wall King Hezekiah is building around our part of the city. He started it several years back. We're rushing to finish before the Assyrians come. We'll be helping with that project, too, now that we finished the water tunnel."

"Do you think the Assyrians will come?" I asked.

"Father seems sure of it," Nathan said with conviction.

Ahead of us was another gate on the other side of the courtyard. The wall was slightly taller and a guard tower rose to a height of about sixty feet beside it. As I looked along the wall, I could see similar guard towers rising at intervals along the wall. I stepped up to the gate and looked out into a steep valley that plummeted away from the fortress walls. It was a long way down. Suddenly the memory from the water tower in Portland, with the ground calling to me, loomed in my mind. But in this odd dream, life seemed too powerful to let go.

"That's the Kidron Valley," Nathan volunteered. "Its steep sides are an important part of the city's defense."

"It's like they built the whole city on top of a mountain," I said.

"That's right. They did." After walking a little farther he

said, "What do you think of Sarah? I suppose you've never met anyone like her before."

I froze for a moment and then had to take a quick step to catch up. "What do you mean?" I said, stalling for time.

"I mean, don't you think she's beautiful?"

I hadn't thought about Sarah that way before, but Nathan was right. "Yeah, I guess so."

Stopping, Nathan reached out turning me to face him. "Okay, now I'm really starting to believe what you say about being from the future. My Joshua would have never said that."

"What do you mean?"

"All three of us grew up together—you, I mean my Joshua, Sarah, and I. Whenever I start talking about how I feel about Sarah I get a lecture about how she's like a sister to us. My Joshua doesn't want me to think about Sarah as a beautiful woman."

"Really?"

In a hushed voice Nathan continued, "I'm going to tell you something I've never told anyone."

I nodded.

"I'm going to see if Sarah and I can become betrothed."

"Does that mean married?" I asked, a little shocked.

"Not exactly. It means promised to each other for marriage."

"Aren't you a little young for that?"

"No. Many men my age are married or betrothed. People my age have children." Nathan grinned and slapped me on the shoulder. "Can you imagine how wonderful it would be to have Sarah as my wife?"

I stared at him speechlessly.

"Come on. We've got to keep moving if we're going to get to the temple before it gets too warm."

Next we came to a steep uphill section of the road. Here the streets were wide and the buildings were huge. Extensive terraces and tall colonnades made them look like monuments.

"Those are tombs for the House of David," Nathan said, pointing to his right as we walked along. "Many of the king's ancestors are buried there."

We went through another gate and emerged onto an open rocky area. It was a steep ridge of exposed bedrock connecting two parts of the city. There were only occasional buildings in this area. The well-used path narrowed as we approached the highest point.

Pointing to what seemed the summit up ahead, I said, "That looks like a flattened mountain top."

"That's what it is," Nathan responded as we made our way up steps cut into the rock. "We call it the Temple Mount. It's also called Mount Moriah."

"What's that?" I exclaimed as a set of giant ornate buildings came into view through a gate at the top of the hill.

"That's the royal palace where King Hezekiah lives," Nathan said. "We're not going there. We're going this way." He turned to the right and took a path at the base of the tall stone wall. Soon we turned left again, going between two massive ramparts that fortified the hilltop. We slowed as we came to a gate in the wall on our left. There, a pair of guards seemed to recognize us and let us enter the gate. Going through, we came into a large courtyard, half-filled with clusters of people. Each group had livestock with them, like bulls, sheep, goats, or cages of doves.

Nathan headed for a set of wooden tables arranged along the base of the wall. As we approached, I saw that the tables held cuts of butchered meat. Nathan went up to one of the attendants and said, "The household of Benjamin, son of Beniah, Levite and servant of the king."

"You may select your daily allotment," the attendant responded, gesturing to the table.

Nathan looked over the table and selected what looked like a large roast. He put it into a cloth bag that hung at his side along with a couple of smaller cuts of meat.

I shifted my position to see where the people with animals were going. The orderly procession led through a gateway into a vast courtyard where I saw a large building that rose nearly twenty stories high. The ornate structure had a massive front entrance flanked by gigantic bronze pillars shaped into stylized palm trees. In front of this enormous temple, in the center of the courtyard, stood a tall stone structure. It was an altar, I guessed, on a raised stone platform. A small bonfire roared on the altar attended by a priest in ritual trappings.

"What is going on in there?" I asked Nathan.

"The priests are performing sacrifice," he answered.

I drifted toward the opening to get a better look at what was causing the din emanating from the doorway. As the scene through the inner door came into view, I saw a priest dressed in a long white gown covered in blood plunge a long knife into a struggling lamb he held bound on the altar in front of him. The blood ran freely down the sides of the altar as the priest, with quick slashes, continued to butcher the creature. I was shocked. The whole place was a giant slaughterhouse. Priests were killing animals everywhere. Blood ran on the stones of the inner courtyard. I must have cried out because Nathan was suddenly at my side helping me to a shady spot near the wall, where I sat down with a thump, my head swimming. I leaned over to lie on the ground, and then darkness came.

Chapter 12

Youth Group

The image of a courtyard covered in blood faded in Monday morning's sunlight. I still felt queasy as I opened my eyes and then jerked awake, thinking I must have slept past my alarm for basketball practice. I was relieved to realize that this was the boys' week for practice after school. Still, I needed to get going or I'd be late.

The first couple of days that week were pretty ordinary. I was disappointed with my play at basketball practice, but Tuesday evening I had another lesson with Sarah after supper.

"On defense, always stay between your man and the basket. Hold one hand up in your opponent's face to distract him." Sarah crouched in a defensive stance in front of me. "Then come from below with the other hand to steal the ball. Now you try it."

I traded places with her.

She dribbled to the left. I moved to stay between her and

the basket and balanced with my right hand up in front of her face.

"That's it, Josh," Sarah encouraged. "Now watch for your chance to steal."

As she picked up the ball from her dribble, she pivoted and brought the ball in front of her body, preparing for a shot.

I snapped my left hand from below the way Sarah had taught me, punching the ball upward. It popped free and I grabbed it with my right hand.

"That's it!" Sarah crowed. "That's exactly right. You are really improving. You're going to be ready for your first game."

***

"Let's see what you've got, city boy," Marshal said under his breath at our scrimmage on Wednesday after school. He faked to his left and drove right.

I shuffled back in my defensive stance, keeping between him and the basket.

Seeing that I had him cut off, Marshal picked up the ball and crouched for a shot. As he brought the ball up, I stepped in and snapped my hand under the ball. It popped free. Grabbing it, I made a quick pass out to Sean at mid-court. He relayed to Eddie, who raced toward our basket for an easy layup and two points for the JV.

"He fouled me!" Marshal shouted.

Coach blew his whistle. "Sorry, Marshal. That was a clean

steal. You need to make more passes instead of trying to force the shot."

Marshal growled his disapproval and silently mouthed an obscenity at me on the way back up the court.

***

"Hey, Cooper, where'd you learn to steal like that?" Eddie said as he, Sean, and I stood at our lockers after practice.

"What I liked was the look on Marshal's face when you caught him flat-footed," Sean said, leaning on his locker.

"That was cool too," Eddie said. "Hey, Sean, I'm sorry about tonight. Mom needs me to watch my little brother and sister."

"Yeah, I understand." Sean's disappointment was evident.

"Maybe you could get Josh here to go as your wingman this week," Eddie said with a laugh.

"What's that?" I asked.

"Eddie . . ." Sean looked a warning at Eddie to no effect.

"Sean developed a sudden spiritual interest in going to church youth group," Eddie said with a mischievous twinkle in his eye.

"Eddie . . ." Sean tried again.

"A spiritual interest?" I asked.

"Yeah. Her name is Ellen." Eddie laughed.

"Come on, Eddie." Sean's galaxy of freckles disappeared into his blush.

"How about it, Josh? Would you help this poor Romeo out

and go to youth group in my place?" Eddie asked me. He was still joking around, but the request was genuine.

Sean groaned, but his glance in my direction looked hopeful.

"What youth group is this and when is it happening?"

"It's over at Wheaton Community Church tonight and they serve dinner, so you can go right on over now," Eddie said.

"Okay," I said. "It wouldn't hurt me to go to youth group, I guess, if you think it will be okay, Sean."

The look of pleasure on Sean's face was reward enough for the decision. "Sure," he said. "That would be great, Josh. Do you know where to go?"

"Yeah, I can get to the church okay, but if you wait at the door I could use some help getting to the right place inside."

"Sure thing." Sean slid his backpack over his shoulder and strode off on his long legs.

Eddie slapped my shoulder and said, "Thanks man." Then he scurried off after Sean.

On my way to the Beast I fished my phone out of my pocket and let Mom know what I was up to.

"That sounds great, Josh!" she said enthusiastically.

"Yeah, sure," I said. "Bye, Mom."

On the way, I drove past the Cenex and saw my Honda sitting out back. The insurance company had called and said it was totaled. Gramps said that I could keep driving the Beast as long as I needed it. I loved driving that old pickup, and Mom's face lit up when we decided to use the insurance money to buy her horses.

"Hey, Josh, Sean," Fred Nicholson called out as we stepped into the church's gathering room. "Come on over here." He was standing in front of a long counter loaded with sloppy joes, chips, fruit, and brownies. "Help yourself. There's plenty, so take two or three sandwiches to get started."

"Thanks!" I said, wasting no time following Sean's example by heaping my paper plate to capacity. Then we went over to a table where a group of students were already eating.

"Hi, Josh," Jean Wilkerson said. "Are you going to join our youth group?"

"Uh," I said, not quite sure how to respond.

"Come on, Jean, give the guy a chance before you pressure him," said Ellen Longfeather. She sat across from Jean. She was tall with long dark hair.

"Once he figures out what a religious nut you are, Jean, he'll probably run the other way," Sean said.

I tensed, but the whole table erupted in laughter.

"If I'm a religious nut, then you're a heathen and a heretic, Sean Johnson!" Jean shot back. I laughed along with everyone else this time around.

***

After dinner, we filed through a door and down a hall to a room with garishly painted walls, old couches, and lounge chairs. Pastor Andrew started the meeting with prayer and then said, "Tonight's Bible study is about faith in a scientific age. Fred Nicholson has agreed to help us with this subject from his perspective as a science teacher. Thank you, Fred. Is there anything you want to say as we get started?"

"I just want to thank you for this opportunity, Pastor Andrew. When I teach science in school, I can't discuss the religious implications of our science curriculum. I know that's a problem for some students, so I'm delighted to be able to talk about things freely."

"Thanks, Fred," Pastor Andrew said. "Tonight we are going to start at the beginning and look at how the Bible presents creation. Can I get a couple of volunteers to read the first chapter of Genesis?"

I wasn't surprised when Jean Wilkerson stepped up quickly, but was caught off-guard when Sean volunteered. Then I saw the impressed look on Ellen's face and it made sense.

"Now, take turns reading what happened on each day of creation, starting with Jean," Pastor instructed. "Then, when we get to the parts that read 'And there was evening, and there was morning,' I want everyone to join in."

It was odd but I heard the Biblical account of creation differently because it was done that way. It was more like a song than a story.

"I have a question," Jean said as the reading finished.

"Go ahead, Jean," Pastor said, looking pleased.

"The Bible clearly says that God created the world in six days. Why does science teach that it took billions of years for the universe to come into being?"

"That's a good question, Jean," Pastor Andrew said. "Lots

of people approach the Bible's first story of creation that way. However, that understanding forces Scripture to answer a specific scientific question. I am certain the Bible shouldn't serve that purpose. I'm worried that it will get in the way of what the Bible is really trying to do."

"What do you mean?" Jean sounded a little irritated.

"Well, did you notice anything when we read the first chapter of Genesis the way we did?"

Silence met his question, but he waited, giving the group time to think.

Finally, Sean responded. "It had a pattern. That's why we could read it together that way."

"Yes, that's it exactly," Pastor said, getting excited. "It's a pattern like a song. Each verse takes one of the days of the week to talk about God's activity in creation. The six days organize the creation hymn in a way that is familiar to us—a weekly cycle. It's not a helpful interpretation to think that the six days, as twenty-four hour periods, tell us how long God took to make the universe."

"Shouldn't we believe what the Bible says?" Jean said.

"Oh, absolutely, we should," Pastor answered. "But the Bible is a compilation of all different kinds of literature. To believe what it says, we also need to consider what it means by the way it says it. In the case of the first chapter of Genesis, the Bible is telling us that God is the one who created the world. Furthermore, it is telling us that the reason he made it was to do something good. The six days are a literary device meant to connect creation to our daily existence. It also helps to establish a reason for the seventh day of rest."

"But how can we be sure that the Bible is not saying that God made creation in six days?" Jean persisted.

"We're sure of the poetic nature of chapter one because the second chapter of Genesis retells the creation account in an entirely different way. It tells a story — a story about Adam and Eve. Its purpose is to help us understand the origin of evil in the world. The details between the Bible's two stories of creation are quite different. If we use these two stories to explain creation scientifically, then we force the Bible to contradict itself. A much better way to understand them is to see that together they help us learn that God made creation and why he did it."

"I'd like to add something, Pastor," Mr. Nicholson said.

"Go ahead, Fred."

"I believe that Pastor's right about the poetic nature of the first story of creation," Mr. Nicholson said as he shifted into lecture mode. "However, the way the Bible sets up the six days produces a scientifically accurate account not understood before the formulation of the current Big Bang hypothesis. Can anyone guess what I'm going to say?"

After an extended pause, Mr. Nicholson went on. "On which day did God create light?"

"The first day," Ellen said.

"That's right. Light was the first thing God created. But before Big Bang cosmology, science understood that light came from the sun and stars. So, according to Genesis one, when did God create them?"

We all bent over our Bibles, scanning the text.

"The fourth day?" Jean said uncertainly.

"Yes. How could you have light for three entire days without sun and stars?" Mr. Nicholson said, lifting his voice a bit theatrically. He waited, building suspense. "Doesn't that look like an error in Scripture? However, the Big Bang completely exonerates the Bible's ordering of events. In the Big Bang, light simply existed for a long time as random particles before the formation of solar systems. I like to say that the Bible understood the truth of the Big Bang thousands of years before science caught on."

After the Bible study, Mr. Nicholson led us in a group game where we ran around the church in the dark. The evening finished with Pastor Andrew leading a couple of songs with his guitar and closing with prayer. The pastor asked God to keep the basketball teams safe when they traveled and help them play well. I wondered about that. If there was a God, would he really care how I played basketball?

***

"Thanks man, I owe you," Sean said as we stood in the church entrance.

"Sure thing, Sean."

Jean emerged with Ellen in tow. "Sean," she said, "I was supposed to take Ellen home, but I've got to go back to school for something. Would you mind taking her? She's right on your way."

Sean's glance at me was unreadable, and I nodded encouragingly.

Then, grinning, Sean said, "Well then, milady, let me escort you to my chariot."

Ellen gave a little laugh as she followed Sean to his car.

"Do you really have something to get at school?" I asked Jean.

"No." She laughed. "Sometimes they just need a little push. Were you Eddie's substitute tonight?"

"Yeah." I smiled sheepishly.

"Well, good work. How's it going with your basketball lessons?"

"Not bad. Sarah is a great teacher, and she sure knows a lot about basketball."

Jean looked at me for a moment and then said, "That's true. So why is it going only 'not bad'?"

"Well, I'm not very good. Sarah has an uphill battle to make anything out of me."

"That's not what she says. She thinks you have natural talent and that you learn fast." Jean folded her arms and leaned against the wall.

"Really?"

"Yeah, and for some reason she's been a lot more pleasant to be around since you started taking lessons."

I decided not to follow that up. After a moment I asked, "What's the deal between her and Marshal?"

"Sarah's pretty tight-lipped about that. But it started about a couple years back when we were sophomores. And incidentally, there's not a shred of truth in what they say about her."

"Yeah, I figured that out."

"I'm pretty sure that Melanie is behind all of that. I wish I could prove it. I'd love to see Melanie get what she deserves."

"That makes two of us," I agreed.

Jean uncrossed her arms and took a step away from the wall. "Well, I'm glad you came tonight. I hope you come back."

"Maybe I will." I smiled.

Smiling back, she stepped out into the parking lot with a wave.

I watched her fish her keys out of her backpack. With a start I realized I had to go home too.

Chapter 13

Cow Ponies

The rest of the week went by in a blur. I stayed up too late Friday night playing video games, so I was deep into bliss-filled oblivion when I heard Dad call up the stairs, "Josh, Josh, did you want to go with us?"

I wondered what he meant until my mind cleared, and I remembered today's horse buying trip. "Sure, Dad," I called out. "I'll be right there." I frantically rummaged for clothes, pulling them on at a run. I burst into the kitchen, surprising the three adults drinking coffee at the table.

"Whoa, Josh! That was fast!" Dad said, setting his cup down.

"I was worried that I was holding you up," I said breathlessly.

"Goodness, no," Gramps said. "We still have to hitch up the trailer. Speaking of which, shall we get to it, Ben?"

"Sounds like a plan, Harlan," Dad said, picking up his breakfast dishes and taking them to the sink.

"You've got time for breakfast, Josh," Mom said, "and to run a comb through your hair."

***

Before long I was in the spacious rear seat of Mom's truck. I stared out the back window across the pickup bed at the horse trailer, as we sped down the open highway. Its white and green paint was faded and there were more than a few rust spots, evidence of its years behind the barn.

"It may not look like much, but it's roadworthy," Gramps said from the other side of the back seat. "I put brand new tires on it last week and had the bearings repacked. We got that trailer for your mom's first horse when she was in third grade. It's nearly as old as she is."

"Yeah, it kind of looks like it," I said.

"Hey, watch it, buster. I heard that!" Mom growled from the driver's seat. But Dad's bark of laughter soon had everyone chuckling.

As we went along, I stared out the window at the South Dakota countryside flashing by. The November day was gray, and the barren trees huddled together in forlorn windbreaks. Everything anticipated the inevitability of winter.

As we passed by Wheaton I looked up at the water tower. Maybe it was higher than I thought—it soared above the little town. In fact, it was the tallest thing for miles and could be seen long after Wheaton itself disappeared over the horizon.

"Are you sure you're okay with getting these horses, Ben?"

Mom's question startled me out of my reverie. I thought the horse issue was settled.

Dad sighed. Gramps and I got really quiet.

Finally, speaking deliberately, Dad said, "Well, Rachel, the financial numbers on using horses for cattle ranching don't really come out very well, but you know that."

Mom kept her eyes on the road but I could see that she was biting her lip.

Dad continued, "But I don't think this decision is strictly about the bottom line."

Mom glanced over at Dad with a ghost of a smile.

"I think horses connect to your life growing up on the farm. But I believe you when you say they'll earn their keep. Since Gramps and Josh cooked up this scheme to fund their purchase with the insurance money from the Honda, I really have nothing to complain about. And having you be happy with our work on the farm is a priority for me, so yes, I'm okay with getting these horses, Rachel."

A beautiful smile lit up the rear view mirror where I was watching Mom's reactions.

"However," Dad paused for effect, "if we get into cash flow problems, the horses are the first thing to go, right?"

A pained look replaced Mom's smile and she said, "Right. That's what we decided."

"And," again Dad paused, "I don't have to ride them, do I?"

"Nope," Mom said quickly. "That's our agreement. You can ride them if you decide to, but you don't have to." Her voice sounded very businesslike, but her face looked hopeful.

Gramps and I shifted into a more relaxed positions. For a time, an extended silence reigned over the continuous hum of the tires on blacktop, broken only by the occasional thumps that characterized the state highway.

After a while Mom said, "Here we are." She slowed the truck and pulled onto a well-graveled lane with white board fences running along each side.

A large sign announced "Equestrian Acres. Horses For Sale."

***

It wasn't long before I was sitting on the top rail of a corral. Dad and Gramps were standing beside me, leaning against the high fence. We were observing the five horses Mom had picked out of the rancher's herd. Three horses were dark brown with white markings on their faces. The rancher called them quarter horses. The other two were called paints and had wild combinations of white and brown all over their bodies.

"How old is that quarter with the dark front stockings?" Mom asked.

"She's 14," the rancher said. "Her previous owner wanted a younger animal for competition. But she's a good cow pony and knows what she's doing with cattle. She's probably got a dozen good years left in her. I'd give you a good price on her."

Mom walked confidently up to the elderly quarter horse and scratched her behind the ear. "I like her. What about the light brown paint? What's the story there?" she said, pointing to a smaller horse with white and tan markings. It was off by itself and kept flicking its ears and snorting.

"That paint's got great bloodlines but has been a bit of a disappointment in competition. The horse has cow sense, but crowds distract him. He's pretty young, only four, but handle him right and I think he'd do ranch work just fine. I'll give you a good price on him too."

Soon Dad and I were helping Gramps load the two horses into the trailer. "The old quarter horse's name is Bonny, so I think we should call the paint Clyde," Gramps said. "Get it? Bonny and Clyde?"

As they shut the doors on the trailer, Mom came back. "We came in about $500 under budget. That'll give us a good start on tack and feed."

"My wife, the cowgirl!" Dad said chuckling. "You're like a different person from a month ago. I love it!" He gave her a hug and a congratulatory kiss.

Mom blushed deeply but looked pleased.

"Hey, you, the one standing there gawking," Mom said to me. "I hope you realize that these horses are going to have a big impact on your life."

I laughed. "Yeah, I know. I get to take care of them. You already told me that."

"Your father and I have been trying to figure out the best way to involve you in the farm work. You can feed them and muck out their stalls when it fits around your school and basketball schedule."

"I don't think that'll be too bad."

"And you can take them out for exercise once you get the hang of riding," Gramps put in. "Maybe we could get Sarah to help you with horsemanship in addition to basketball."

"We should stop and show Sarah the horses on the way home. What do you think, Gramps?" Mom said.

"I think that's a splendid idea, Rachel."

Dad looked uncertainly from his wife to his father-in-law. "I'm not so sure that's a good idea. Won't that just make Sarah sad, since she doesn't have horses any more? I still think we should move slowly with her."

I clenched my fists.

Mom glanced at me and said, "Ben, I don't see how it would hurt. Sarah already knows we were going out to buy horses today. We'll stop for just a minute."

Dad looked up from the spot on the ground he'd been staring at. "Harlan, you told us how everything from their farm went in the bankruptcy auction. Do you think she'll be okay?"

Gramps nodded.

Dad look at me and then said, "I suppose it's all right. Okay."

***

About forty-five minutes later, I stepped out of the truck into the Dirks' yard. Sarah saw us coming and eagerly followed Mom and Gramps around the trailer for a look at the horses. A rusted out Mercury sedan I'd never seen before was parked beside Sarah's pickup. Just then, the screen door on the Dirks' back porch squeaked open and then banged shut. A tall, raw-boned man stood on the stoop with his dark hair going all directions over an unshaven face. His paunch was an unattractive addition to his otherwise athletic build. He took a pull from a long-necked beer bottle before he called out in a loud voice, "Well, if it's not those meddling neighbors! What's the matter Neilson? Are you getting too old to find your side of the fence?" He slurred his speech and swayed precariously.

"Dad!" Sarah squealed. She came quickly around the trailer and headed for the back porch. Forcing calm into her voice, she said, "You're missing the Michigan basketball game. You know how disappointed you are when you don't catch those critical moments. Come back in and I'll get you a fresh beer." She took his arm and led him through the door without a backward glance.

We all stood in the driveway looking at each other, not sure what to do. After a few minutes, when Sarah did not return, we got back into the truck and drove home in silence.

Chapter 14

Thanksgiving

On Thanksgiving morning I sat in Gramps' old stuffed rocker. Dad and I were watching the Chicago Bears battle the Detroit Lions. Mom and Gramps were in the kitchen noisily preparing the holiday dinner with occasional loud "discussions" about how to cook it. Sometimes Dad and my whoops brought them running into the living room to see what was happening in the game.

"Time for dinner," Mom called out, as Gramps placed a platter of sliced turkey in the center of a dazzling culinary display.

"Perfect timing," Dad said, switching off the television.

"The Bears won 23 to 16. Not that anyone cares, but it was a good game," I reported.

"Well, if it had been a Vikings' game, you'd all still be waiting for dinner," Gramps said, laughing.

"Looks like we're all winners here," Dad said, breathing in the rich aromas.

"I'm not sure it's up to Grandma Izzy's standards, but we did our best," Mom said. "Would you say grace for us, Gramps?"

My mouth began to water as I folded my hands and bowed my head.

Gramps' prayer was long, thanking God in detail for our new shared life in South Dakota. As he prayed, Gramps' voice broke slightly. "Lord, you know how much we miss those not with us today, Isabel and Nathan. Help us to continue to entrust them to your tender care. We give you thanks on this special day for the food we are about to eat. Amen."

Following the prayer, the only thing breaking the silence was the scraping of chairs and the clinking of dishes as we passed the feast around the table. It hurt to have Gramps name Grandma Izzy and Nathan in the prayer, but it felt right too.

"It's been five years since Grandma Izzy died," Mom said. "You brought boxed turkey dinners up to the hospital cancer unit for Thanksgiving that year, Gramps."

"I remember that," Gramps said. "It was just the three of us because Ben and the boys were still traveling from Portland. Izzy didn't eat any of hers, but she said it was the best Thanksgiving she'd ever had."

"I'm thankful we made it in time," Dad said. "I'm not sure I'd ever take that risk again, whether the boys were in school or not. We're lucky we got there in time to say good-bye."

"We ended up missing school anyway," I said, "for the funeral. Nathan and I spent a lot of time out in the barn.

Nathan loved this farm." My eyes burned, matching other eyes that glinted with unspilled tears.

"He sure did, Son," Dad said. "He sure did."

There was silence for a while. Then Mom said, "What time do you need to be at school tomorrow to catch the bus, Josh?"

"Coach said the bus leaves at 7:00 a.m. sharp. I wonder why we have to leave so early. Our first game isn't until 11:00 a.m."

"The girls have their first game at 9:30 a.m," Gramps said.

"Oh. I forgot about the girls' game. It's hard to remember that our whole school can travel on one bus."

"I grew up with that," Mom said. "But I imagine it's different for you, Josh. Riding the team bus can be fun. You didn't get to do that in Portland."

"Yeah, I know." I wasn't sure how I felt about riding the team bus.

"I'm looking forward to watching your first basketball game tomorrow, Josh," Dad said enthusiastically.

"Me too!" Gramps and Mom chorused.

"I suppose tomorrow is the first game of the season for Sarah too," Mom mused. "Dad, what's the deal with Paul Dirk? I used to know him when we were kids. I never thought he would act like he did when we stopped by with the horses."

"He's been different since he came back from Desert Storm."

"He was a soldier?" Mom asked.

"He enlisted right after graduating from high school. I know he saw quite a bit of action."

"It's odd to think of Paul as a soldier. He was such a

goof-off in school. About the only time he was ever serious was when he was on the basketball court."

"I think he was serious about military service. He was awarded a couple of medals," Gramps said. "Things got serious when Paul met Sarah's mother in Kuwait. What was her name? Sabra, I think. She worked for the army as an interpreter. When Paul finished his tour of duty, they came home married, with baby Sarah."

"Weren't they pretty young for all of that?" Dad said.

"They certainly were," Gramps said. "I think Paul was barely twenty-two when Sarah was born. After his military service, Sabra and Sarah lived with Paul on the Dirk family farm. I'd never seen Elias so happy.

"Who's Elias?" I asked.

"Elias was Paul's father. Elias was probably the most respected civic leader in Wheaton. There was talk about him running for county commissioner. With Paul's help on the farm, a campaign and term of office would've been possible."

"Did he run?" Mom asked.

"No," Gramps answered. "It was about then that Elias got cancer. His health was bad for years while he battled the disease. When he died, he left the family with a hopeless financial situation. Paul worked hard to hang on to the farm, but they finally had to give it up and declare bankruptcy."

"That's so sad," Mom said.

"And to top it all off, Sarah's mom went back to Egypt to live with her family," Gramps continued. "I don't know if they got a divorce, but she's not been around here for a long time."

"Poor Sarah! I had no idea how bad things were for her," Mom said.

"They were able to hang onto the house, but everything else went in the auction. With help from friends Paul managed to get into truck driving. I think Sarah spends a lot of time alone. I've heard rumors about Paul's drinking, but nothing like what we saw last Saturday. That was bad."

"I'm sure Sarah was horribly embarrassed," Mom observed.

"It might explain why she's weird about when I can come for basketball lessons sometimes," I put in. "Her father's never been there."

"Yeah, that's what has me worried." Dad said. "With the talk going around I don't know if you should be over there with her alone so much. It could make things worse."

I put my fork down and stared at my plate.

"Ben, we agreed to let Sarah help Josh with his basketball. I think poor Sarah needs the companionship as much as Josh needs the coaching." Mom said.

Dad turned to look at Mom. A tense silence stretched out for several seconds. Then Dad said, "I was thinking of Sarah too. It's not going to help her if people find out how much time she spends alone with Josh."

"Dad, if you care so much about Sarah, you should be trying to help her, not just protecting my reputation." I couldn't keep the anger out of my voice.

I saw a flash of rage on my Dad's face. I could see him counting to ten before he spoke. "So, what would you suggest I do to help her?"

In the height of my fury, I was afraid to say anything.

Gramps came to my rescue. "We could start by cheering for her at the tournament tomorrow. She's a real talent, so that shouldn't be too hard."

Dad turned to look at Gramps.

Gramps shrugged. "Just a suggestion."

"It's a good suggestion," Mom said quickly. "You're right. A little public support for her might help people change what they think of her."

Dad looked from Mom to Gramps for a minute and then sighed. "Okay. I can do that."

The tension in the room dissipated noticeably.

Then Dad turned to me with a serious look. "Josh, you're 16 now, you'll be 17 in April. Sarah is already 17. I suppose it might be time to let you fight your own battles. But, would you do me a favor and be careful?"

Amazement replaced anger. "Okay, Dad" was all I managed to say.

***

Dinner concluded with a full court press on the dishes. Everyone pitched in and the kitchen was soon spotless, with the dishwasher humming and sloshing away at its appointed task. Gramps stretched out on the couch in front of a mindless fishing show. Dad pulled on his coat and boots to check the livestock. Mom disappeared into the bedroom, leaving instructions to wake her in a couple of hours if we didn't see her by then.

I climbed the steps to my room slowly. I thought about playing my Xbox, but instead grabbed Mom's old laptop and flopped down on the bed. I googled "King Hezekiah." I clicked the link for the Wikipedia article and learned that he was the thirteenth king of Judah and was considered their most righteous ruler. The article said that the Biblical accounts about him were in Second Kings, Second Chronicles, and Isaiah. I clicked on the link for Second Chronicles. There were several chapters about Hezekiah. As I skimmed through the archaic verses, I started to nod off. Most of it was about Hezekiah reforming Judah's worship. I pushed the computer onto the bed and curled up around it. Just as I was drifting off, something caught my attention. The reference note said it was from II Chronicles chapter 32 verse 2 and following. I struggled a little to understand the archaic King James Version. But the message matched my dream about the cave in and the terrifying situation in ancient Jerusalem.

"And when Hezekiah saw that Sennacherib was come, and that he was purposed to fight against Jerusalem, he took counsel with his princes and his mighty men to stop the waters of the fountains which were without the city; and they did help him. So there was gathered much people together, who stopped all the fountains, and the brook that ran through the midst of the land, saying, 'Why should the kings of Assyria come, and find much water?' Also he strengthened himself, and built up all the wall that was broken down, and raised it up to the towers, and another wall without . . ."

Chapter 15

Broad Wall

"Hey, Josh! wake up!" Nathan said, shaking my shoulder.

My pillow was gone, replaced by a rough stone wall. Instead of lying on my bed, I was sitting on a pile of rocks.

"How can you fall asleep so fast?" Nathan continued. "The supervisor only gave us a short rest. We'll be finishing our shift in an hour."

"Nathan?" I asked uncertainly.

A look of concern crossed Nathan's face. "Joshua, are you okay?"

"Uh, I'm not sure. Give me a minute."

"Here. Drink some of this," Nathan said as he pressed a water skin into my hands.

The water was disgusting, but it helped clear my head. "Where am I?"

Nathan just stared at me.

"Nathan, it's me—Future Joshua," I said softly.

A look of startled recognition passed over Nathan's face. "Oh!"

A thin musical blast, like a breathy trumpet, echoed around us.

"Joshua, that's the supervisor's shofar. We have to get back to work."

"I have no idea what we're doing here."

"Only an hour to go and we can talk. Until then, you should follow my lead," Nathan said, shouldering a wooden yoke that had a wicker bucket hanging from each end. He pointed to a similar contraption to my left. "Pick that up and follow me."

It took a couple of tries to get the yoke adjusted on my shoulders. The buckets were heavy, since they were filled with stones. As I followed Nathan along a path between piles of rock, I took in my surroundings. The building looked bombed out. The walls were half gone, and piles of rubble were everywhere.

We emerged from the building into the late afternoon sunlight. It was hot but not uncomfortably so. I had to look down at Nathan's feet to see where to go through the blinding sunlight.

As we came into the shade, I saw scaffolding attached to the structure. A crew of men was on the top level with sledgehammers and pry bars. Suddenly I realized that these workers were tearing the building down.

Following Nathan, I crossed an open space filled with rubble. Men with shovels and brooms were cleaning the area while another crew laid paving stones. Glancing to the side I realized that this area was becoming part of a street that ran beside the massive wall we were approaching.

When Nathan reached the wall, he turned to his left and started up a rickety set of steps built into a large scaffold. As we got farther and farther above ground, I had to maneuver my yoke and buckets around the scaffolding carefully — the whole thing shook as we ascended. Worse yet, there were several people with yokes and buckets using the stairs in front of us and behind us. How much weight could this flimsy contraption bear?

Finally, we stepped off the stairway onto the wall itself. I was stunned by the scene before me. The wall was gigantic. It extended thousands of feet to the south before it curved back to the east. It was like a highway, over 20 feet wide, running five stories above the ground.

The top of the wall was a beehive of activity, with people moving all over it. I couldn't make out all of what they were doing. Large contraptions like wooden cranes were lifting gigantic stones along the sides of the wall. Whole crews with bulging muscles, dripping with sweat, worked in rhythm at the ropes. Long lines of people with yoked buckets carried stones.

"Joshua!" Nathan called out sharply. "You can't stop. The line has to keep moving."

I shuffled ahead, closing the gap that had opened between

us. At the top, a man directed us to dump our buckets of stones. A ram's horn shofar, slung by a rope over his shoulder, identified him as the supervisor. The minute we dropped our stones we were off again, descending the wall on a different rickety stairway.

When we reached the bottom, Nathan led the way as we quickly filled our buckets with stones from the piles of debris. Then we repeated the cycle back to the top of the wall. I was sure that my strength would give out, but my body in Jerusalem seemed adapted to this kind of hard work. Finally, the blast of the supervisor's shofar marked the end of our shift.

As we made our way back through the streets of Jerusalem, I asked, "What was all that about?"

"King Hezekiah is trying to protect the new part of the city built outside the old walls. We call it the Broad Wall because it is thicker than any other city walls. The King started this project years ago to protect the new city. Now that the Assyrians are coming, the Broad Wall has become our main priority. Everyone is working in shifts to finish it. We are even tearing down residences along the wall to provide material to speed construction. Our supervisor says we will be able to complete the length of the wall next week, and we'll be able to raise it to full height in a month. I hope we have that long."

"Didn't the tribute the king sent to the Assyrians save the city?" I asked.

"We still don't know," Nathan said. "Some of Father's spies have reported that there are large scale movements of Assyrian troops in the north. It doesn't look good."

***

We arrived at a set of apartments I recognized. Nathan led the way up a stone stair and through an archway into the building. Wooden stairs led up to a door that Nathan opened.

A voice called out, "Wait by the door. I don't want you tracking in all that dirt on my freshly swept floor."

Nathan's smile broadened as we closed the door and waited obediently. After a short time, Sarah came down the hall carrying a lamp, a large basin, and a stack of towels, with a clay water jar on her head. She looked like a juggler in the circus. Sarah gracefully set everything down. Pouring water into the basin, she slid it in front of me and knelt. After an awkward moment, Nathan said, "Sarah, could you start with me? I think Joshua got a little sun-dazed at work."

Sarah slid the basin in front of Nathan with a shrug. Nathan untied the laces on his sandals. He put a foot in the bowl of water. Sarah washed it quickly and then dried it with one of the cloths. Then she did his other foot. I noticed the look of pleasure on Nathan's face at her touch.

By the time Sarah slid the basin in front of me, I had managed to get my sandals undone. I put one foot and then the other in the water for Sarah to wash. The water was dark with mud and I realized how grimy my feet had been. Sarah was businesslike in her work, but the process was surprisingly intimate.

"Now you won't mess up my clean floors," Sarah said as she finished. "Leave those dirty sandals by the door and I'll clean them later."

Nathan led me through the apartment. Things were starting to feel familiar, especially when we entered my bedchamber. After lighting a couple of lamps, Nathan helped me find a clean tunic and robe. Nathan left to go to his room while I changed but he reappeared shortly.

"We can't talk in the house," Nathan said. "It's too easy to be overheard. But Mother has made some bread for the scribes. I said we would take it to them before supper. We can talk on the way."

***

Soon, the two of us made our way through the narrow pathways of Jerusalem. There were as many stairs as streets. Modern vehicles would be useless here.

"How long has it been since I was here last?" I asked.

"Almost two weeks," Nathan said. "My Joshua was surprised when he woke up at the temple after you left last time. He had no idea how he'd gotten from his bed to the temple. What happened to you?" he asked. "One minute you were staring wide-eyed through the temple gates, and the next you were face down on the pavement."

I felt a wave of nausea as I remembered. "All that blood. It was everywhere."

"Oh, the sacrificing at the temple is bloody. My Joshua doesn't like it either, but I don't think he's ever fainted before."

We walked in silence for a while and then Nathan asked, "How does this traveling to the past happen?"

"I don't understand how it works at all," I answered. "I just wake up here."

"I wonder where my Joshua is while you're here."

"Uh." I hesitated thinking about the other Joshua sleeping in my room surrounded by all my twenty-first century stuff. I sure hoped he wouldn't wake up. It'd scare him to death. "Has your Joshua ever remembered anything from the other times I've been here?"

"No. He just thinks he's been asleep."

"Then he's okay. I'm sure of it," I said. "I was in a safe place when I fell asleep. He's probably there."

"I sure hope you're right."

Nathan took my arm and led me through an archway. "We're here."

Evening darkness crept across Jerusalem as we entered a short, dimly lit hallway. A large wooden double door opened as we approached, and a young man emerged carrying a lamp.

"Hello!" he said cheerfully. He set the lamp on a shelf beside the door where it lit the entryway.

"On lamp duty, Oren?" Nathan asked with a wicked grin.

"Yes, you dog. It was supposed to be your night, but Jamin passed it to me because you had a shift on the wall. Say! Do I smell what I think I smell?"

"Yes. It's some of Mother's fresh bread. And I'm taking it straight to Jamin. Don't get any ideas about sampling it," Nathan said firmly.

"Alright, alright" Oren chuckled as he held the door for us to enter.

Inside, we entered a huge room. I'd guess it must have been over ninety feet long and nearly thirty feet wide. The walls were stonework, with massive beams supporting the ceiling twenty-five feet above them. Lamps hung on chains and sat on wall sconces throughout the Scriptorium. I suddenly realized how busy Oren would be putting oil in all of those lamps.

Large tables filled the main room and I could see about a dozen people working. Some people read scrolls and others wrote on them. At one table a couple of younger men, probably apprentices, were grinding bits of charcoal with a mortar and pestle and mixing the resulting dust with various liquids.

"They're making ink," Nathan said under his breath. "And over there they're making parchment." He pointed to an open area at the end of the large room where an apprentice was scraping animal skins stretched on wooden frames.

Halfway down the room we approached a raised wooden platform. On it sat a man at a small table piled with scrolls, flanked by lamp stands. He looked up with a frown and said, "What are you doing here? I thought you were on the wall today."

"We just finished," Nathan said, slightly flustered. "Mother sent some freshly baked bread for the scribes' evening meal."

"All right. Please extend our gratitude to Rachel. She's a dear woman. Remember, you're working tomorrow morning. We need to get that new set of Origins scrolls copied for the royal archive soon since the king ordered it."

"Yes, sir," Nathan said, but Jamin was already turning

away as another scribe approached the dais carrying an arm-load of scrolls.

"Come on," Nathan said as he picked up a lamp and led us away. "I want to show you what I'm working on."

We headed toward a series of low arches that flanked both sides of the Scriptorium, each leading into dark chambers. At the base of the archways stood large clay jars filled with sand. Nathan took a lamp from a sconce and entered one of these dark chambers.

Following I said, "What are those?" I pointed to the clay jars.

"They're for putting out fires," Nathan explained. He set the lamp on a stand in the center of the room. "Fire is our worst enemy in the Scriptorium. We have to be careful all the time, or we could quickly lose this treasure that has taken years to make." He gestured with a sweeping motion around the chamber. "Water would damage the scrolls almost as badly as fire, so we use sand."

Diagonally slatted wooden structures covered every inch of the wall inside the chamber, like giant wine racks. The cubby holes that resulted stored hundreds and hundreds of scrolls.

Nathan set the lamp on a table in the center of the chamber. He pointed to a tall rack of scrolls in front of us. "Those scrolls are the Origins project Jamin has me working on. It tells our people's story from the creation of the world through the lives of our ancestors, Abraham, Isaac, and Jacob."

I felt an electric shock as I realized what I was seeing. "Did you include two different stories of creation?"

Nathan turned and stared at me. "How did you know that? The scribes debated that issue for months."

"Were they worried that the two different stories would confuse people about how God created things?"

"Of course not. Nobody knows how God created the world. The debate was over which of all the various creation stories to include. They ended up limiting it to two. The first is a praise song we often use in festival worship. The second is a story parents tell their children to teach right from wrong."

I looked around, amazed. They were writing the Bible here.

As we left the Scriptorium and made our way through the streets of Jerusalem, I asked, "Why is the Scriptorium recording your people's stories?"

"It was King Hezekiah's idea. He has worked to restore the true worship of God among our people during his whole reign. The Scriptorium's chief purpose was to record the business of the king. However, King Hezekiah also wanted the traditional stories of the Hebrews collected and written down. So that's what we are doing. Why does the Scriptorium's work seem so important to you?"

"It's related to the business about the Bible, so we probably shouldn't talk about it," I said and then decided to change the subject. "Last time I was here you said you were getting serious about Sarah. Has anything happened with that?"

Nathan, startled, stopped and stared at me. "I forgot I told you that."

"Well?"

"Uh, yes, I talked to Sarah about it . . . about a betrothal."

"What did she say?"

Nathan started walking again and I hurried to match his pace. After a few steps he said, "She reacted the way I expected. She told me that she loves me and that she'd like to be my wife, but she's worried about marrying her master's son."

"But your parents love her like a daughter," I said.

"Too much of that would make her our sister. I'm not sure you're helping here, Joshua."

"Oh, right." I waited for him to continue.

He said, "You've seen how practical Sarah is?"

I nodded.

"She suggested that we wait to bring it up with Father until after this Assyrian matter is resolved. I sure don't feel like waiting, but she was pretty adamant, so I agreed."

Sarah met us at the door again and I noticed the special tenderness between her and Nathan. I felt a peculiar emotional twinge, but didn't have time to analyze it because we were late for dinner.

The evening meal felt like a family meal back in Portland with Nathan there. Sarah's presence made me think of South Dakota. I was finally getting the hang of lying down to eat too. Toward the end of the meal I started to feel dizzy.

"I must be exhausted." I stood up shakily. "I think I'd better go lie down."

"I'll help you," Nathan volunteered, guiding me back to the now-familiar bedchamber.

We barely made it back before I started to black out.

"Are you all right?" Nathan asked.

"This is the way it feels at the end of my dreams, or time travels, or whatever this is."

As Nathan helped me to bed, he said, "I suppose it will be our Joshua who wakes up here tomorrow morning."

"Who knows?" Then the world winked out.

Chapter 16

The Season Starts

Early Friday morning, the bare light bulb in the barn struggled to drive back the darkness. I counted scoops of grain into Bonny and Clyde's feed buckets. I moved them out of their stalls and tethered them to one of the barn's big support posts. They happily munched on the sweet-smelling mixture, while I mucked out their stalls. The horses weren't going to get much exercise today or tomorrow while we were all in Sioux Falls for the Thanksgiving Invitational Basketball Tournament. I told them I'd have to make it up to them later.

It was just starting to get light when I drove slowly past the bus parked by the gym door. I pulled up next to Sarah's ancient Dodge pickup. Together her truck and the Beast looked like an antique auto show. Grabbing my gym bag, I headed for the bus. The driver swung the door open as I approached. Mounting the steps, I looked down the long aisle at the half-filled seats. Loud laughter came from the back where Marshal and Allen were entertaining a little group. Melanie was sitting with Marshal and egging him on. Shelly Waters, Ellen Longfeather, and, surprisingly, Jean Wilkerson were part of the group as well.

Sarah was sitting in a seat by herself about halfway back. I wondered if I should sit with her. That was what I wanted to do. It would make it easy to talk to her. The laughter died away as the group at the back noticed me. Sarah pointedly ignored me and looked down into her lap. I dropped into an empty seat near the front of the bus.

The loud laughter resumed as the bus continued to fill. Eddie slid into the seat beside me. "Hey, Josh! First game, eh?" he chattered. "Are you pumped?"

"Yeah, I guess."

"You're a lucky upperclassman, getting to suit up for all the games," Eddie said. "There's no JV game at this tournament, so us underclassmen have to take turns. I'm in the second game."

A blast of cold air caught us as the bus doors fanned open.

"Hey, Sean!" Eddie gently slugged the tall redhead's shoulder as he climbed the bus stairs. He dropped into an empty spot directly behind us.

"Didn't Coach say everyone would get some playtime?" I asked.

"I'm counting on it. My whole family is going to be at the tournament. They think I'm a rising star," Eddie laughed.

"You're a basketball phenom in your own mind, Eddie," Sean laughed, leaning forward to join the conversation.

Eddie's banter continued as the bus pulled away from the school. Eddie, Sean and I talked for the whole trip.

I kept glancing back at Sarah. I couldn't tell how she was feeling. There was a bubble of silence around her, and she had her game face on, but I thought she looked sad. Once, when our eyes met, and she quickly looked away. I wondered if she was still embarrassed about her dad.

As I descended the bus steps I said, "I'll catch up with you guys later."

"Let's sit together during the girls' game," Eddie said as he headed for the sports complex entrance.

I slapped Sean on the shoulder as I stepped aside to let the flow of students pass me. When I saw Sarah coming out of the bus, I fell into step beside her. "Hey, Sarah, are you ready for the game?"

She seemed startled but recovered quickly. "Hey, Cooper, aren't you afraid to be seen with me?" she said softly, but her expression was angry.

It was my turn to be startled. "Uh, no."

We walked along in awkward silence with me stubbornly matching her pace. Finally, as we went through the door, Sarah slackened her pace and stepped aside from the flow of students. I circled and came to stand beside her. I looked at her and waited. Sarah bit her lip. "I'm sorry you had to see my dad like that last Saturday." I could see the faint red flush under her dark skin.

"Sarah, don't worry about that. I wasn't offended, and our

whole family understands. We're all looking forward to seeing you play basketball."

Sarah didn't answer, but she looked relieved.

"Hey, Cooper!" Marshal said as he came through the door. "Looking for a good time?" He laughed cruelly.

"Hubba! Hubba!" Allen called out while making a crude gesture. Their group broke into nervous giggles, except for Jean, who stared angrily at Marshal, then Allen.

I pivoted to look at Marshal, but when I turned back, Sarah was striding rapidly toward the women's locker room.

***

Jean Wilkerson crouched in the center circle as the referee threw the ball up to start the game. Anticipating Jean's tip, Sarah broke toward the Wheaton basket to execute a perfect layup, putting the Rockets quickly up 2-0.

"Way to go, Sarah!" my dad boomed from the spectators' seats behind me. The crowd was light for the early morning game, so Dad's voice stood out. I was not sure whether to be embarrassed or proud.

The smile on Sarah's face as she ran back down the court pushed me toward pride.

My pride swelled as the Wheaton girls, led by Sarah, steadily built their lead. I was on my feet, cheering more than sitting. Once, when I sat back down, I noticed Ellen Longfeather sitting beside me. She had taken advantage of Eddie's departure for the bathroom to slide between me and Sean. She focused most of her attention on Sean, but after a bit, she turned to me.

"Thanks for being at youth group, Josh," Ellen said. "It's very encouraging to have boys like you and Sean come. We always have more than enough girls."

"Sure thing," I said awkwardly. "It was, uh, an interesting evening."

"Do you think you will be coming back?" Ellen flipped her long black hair over her shoulder.

"I might."

"Good." Ellen's expression looked pleased. Then a shadow passed over her features. "I feel like I should warn you about Sarah. I like her and everything. I know she's had a tough life. And maybe what they say about her isn't true. But you should be careful about how much you're around her."

I looked straight at Ellen. "Really," I said, "Sarah's not like that."

"Maybe," Ellen said.

I decided Ellen was just trying to be helpful, but I was angry. "How did those stories about her get started?"

"About a year ago Allen started claiming that Sarah had let him," Ellen paused, "you know. Ugh! Allen is disgusting! I can't imagine that Sarah would come within a mile of him. Then Melanie sent out some Instagram posts saying Sarah had tried to get her hooks into Marshal. That was just after she and Marshal started going steady. Then a couple guys from the football team said Sarah had done some stuff with them too. Like weird stuff."

"Why does anyone believe those stories?"

"Sarah's never said anything to defend herself. And it's not like it's just one guy. If it were just Allen . . ."

"That's not much to go on." I was sure Ellen could hear the anger creeping into my voice.

"I suppose," Ellen conceded. "But I just thought you should know."

Eddie came back and Ellen stood to go. "Bye, Sean."

As I watched her leave I decided Sarah needed a friend as much as I need help with basketball.

The girls' game finished with Wheaton winning handily. Sarah scored sixteen points, and her passing helped Jean and Shelly score in double digits too. The Rocket women looked unbeatable.

It did not go nearly as well for the Rocket men. I spent the first half of the game watching from the bench. Coach tried hard to get the starting team to respond to the beating we were taking, but the Rockets were down by fifteen points going into halftime.

"Marshal, you've got to stop taking so many risky shots. They have us beat on the boards with those two six-foot forwards. We need to make our shots count," Coach said while the team stretched out on the locker room benches during half time.

"Nobody's doing anything, Coach," Marshal said defensively. "I'm just trying to get some points on the board. Besides, I'm already scoring in double figures."

"Then maybe it's time to give someone else a chance. Cooper, you're starting second half in Marshal's place."

"What?" was all that Marshal said. He stopped talking when he noticed the thunderstorm brewing on Coach's face.

I took my place for the second half jump ball. The other team won possession, and I dropped back, picking up the man I was assigned to guard. Allen managed to intercept a pass, but his slow dribble back up the court forfeited any chance we had for a fast break. As the team came down the court, Allen made a pass to me, but the ball came low and hard, and I fumbled it out of bounds.

"Way to go, loser!" Allen said under his breath as he ran past me on the way back up the court.

The opposing team scored, lifting their lead to seventeen.

The next time down the court Carl Bolstad, our center, passed the ball out to me on the side of the court. I faked a set shot and snapped a bounce pass back to Carl as he came down the lane. He made an easy layup and cut the lead by two. The other team seemed stunned by the crisp play.

When the opposing team missed their next shot, Carl got the rebound and passed to Roger Whitfield, who moved the up the court fast, putting pressure on the defense. He made a sharp pass to me on the baseline. Relaxing my hands, just as Sarah had taught me, I drew it in and started a drive toward the basket. As two opposing players moved quickly to stop me, I made a quick shovel-pass directly off the dribble back to Roger, who swished a ten-foot jump shot.

The whistles blew loudly as the other team took time out.

"Great job, Cooper. Keep making those assists!" Coach said.

When I got back out on the floor I was being guarded by a different player. The boy who shadowed me moved like lightning and was always in my way when I wanted to pass. The other team soon recovered their momentum. By fourth quarter both sides had their second teams in the game as it ground to an embarrassing loss for the Rockets.

After the game I said to Coach MacAllister, "Sorry, Coach. I just couldn't get a pass around that guy."

"Cooper, that guy made the all-state team last year. The opposing coach paid you quite a compliment by shifting coverage that way. Don't worry. You did well."

I told my parents what Coach said while riding home with them Friday evening. I decided not to ride back on the bus. We lost our second game in the afternoon and were out of the tournament. Our mortification deepened when girls' team won their evening game, putting them in the championship the next night.

"I think you did well in your first couple of games," Gramps said.

"We're extremely proud of you," Mom agreed.

"I think Nathan would have been pleased, too," Dad said. "I know you haven't had the same desire to play as Nathan, but you've stepped up. This school needs you. Good job, Son!"

I wondered if Nathan would be pleased.

Chapter 17

Take the Shot

"Better get going, Josh," Gramps said, up to his elbows in dishwater after dinner on Sunday. "You shouldn't keep a lady waiting. I can dry these last two pans myself."

I was out the door and in the Beast practically before he finished his sentence. Sarah emerged from the back porch in sweats, with a basketball under her arm. Evidently she had been watching for me. I looked around the yard. The only vehicle there was Sarah's orange Dodge. I relaxed and followed Sarah into the barn.

As Sarah turned on the lights, I said, "You were great in the tournament. Eighteen points."

Sarah shrugged. "We won, and that's what counts. Everyone had a good game."

"Did your dad get a chance to watch you play last night?"

Sarah stiffened. "Sort of . . . he was going to come. He made it as far as Joey's Bar. He said they had the game on, so he decided not to waste the gas driving into Sioux Falls."

"What did he say about your game?"

"Not much," Sarah said, tight-lipped. "He thought I was hogging the ball. But he was in a hurry this morning to get to work. He has a run to Saint Louis today."

I took the hint and dropped the subject. "Sorry I didn't play better on Friday. You've helped me a lot. I should have done better."

"Josh, you did just fine. That's why I wanted to get together this afternoon. You're ready for the next step."

"What do you mean, fine? I was making passes as you taught me, but then I totally flubbed it."

"If they hadn't popped that all-stater on you, you'd have given them a run for their money. Marshal is such a show-off – he missed opportunities by not passing off. When you got in, things started working."

"Why was that guy able to shut me down?"

"That's why we are here now. When he figured out you were uncomfortable taking a shot, he just loosened up his coverage and shut down your passing. Being able to make a basket or two will fix that. I need to show you some stuff, and then we need to work on your shooting."

"Okay," I said uncertainly.

"Start by guarding me."

I assumed a defensive stance within reach of Sarah.

"Now watch this." Sarah feinted to the left. As I leaned to cover, Sarah brought the ball back across her body and bounced it beside my left foot the way she had taught me to pass. But this turned out to be a pass to herself as she flashed past me and made an easy layup.

"Okay, let's try that again."

"Pretty bad, huh!" I said.

Sarah made precisely the same feint she had before. When she brought the ball across her body, I stepped backward to the left, hoping to prevent the drive. Sarah rose in a perfect jump shot that swished the net. I was too far away to check the ball.

"What did you learn?" she asked.

"That you can beat the tar out of me. But we already knew that."

"Josh, stop that. Think. What just happened?"

"You had me coming and going. If I guard you too closely, you drive past me. If I slacked off to prevent the drive, you have room to shoot."

"Passing opportunities are the same as driving. You want the defender up close to you so you can easily pass through them. If they fall back to cut off the pass, then you have the opening to shoot. Try it." Sarah handed me the basketball and moved into a defensive stance between me and the basket.

I faked to my left and then shifted my weight to drive right. Sarah dropped back to cut me off. I crouched to shoot and released the ball from the top of my jump, just as Sarah had taught me. Sarah moved to check me, but she was too far away to stop it. The ball sailed over her outstretched arms and bounced, scoreless, off the rim.

"That's it, Josh!" Sarah called out enthusiastically.

"But I missed the shot. Wouldn't it be better to get the ball to someone who can make the shot?"

"No! When you have an open shot like that, you need to take it. First, it creates opportunities for you in the future by keeping your defender honest. Second, if you can manage to hit the rim or backboard, there's a fair chance our team will pick up the rebound. That's as good as a pass and often leads to a score. And finally, you might make the basket." Sarah laughed.

"How is that different from what Marshal is doing?"

"Marshal is so focused on shooting the ball that he is not watching for passing opportunities. He forces it by taking a shot when he isn't open. He cuts off our team's opportunity to work for an open shot."

"I think I understand but I sure wish I could put my shots in."

"That will come with practice. Here. I noticed something that might help. Bring the ball up like you're going to take a shot and just hold it there."

As I brought the ball up into shooting position, Sarah put her hand on the small of my back. "Straighten your back. Don't hunch." Then stepping in front of me, she put her hands over mine to raise the ball about six inches.

I felt myself starting to blush at her touch. Nathan thought Sarah was beautiful and I saw what he meant. Thank goodness I was already red in the face from exertion.

"Now try taking a jump shot from that position," Sarah said. I remained motionless. "Josh?"

"Oh!" I jumped and took the shot, and it bounced around the rim, falling in. That was better. I could feel it.

"That's it, Josh! Great!"

We spent the next hour in concentrated practice, and despite the chill we were both sweating.

"You're getting better," she said. "Five more shots?"

I nodded, pushing back my damp, sweaty hair.

She grabbed the ball and froze. "Hold it!"

I looked at her quizzically. "What is it?"

"Shush!" she said, holding her finger to her lips.

Then I heard it. A car was pulling into the yard. It knocked loudly as the driver shut it off, hissing noisily as the engine died.

I looked at Sarah. She stared back with big round eyes. "I think," she said, "you are about to meet my dad for real." Sarah looked nervous as she walked to the big barn door and slid it partially open.

Paul emerged from the rusted-out Mercury sedan. Last time I'd seen him he was yelling at my family. Now he had a case of beer tucked under his arm. But his neat appearance, with hair combed and face shaved, was a radical change. A grin split his face and his eyes twinkled as he saw his daughter step out of the barn.

"I thought you had a run to Saint Louis," Sarah called out as she walked toward her dad. I stood in the doorway to see what would happen.

"Thought you'd get some time alone with your boyfriend, huh?" Paul Dirk laughed.

"Da-ad! Stop that!"

Paul set the case of beer on the ground and threw his arms around his daughter, drawing her close in a gentle hug.

I saw a look on her face that I'd never seen before. She looked happy.

"They canceled today's run and rescheduled it for tomorrow. I'll have to go to Kansas City on the way." Paul snatched the basketball from Sarah and strode vigorously toward the barn door. As he approached me, he held out his hand. "You must be Josh."

"Yes, sir."

"Save the 'sirs' for damn officers, son. I'm Paul. That's my name, and I want you to use it!" He laughed again.

This time I couldn't help laughing along. "Okay . . . Paul."

Paul marched energetically by me into the barn. "I hear Sarah has been teaching you a thing or two about basketball. She's pretty good . . . for a girl."

"Dad!" Sarah huffed as she came up behind me.

Paul laughed again as he dribbled the basketball into a far corner, turned, jumped, and with a flick of his wrist, rocketed the ball twenty-five feet to swish through the hoop.

"Mom said you used to play basketball for Wheaton," I said.

Paul loped toward the basket, picked up the ball on its first bounce, and executed a perfect under the rim layup that was almost a dunk.

"Yeah," he said, "I do love basketball. I made the team at Dakota State. Then I got a wild hair to enlist and Desert

Storm ended my sports career." Paul tossed the ball back to Sarah. "Say, how is Rachel? I haven't seen her for years."

I looked at Sarah, who met my eyes. "Mom's doing great. Farming is good for her."

"I always liked Rachel. She was a couple of years ahead of me in school, but she was kind to me as a lowly freshman. Say hi to her for me."

"Sure."

Paul moved toward the open barn door. "It looks like I'm going to get to see that Vikings–Packers game after all. I suppose I should start getting ready." He chuckled to himself as he picked up the case of beer and headed for the house.

Sarah and I stood in silence, watching him until he went inside. Then Sarah dribbled out onto the court and sunk a twelve-foot turn around jump shot.

"I suppose I should go," I said.

"Don't go just yet," Sarah said softly. Then she took another shot that bounced off the front rim. She lunged to retrieve the ball before coming back to stand near the barn door. It was silent except for the occasional bouncing of the basketball.

"I like him," I said finally.

"I do too," Sarah said quickly. "I just . . . don't like some of the things he does."

"Like when we came to show you the horses?"

Sarah nodded and then looked away. She scrubbed her face.

I wondered if she were crying.

"I like your folks too," Sarah said. Her voice was a little husky. "Especially your mom. She's kind, just like Dad said. And I like your grandfather and dad too."

"They're sure your fans. It was a little embarrassing at the tournament. I mean, you deserved it, but they got kind of loud."

"Yeah, I heard them. It meant a lot to me."

More silence.

"Joshua . . . thanks."

"For what? You're the one who's helped me. I should be thanking you."

Sarah bounced the ball off my head. "Guys are so clueless!" She laughed. "Never mind," she said, in answer to my puzzled look.

She stepped out into the yard. I followed her through the barn door, which she closed behind us.

"See you tomorrow, Josh!" Sarah called out cheerfully as she strode toward the house.

I took the hint and headed for the Beast.

***

The next week was routine until Friday. The boys were on early morning practice. Coach substituted me in with the varsity starters several times during scrimmages. I was starting to feel more confident. Even though Carl and Roger grew friendlier, Marshal and Allen never missed a chance to take me down.

Friday started okay, with the usual sense of relief because

the weekend was near. Practice was light because we had a game that evening. Mr. Nicholson asked me to stay after school and help set up some equipment for physics demonstrations he had planned for the next week. I was happy to help, especially since it gave me an excuse to hang around until Sarah finished her practice.

As Sarah and I were walking out together, we noticed that there were quite a few people in the parking lot. They were huddled in little groups. Some were laughing and pointing, but most of the expressions were unreadable.

At first I couldn't find the Beast, but then I saw it. It had been rolled to the center of the parking lot. Cardboard had been hung around the front and sides of the cab. On the cardboard, letters in orange paint read "Take a ride in the Wheaton Pimp Mobile." The paint had been applied haphazardly and a lot of paint spray was on the windows and the cab of the truck. Wooden stakes had been inserted into the pockets along the truck bed. From the stakes hung pink frilly curtains. To the curtains were attached several gross pornographic pictures with Sarah and my faces photoshopped into them.

Sarah and I walked around the truck in stunned silence. When we got to the back where we could see into the bed, there was a full-sized sex doll arranged on a blanket. Around its neck hung a sign that read "Hey Big Boy! I'm Sarah! $5 for a party!" We stood there staring for a minute. I could feel the other people shifting behind us trying to get a better look at our reactions.

I turned to look at Sarah's expressionless face. "Sarah, I'm so sorry . . ."

She cut me off with an upraised hand. "Don't be. You did nothing wrong." She turned and seemed to teleport to her truck. She came back pulling the biggest hunting knife I'd ever seen from its sheath. She vaulted into the truck and a loud pop signaled the end of her plastic doppelganger.

When she returned to the ground she was still brandishing the knife. The spectators abruptly got into their cars and drove away.

"Please put away the knife, Sarah," Kathryn Longfeather, the school principal, said as she approached us. She was the adult version of her daughter Ellen—willowy and tall, with long dark hair.

A grim-faced Mr. Nicholson was a step behind her.

"Fred, we are going to have to get to the bottom of this. We can't have bullying and vandalism."

"I've got a pretty good idea who's responsible for it. I've seen it coming for some time."

"Take some pictures, Fred. We're going to have to contact all the parents and get the story straight." Then the principal turned to us. "I'm so sorry this happened, Josh, Sarah. Do you know who did it?"

Sarah and I looked at each other.

"I mean, did you see anyone doing it?"

"No," I said, and Sarah shook her head.

"That figures," Mrs. Longfeather said. "But, I'm pretty sure someone saw them. I'll find out sooner or later. Fred, after you get some shots of this, let's help Josh get his truck cleaned off so he can go home."

Chapter 18

Snowmobile

It was the start of Christmas vacation and I'd just come in from doing my chores. I had the whole day to myself except for basketball practice late in the afternoon. I looked at my Xbox and then decided to sit down at my computer.

I typed "time travel" into Google and studied the results. Wikipedia's explanation was soon over my head with its talk of general relativity and quantum physics. Everything was about physically traveling from one time to another. As real as my odd dreams of Jerusalem were, I had only traveled in my mind, not physically.

Next I typed "mental time travel" and discovered that it was called chronesthesia. There was quite a bit of stuff about it, including some scientific studies. But as I looked closer I realized it was only intense remembering.

Nothing seemed to connect with my experience. Growing bored, I spun the mouse wheel and paged through the Google results. A phrase caught my eye—"matching family pattern forms a temporal connection." I clicked on the link and found myself on an ugly, home-grown website called "My Trip to the Nineteenth Century".

The author claimed that he had engaged in mental time travel to France in 1804 where he was a minister for Napoleon helping with the sale of the Louisiana Territory. He insisted that what enabled this temporal transmigration was the exact duplication of his family. His wife and children were precisely the same in the past as they were in the present. His best friend and business partner was also identical in both time periods and worked with him on the deal with the United States.

The website detailed a phenomenon it called Historical Congruence where an exact family pattern match occurring in two different time periods enabled mental travel through time. Many of the comments on the website suggested that the author was either a phony or a kook. But a couple of comments suggested that others had similar experiences. I was mesmerized, but clicked it off quickly when I heard footsteps on the stairs.

"Here you go, Josh." Gramps handed me a big steaming cup of hot chocolate. "Careful. It's hot. I just made it. Thought you might like to have some."

"Thanks, Gramps."

Gramps took his cup over to my big window and looked out over the yard. I joined him to watch the snow come down in big fluffy flakes. Mostly it gusted sideways.

"Did you get Bonnie and Clyde taken care of?" Gramps asked.

"Yep."

"Christmas vacation starts today. So enjoy it. Do you have basketball practice this afternoon?"

"Will they have it in this blizzard?" I asked.

Gramps laughed. "Josh, this isn't a blizzard. It barely qualifies as a snowstorm."

I looked at Gramps to make sure he was serious. "There are already six inches on the ground and it's just getting started. If we had a storm like this in Portland, the whole city would shut down for a week."

Gramps laughed again. "I suppose you're right. But in soft snow, your Mom's truck can easily handle a couple of feet. Besides, the highway department will keep up with this. We'll get you to basketball practice."

"Gramps . . ." I started.

"Yes, Josh?"

"I'm sorry about that orange paint on the Beast."

Gramps was quiet for a while, evidently thinking about how to respond. "You shouldn't be sorry for that, Josh. You had nothing to do with it. Unless your rapidly improving basketball skills may have inflamed someone's jealousy."

"Do you really think that's what caused it?"

"It makes sense. People know Sarah is helping you. Your play has improved so dramatically that it'll threaten varsity starting spots. My guess is that Marshal James and Allen Osgaard are responsible. That's the talk about town."

"Yeah, that's what I think, Gramps. They were laughing the loudest."

"Mrs. Longfeather called and assured me that the school insurance will take care of the cost of fixing the Beast's paint. She was also confident that they'll catch the culprits." Gramps took a long drink of his cocoa.

"I sure hope so." I sipped at my cup. "Mom said they sent out an email to all the parents with pictures."

"That should bring results." Gramps seemed confident.

"Sarah is still so mad that she won't even talk about it."

"How are you feeling, Josh?"

"Uh." I looked at Gramps. "I'm mad too, I guess. I'd like to punch somebody, but I don't know who."

"I can understand why you'd feel that way, Josh. But you need to be careful." Gramps finished his mug.

"Yeah, I know."

Just then the back screen door banged shut. I looked out through the snow-filled air. "Hey! That's Mom and Dad. It looks like they are heading for the shop. I wonder what they are up to?"

"Beats me," Gramps said, but he had a mysterious look on his face. "Hey, Josh, you want to help me get out my old snowmobile? I want to tune it up and get it out in this snow today."

"Yeah! Let's go!" Some of my favorite memories involved riding that snowmobile when Nathan and I had visited Grandma and Gramps over past Christmas vacations. I drank the last of my hot chocolate and said, "I'll get my coat on."

＊＊＊

I was puzzled a few minutes later when Gramps ushered me into the dark interior of the shop. I wondered where Mom and Dad were and why the lights were off.

As Gramps snapped on the light, my parents yelled, "Merry Christmas!" They had been standing there in the dark, waiting beside a brand new Polaris snowmobile with a huge red bow on it.

I froze in my confusion.

"Come over here, Son, and look at your new snowmobile," Dad said.

"My snowmobile?"

"I know it's not Christmas yet," Mom said, "but we wanted you to enjoy it for the whole vacation. Since it snowed today we thought we'd give it to you now."

I approached the shiny machine slowly. I couldn't believe it.

"It's all yours, Josh," Dad said, "but your mother and I hope you'll let us borrow it sometimes to help with winter farm work."

"No problem." I swung my leg over the seat and put my hands on the grips. I was shaking with excitement.

"And here is something to go with it." Mom set a basketball-sized box wrapped in Christmas paper on the seat in front of me. I tore the wrapping off to reveal a helmet, goggles, and thermal gloves. "You will be wearing these whenever you ride." Her tone was uncompromising.

"Yes, Mom."

For the next forty-five minutes, I ran the new snowmobile around the barnyard and out into the back pasture. Gramps got out his snowmobile. Soon the two machines were buzzing around the farm. I'm sure it was evident to everyone that I loved my new snowmobile. When we went into the farmhouse for lunch, I had a hard time leaving it behind in the shop. I had an overwhelming desire to share it with someone, but who? Sarah was the first name that came to mind.

As I took my dishes to the sink after lunch, I said, "I think I'll buzz over to show Sarah my new snowmobile."

My parents looked at each other and a grin split Gramps' face. He said, "Sounds like a good plan, Josh!"

"Be sure to give her some warning that you're coming," Mom said.

As I dug in my pocket for my phone, Dad chuckled in spite of his serious look.

***

Speeding across the front pasture was much faster than going around by the driveways. The falling snow was over a foot deep and it sprayed out around me.

At first I thought the figure standing in the driveway wearing thermal overalls, Carhartt jacket, and stocking hat was Paul Dirk. But as I pulled up, I recognized Sarah. She said something I couldn't hear. Shutting down, I said, "What's that?"

"Cool snowmobile!"

I hopped off the snowmobile and walked around it, admiring its sleek lines. "Do you want to take it out for a spin?"

"Sure do!" Sarah hopped on before I could say anything more.

She blasted out of the yard into the pasture so fast that I didn't get a chance to give her my helmet. She could really make that thing go.

Sarah rode the snowmobile for a full twenty minutes, and I was starting to wonder if she'd ever come back when she roared up, spraying me with snow, bringing the snowmobile to a skidding stop. She laughed as she shut the engine down. "That was fantastic! This bugger goes!"

My momentary irritation vanished as I saw the joy in her sparkling eyes and the smile that threatened to burst her rosy cheeks. I said, "You know how to drive one of these things."

"Dad and Mom used to have snowmobiles. I grew up riding them. But when we lost the farm they went into the auction. It's terrific to ride again."

We stood there in silence for a bit as Sarah's familiar sadness came back.

"Josh," Sarah said softly.

"Yes?"

"I don't suppose you'd be willing to do me a favor?"

"Of course," I said, lifting my head to look closely at Sarah.

"I need to check my traps before basketball practice today, otherwise I'll have to do it in the dark. Tramping through this snow will be slow, but if you took me on your snowmobile, I'd be done in plenty of time."

"I can do that," I said.

"I'll get my pack." Sarah turned toward the barn.

Sarah emerged from the barn's small side door with a large-frame pack on her back. She wore chest waders over her coveralls and carried a rifle in a canvas sling. She tied the sling to the snowmobile, swung her leg over, and sat down. I stood with my helmet under my arm, staring at her.

"What?" Sarah laughed. "Haven't you ever seen a trapper before?"

"Yeah, in the movies—coonskin hat, flintlock rifle, that sort of thing."

"What? A girl can't hunt and trap?" Sarah said in a low, even voice. "I fish too. Want to make something of it?" The menace was convincing.

"I'm not saying that. It's more like culture shock. I'm still a city boy."

"Oh, that. I can beat that out of you too."

"Where to, boss?"

I started the snowmobile and followed Sarah's directions across the fields down to Benton Slough. As the way got a little rougher down in the breaks, Sarah put one arm around my chest, bracing her pack with the other.

"Slow down here," she yelled in my ear as we went along the edge of the frozen water.

"Don't go out on the ice because it's still too thin," she shouted. Then, pointing to something red sticking up through the snow, she shouted, "Stop there!"

She went over and dusted off the red flag that marked the site of her trap. It hung on a stiff wire that had been inserted through the ice into the bottom of the pond. Taking a hatchet from her pack, she broke the ice around the flag. She pulled on a pair of long-sleeved rubber gloves and reached into the water, feeling around carefully. Then with a shout of joy, she lifted a metal contraption from the water. The dead body of a small furry creature was in it.

"What is it?" I asked.

"A muskrat," she explained.

"Oh." I wrinkled my nose as Sarah held the muskrat in front of my face. It smelled odd and it looked like an overgrown rat.

Sarah reset the trap and directed me toward the next flag.

After about forty-five minutes, Sarah told me to stop at the base of a hill that rose well above the wetlands. She took the rifle from its sling and motioned for me to follow. She crouched as she made her way to the top of the hill and then crawled over the crest, making her way to a high bluff overlooking the river. I imitated her movement. Lying in the snow, Sarah brought up her gun and peered through the telescopic sight. She scanned the horizon carefully in a 180-degree arc. Finally she relaxed and sat up, holding the rifle across her lap. I looked down to the boulders along the stream 30 feet below. The ground called to me here too. Even though the drop was 100 feet short of the drop from the water tower in Portland, a fall would probably be lethal.

"I shot a coyote here a week ago and a fox two weeks back. Their pelts are hanging in the barn right now," she said.

"Sarah, I know you said you do this to save for college, but wow! It's brutal."

"I suppose." Sarah followed my gaze to the rocks below.

"Doesn't it bother you to kill these little animals?" I asked.

"Sometimes it does," Sarah said somberly. "Every year this area produces more fur-bearing animals than the land can support. I believe that the ones I kill make way for others to live."

We sat in silence for a while staring down over the precipice. I blurted, "Do you ever think of just offing yourself?"

There was a long frozen silence. It was too late to take it back.

Finally Sarah said, "Yeah, a couple of years ago, when I figured out that my mom wasn't coming back, I was sad," she paused before she continued, "and angry. I thought about it. Why do you ask?"

"Uh . . ."

"Are you thinking about it . . . now?" Her voice filled with concern.

"Um, not now . . . not at the moment."

Sarah seemed to relax a little. She shifted so she was facing me, but she remained silent, waiting.

Finally I said, "Last summer the sadness in our family was

tearing Mom and Dad apart. I couldn't face living without Nathan or without Mom and Dad being married. It seemed hopeless. What was the point?" I looked down at the boulders.

"I can see how that would make you epically sad. But I'm glad you didn't." Sarah continued to sit quietly.

I could feel her eyes on me, but I couldn't look away from the boulders far below. A long moment passed and then another. Finally I sighed and turned away from the edge and looked at Sarah.

She said nothing, only returned a steady gaze. Then, grunting, she stood up.

The silence continued as we returned to the snowmobile and packed to leave. Nothing had changed about Sarah. Her movements were confident and quick. She had that same little smile that had adorned her face all afternoon. Just as I was getting ready to start up, she leaned forward and said into my ear, "Thanks for being here, Josh."

As I sorted through the layers of meaning, I felt understood and decided that was enough.

***

The light was starting to fade by the time we got back. As Sarah untied the sling, I picked up her pack and followed her into the little shed attached to the back of the barn. The strong smell of muskrats assaulted me as I stepped through the door.

"Put the pack over there," she said. "I'll take care of them later. You need to get going since the boys practice first tonight. Thanks for your help."

"No problem," I said, turning to leave. "What's this?" I gestured to a table holding a bulletin board and several plastic containers. Pinned to the bulletin board was a large sign that read "The Life Cycle of Muskrats."

"Yeah, I'm doing a project on the life cycle of the muskrat for my science fair project," Sarah grinned.

"I heard Mr. Nicholson talking about science fair projects in physics. But I think I came too late in the year to start one."

"I don't think that's true, Josh," Sarah said in a serious voice. "Why don't you talk to Mr. Nicholson when school starts? I'll bet there is still time to enter."

"I might do that. It sounds like fun," I said, surprised that I meant it. "I better get going."

Sarah went with me as I headed toward the snowmobile. She said, "I guess I'll see you on Tuesday. Your mom invited Dad and me for Christmas dinner."

"Yeah, I heard that," I said with a grin. I stood, trying to think of something else to say. Finally I added, "If you want I can take you around your trap line during vacation."

"Wow! That'd be cool!"

"Give me a call," I said as I started the snowmobile. Sarah just smiled and waved as I flipped on the headlamp and sped across the front pasture.

Chapter 19

Spear Training

MY HEAD HURT. I TRIED TO OPEN MY EYES WITHOUT
SUCCESS.

"Joshua! Joshua! Are you okay?"

Nathan's voice. I felt like I'd been beaned with a fence
post.

"Joshua, wake up! Bring me that bucket of water!"

Suddenly my world was very wet. Spluttering for breath,
I opened my eyes to the bright Jerusalem daylight. Nathan's
concerned face filled my field of vision.

"Wha . . . Wha . . ." I was having trouble forming words. I
squeezed my eyes closed to shut out the daytime glare.

"Just a minute, Joshua. Here, help me get him into the
shade."

I felt hands helping me stand. After a short, stumbling walk I
plopped down with my back to a wall. This time when I opened
my eyes Nathan's worried features came into sharper focus.

"Look! There's a dent in his helmet. You whacked him good, Nathan," someone said.

"I'm so sorry, Joshua. I didn't mean to hit you that hard. After you swept my legs, I had to prove that . . . I got carried away."

"Uh . . ." I tried to speak again, but I still couldn't get much out. "Nathan . . ." I finally managed to say, but my voice was thin and raspy.

"Drink some of this, Joshua." Nathan pushed the open end of a water pouch into my mouth and squirted the warm, foul-tasting contents down my throat.

I choked and coughed, but found that I could speak. "Nathan, what's happening? Where are we?"

"Don't you know? You are really hurt!"

"Nathan! It's me." I clutched Nathan's arm, pulling him closer. In a whisper, I said, "I'm Future Joshua."

"Oh!" Nathan stood up in surprise, looking down at me.

A burly man came up to us. He wore a pointed metal helmet and a heavy mail coat that hung to the middle of his thighs. He carried a thick wooden shaft, which ended in a long blade glinting in the sun.

"What's going on here?"

"Captain," Nathan said as he straightened and brought his fist to his chest in salute. "I hit my brother too hard. I think I knocked him out for a minute."

"It's a good thing we give you recruits practice sticks. If you had real spears, there wouldn't be any of you left to man the walls against the Assyrians." Then in a slightly softer tone, the captain said, "Is he all right?"

"Yes, I think so," Nathan said. "He's just dazed at the moment."

"Okay. We're nearly finished for today anyway. Why don't you take Joshua home," the captain said. "But you both need to be here at dawn tomorrow."

"Yes, sir!" Nathan said to the captain's back. The captain was already returning to the clatter of recruits practicing with wooden staffs. Nathan watched him march away and then he turned back to me.

"Is it you? You're Future Joshua?"

"Yep. Oh, my head hurts."

"Sorry about that. But you should have parried better."

"What's a parry?" I asked.

"You missed blocking my blow."

"I had nothing to do with it."

"I suppose that's why you're here. My Joshua got knocked out and you changed places while he was unconscious."

"I hope I don't end up fighting Assyrians. I wouldn't have a clue what I was doing."

"That wouldn't be good."

"I take it that the news about the Assyrians is not good," I said.

"They took the tribute but they are coming for us anyway. Father's spies report a huge army moving toward Jerusalem."

"What does that mean?" I asked.

"They plan to put Jerusalem under siege and probably to assault the walls. If they get in they will destroy the city.

That's what they've done everywhere else they've gone." Nathan slumped down to sit beside me.

"That's bad, isn't it?"

"When the army drafts apprenticed scribes, it's serious. Eli let Sarah start training with the archers. There are quite a few of the young women with her."

"I remember her saying that she would rather die on the walls than face triumphant Assyrians," I said.

"It doesn't go well for the women when an enemy breaks through." Nathan put his head in his hands.

"Why?"

Nathan's head snapped up to stare at me for a minute. "Don't attackers rape the women when they conquer in the future?"

"I . . . don't know." I suddenly felt sick. "I mean, not our troops, I think. But maybe other places. It's hard to explain and I probably shouldn't try anyway." Then after a short silence I asked, "Are you afraid, Nathan?"

Nathan drooped again with his arms braced against his upraised knees. "Everyone is. The Assyrians have never lost, and they destroy every city they attack. God is greater than all the Assyrian gods put together. The greater god should always win in war. But still . . ."

I looked carefully at Nathan. "What does God have to do with this?"

Nathan raised his head in surprise. "War is the game of the gods. The nations strive in warfare to prove which god is the greatest."

"But didn't you say that Jerusalem's God is the greatest?" We had not covered God and war in Sunday school.

"Israel's God is the only true God." Nathan turned to look at me.

I met his eyes and then focused back into the distance. "What does that mean?"

"God, Yahweh, is the God who created everything. Have future people forgotten? The other gods may be real, but they aren't true gods. They're angels or demons or spirits. God created them, as he created everything. Those gods love war."

"But if God is so powerful, why does he let war happen at all?"

"I don't know. I've heard Isaiah teach that no one can know or understand why God does what he does."

"You know Isaiah, the prophet?"

"Everyone in Jerusalem knows him. He's not popular because he keeps telling people things they don't want to hear. But the king likes him. Isaiah says we can't know why God does what he does. It's like when the northern kingdom rejected God—God let the Assyrians utterly destroy the ten tribes of Israel in the north. The true Lord of the universe doesn't play the game of war, but he uses it for his purposes. Now they're coming for us. We don't know what will happen. Jerusalem has been faithful to God since Hezekiah became king. But there's a history of unfaithfulness by the kings before him." Nathan looked worried.

"You think God wants to destroy Jerusalem?" I said. "How

can you believe in a God like that? Maybe you can't under-stand what God does because there isn't a God. Maybe it's all just chance. And people just die and that's the end of it."

"The songs of King David say that the wicked pretend there is no God so that they can hide their evil desires from themselves. I can't believe that you have become wicked, Joshua." Nathan said it with a laugh, but a look of concern was in his eyes.

"God let my brother Nathan die in the future. How could he do that? How could a good God do that?"

Nathan was quiet for a long time. "You're like my Joshua in this. Your heart is so loud you can't hear your mind. You blame God for letting your Nathan die. You can't do that and stop believing in him at the same time. You believe in God deeply. The problem is that you are angry with him." Nathan looked convinced.

I moaned, only partially from the blow to my head. After a while, I asked, "But, how could God let the Assyrians destroy you? Aren't you the only people who believe in him?"

"Father says that God has a plan for his people, some-thing great that he's doing in the world through us," Nathan explained. "Whether the Assyrians destroy Jerusalem or not, God's plan for us will continue. Father says we need to trust God to do what he thinks is best, even if it seems terrible to us."

"I'm not sure I can do that."

"To be honest, I'm not there either," Nathan confided. "But for now I'm willing to hope that God will deliver us from this disaster."

"I hope you're right, Nathan. Man, do I hope you're right."

"Let's try to get home now. Are you feeling any better?" Nathan asked.

"Maybe a little." I did feel more clear-headed, but still weak.

"Can you walk?"

"I'll try."

Nathan helped me to my feet and I took hold of his arm to steady myself. We made our way slowly through Jerusalem's paths.

"How are you doing now?" Nathan asked as we came to the top of a particularly long set of stairs.

"I think I'm doing better." Then I moaned as a spasm of pain shot through my head.

"Let's sit and rest for a minute," Nathan suggested.

"Good idea." I plopped down on the stairway we'd just climbed. We could see the broad new wall over the roofs of the houses it penned firmly inside. "How is the construction of the wall coming?"

"It's mostly finished," Nathan said, sitting down beside me. "When we learned that the Assyrians were marching, we started working through the night. Now all that's left are some things the army commanders want, like breastworks to protect the archers when they are shooting from the outer edge of the wall."

"Why is the air so smoky?" I asked.

"They've set up forges everywhere," Nathan explained.

"Blacksmiths are beating every non-essential metallic thing into weapons and arrow points. Father says that keeping everyone busy helps them not to panic."

I noticed a group of people working on a rooftop below us. "What are they doing over there?"

Nathan looked in the direction I was pointing. "They are making water pots on those big pottery wheels. And those other workers are preparing the clay to be thrown on the wheel. That's the other reason that the air is smoky—every kiln in the city is fully stoked."

"Why?"

Nathan gazed somberly at me. "We'll fill the pots with water and set them all around the city to help put out fires. It will also give us a better store of water. The water tunnel is still new and we don't yet know if it will provide enough water for a long siege. Tell me, is there no war in the future?"

I shrugged. "Not like this. Not where I live."

We sat looking out over the city in silence for a while longer. Several times we had to move aside to let folks through. People were carrying stuff everywhere. It reminded me of the ant farm I had in third grade.

"I think I'm feeling well enough to go on," I said after a while.

"Okay, let's try it."

***

Even though some things were starting to look familiar, I would have been lost without Nathan. Finally, we came to an archway I recognized.

"Here we are," Nathan said, as we went down the dark hall lit by a single lamp. He worked the latch and pulled the door open.

"You two are back early," Mother said. "What happened?"

"Well," Nathan said hesitantly, "while we were sparring, I hit Joshua on the side of the head. I meant to hit him, but not that hard. He had a helmet on, but I think he was unconscious for a little bit. The captain sent us home to make sure everything was okay."

"Here, let me look at that," Mother said, concern filling her voice. She guided me over to a lamp on a niche in the wall and gently probed my head.

I was startled at how familiar it felt. Those were my mother's fingers. That is how she always touched me. She even smelled like Mom.

"This is going to be a pretty good-sized bump for a while, Son. We should get a cool cloth on it." She turned her head and called out, "Sarah!"

Sarah appeared almost instantly.

"Joshua has been hurt. Go wet some cloths with the cool water in the storeroom," Mother instructed her. "Bring them into Joshua's bedchamber. I'm going to have him lie down. Nathan go help her."

"Let's get you back to your bed, Josh," Mother said, gently taking my arm. As I lay down, and she sat on the edge of my bed and said, "Are you cold or hot?"

"No, I'm fine. Don't worry, Mother."

She reached out and laid the back of her hand against my forehead in another familiar gesture. "You feel the right temperature." Concern choked her voice.

Sarah entered the room followed closely by Nathan who was carrying a lamp.

"Here," Sarah said, handing the damp cloths to Mother and sitting down beside her. "How is he?"

Nathan set the lamp down. "Pampered. That's how he is." Nathan laughed.

Rachel folded the damp cloth and laid it over my forehead. "Stop it, Nathan. This accident is your fault. You're supposed to take care of your little brother, not beat him up." She chuckled a little, taking some of the sting out of her words.

"Mother, it wasn't Nathan's fault. I was supposed to have parried or blocked or something," I said, with a mixture of feelings. I wanted to defend Nathan, but my mother's caring attention was delightful.

"Let's pray that God delivers us. I don't think either of you is a match for Assyrian soldiers. Or you either, Sarah. Although I think you might get in your share of damage before they scale the walls." Mother laughed weakly, but nobody joined her.

Suddenly it felt real. These people were facing terrible danger, suffering, and possibly death. Dread hung over Jerusalem like the smoke of its preparation.

"I think he's going to sleep," I heard Mother say. I'd drifted off for a second. I hadn't noticed when she and Sarah stood up. Mother covered me up with a linen blanket. "Let him rest for a while. Nathan, bring that lamp when you come."

Nathan looked down at me for a long moment, then he picked up the lamp and tiptoed from the room. Everything went dark as Nathan left.

Chapter 20

Christmas Dinner

"I THINK THEY'RE HERE," Gramps said, as he looked out the kitchen window upon hearing the sound of a vehicle coming into the yard.

"Go let them in, Josh," Mom called from the back bedroom.

I made my way through the living room. The lights on the tree sparkled in a preset rhythm. We had cut the tree from Gramps' Christmas tree garden across the back pasture. I went into the front hall, where I waited by the door for the Dirks' knock. It never came.

"Well, hey, Paul, Sarah!" I heard my grandfather say as the back door opened with its characteristic rattle. "Welcome! Welcome!"

How could I forget that farm folk always come to the back door? I arrived in the kitchen in time to see Paul Dirk presenting Gramps with two large bottles of wine. "One white and one rosé," Paul explained with a laugh. "Just to make sure the wine fits the cuisine."

"How thoughtful," Mom said as she walked into the kitchen, raking a strand of her chin-length hair back over her ear. Her broad smile spread across her face as she firmly shook Paul's hand and then hugged Sarah. "Good to see you, dear."

Sarah brightened.

"Let me take your coats," Dad said, reaching to shake Paul's hand. As he gathered the pair of Carhartt jackets, he said, "That was some game last Tuesday night, Sarah! They gave you a run for your money. Glad you girls were able to hold out."

Sarah's smile seemed oddly shy.

Everyone sat down at the dining table. Dad prayed, and after the usual small talk, Paul and Mom started reminiscing about their high school days. After the eating slowed and the conversation lagged, Paul took a big drink of his wine and said, "I was kind of surprised you folks invited me over after what I said the other day."

Sarah looked stricken.

Gramps set his fork down and looked evenly at Paul. "We were caught off guard, but your dad was my oldest and dearest friend. I'm not going to let a few words stand in the way of being a good neighbor to his son."

"Thank you for that, Mr. Neilson," Paul said solemnly. "I want to apologize."

There was a general murmur of acceptance around the table. In the awkward moment that followed, Paul reached for a bottle of wine and refilled his glass.

"Sarah," Mom said, looking up from her plate. "I'm thinking of taking advantage of Haegle's after-Christmas sale to shop for a new pair of boots. Would you like to go along?"

"Absolutely!"

"We could also look at some new tack for the horses. I haven't gotten them anything for Christmas yet."

"That would be fun." Sarah's relieved smile lit up her face.

"That's right! You're a real cowgirl, Rachel," Paul said, sitting back and sipping at his glass. "What was it that you did in the rodeo?"

"Barrel riding."

"Oh yeah, that's right. You were pretty good if I remember right." Paul poured the last of the wine from the bottle into his glass. "No point in letting this go to waste." He lifted his glass in a mock salute.

"I did okay," Mom followed up.

"Naw, I heard you were fantastic! Didn't you beat the crap out of everyone at the Mobridge whatchamacallit rodeo?" His words slurred as he raised his voice theatrically.

I noticed Sarah's worried glance at her father.

"Yes, I did fairly well a couple of years at the Sitting Bull Stampede. Let's have some dessert. We've got cherry and apple pie. You can have it with or without ice cream."

While Mom took dessert orders, Dad and Gramps cleared away some of the dishes. Sarah got up to help Mom dish up the pie and ice cream. While finishing the last of my mashed potatoes, I glanced surreptitiously at Sarah's dad. Paul was staring at the empty wine bottles with a mournful look on his face. I thought his face looked flushed.

As we finished the pie, Sarah said, "Dad, we need to leave pretty soon if you want to catch the Celtics Game."

"Don't be rude, Sarah," Paul said loudly. "These nice people have just served us a lovely meal. We need to thank them before we go." He surveyed the table with glassy eyes and a pasted-on smile.

"Yes, thank you Rachel, Ben, and Mr. Neilson," Sarah said rapidly. "It was a wonderful meal and we appreciated the invitation."

"You are most welcome, Sarah, Paul," Mom said brightly.

"Now, Dad, you know you always get grouchy when you miss the opening tip-off. Maybe we should get going?"

"Okay, okay. I suppose you're right. Thanks, folks, for this splendid meal." Paul Dirk rose unsteadily from his seat.

Dad popped up to retrieve their coats. Everyone accompanied them to the door. As they went out, Sarah dropped her grip on her father's arm to come back and give Mom a silent parting hug. We all stood in the doorway watching Sarah load her father into the passenger's seat. The rusted-out Mercury sedan slowly crept down the driveway.

"Was he drunk?" Dad asked.

"Yeah, it looked that way," Gramps said.

"I don't see how. Paul didn't drink that much wine, did he?" Mom observed.

"No, but he probably had something before he got here. I thought I smelled it when he first came in. It adds up." Gramps started organizing the dishes for washing.

"Poor Sarah," Mom said wistfully.

Chapter 21

A Science Fair Project

It was the first Saturday after we went back to school following Christmas. I steered the Beast toward a small cluster of cars near the main door of Wheaton High School. I drove carefully across the ice-covered parking lot, stopping by a massive pile of snow. Since the accident in November I was skittish about driving on slick surfaces, even when parking.

I yawned even in icy January air. For the sake of science I was sacrificing my one chance to sleep in this week. Mr. Nicholson had told me there was still time to enter the science fair, but I needed to come to a meeting this morning.

Stopping at my locker, I dug out a notebook and a couple of pencils before heading to the science room. Noticing how empty the hallways were, I checked my phone and saw that I was five minutes late. I was going to be making an entrance. Ugh.

"Joshua, great!" Mr. Nicholson said as I entered the room. "I'm so glad you were able to make it this morning. Wonderful! Find a seat. We're just getting started."

I looked around the room. Most of the black-topped science tables had two or three students sitting at them. Sarah sat alone at a table near the back of the room, looking down as she paged through her notebook. I felt the eyes of the room following me as I walked defiantly to Sarah's table and sat down across from her. She looked surprised, but her tight smile seemed grateful.

"Shelly, Melanie, let's hear a progress report," Mr. Nicholson said, interrupting a small storm of whispers. "The science fair at SDSU is coming up next month. How is your project coming?"

Melanie Crawford tapped at her laptop computer and then said, "Shelly and I are working on a project about amino acids, which are the building blocks of life. We want to demonstrate how they formed when lightning struck the earth's primitive atmosphere."

"Yeah!" Shelly Waters said. "We're going to prove that the universe doesn't need God to create life."

Mr. Nicholson cleared his throat. "Ah, Shelly, please leave the theological issues out of your project. You need to focus on science for this project. Okay?"

"Okay, Mr. Nicholson," Shelly said sullenly.

"Melanie," Mr. Nicholson continued, "I take it that you will be reviewing the work of Dr. Miller at the University of Chicago."

"Uh, no, the name we were researching is Dr. Harold Urey. He's a Nobel prize winner who theorized that earth's primitive atmosphere would have formed just the right kind of . . ." Melanie scrolled her computer screen. ". . . prebiotic soup required for organic compounds to emerge."

"That's a good research path, but you will want to look into the work of Dr. Stanley Miller also. He did the actual experiments, applying electric shocks to a mixture of methane, ammonia, and hydrogen. Dr. Urey was his Ph.D. adviser." Mr. Nicholson wrote the chemical symbols for methane, ammonia, and hydrogen on the white-board. "Incidentally, handling these chemicals can be dangerous. Let's schedule a day to visit the Chemistry Department at SDSU to get a little help with any experiments you are planning for your project."

"Can we do that?" Shelly asked enthusiastically.

"Absolutely," Mr. Nicholson said with a broad smile. "I have a buddy who works in that department, and I'm sure he'll be glad to help us."

"Mr. Nicholson, what's the point of doing this project if we can't say that it proves that the origin of life was purely accidental? That's the big deal about Urey's theories," Shelly said with a pout.

"Of course, Shelly, you can include the cultural impact of the scientific work as part of your project. But you must make your points from an accurate scientific perspective. The social response to the Miller–Urey experiments is extraneous information. Not only that, you must be careful to weed out your own religious convictions."

"I'm an atheist, Mr. Nicholson. I don't have religious convictions."

Mr. Nicholson looked at Shelly thoughtfully for a moment. "I understand what you are saying. But from a scientific perspective, any statements about God, including the non-existence of God, are religious convictions."

"True science makes it clear that there can't possibly be a God," Shelly blurted out.

"How can you say that, Shelly?" Jean Wilkerson broke in angrily. "Good science proves the existence of God through the findings of Intelligent Design!"

"Ladies!" Mr. Nicholson's voice cracked through the room. After a significant period of silence he continued. "Both of you are making the same mistake. If you are going to be a successful scientist, you need to correct it. Jean, if you do scientific research to prove a tenant of religious faith, then you are destroying the objectivity necessary to all true science. I find the work in Intelligent Design very interesting, but I'm suspicious of its scientific objectivity."

"But, Mr. Nicholson . . ."

"Let's talk more about this later, Jean. Right now, I need to focus on Shelly and Melanie's project. Okay?"

"Okay," Jean said, with glum resignation.

"Now, Shelly, you're making a similar mistake," Mr. Nicholson said, raising his hand to forestall her outburst. "Trying to show that God doesn't exist is just as damaging to scientific objectivity as attempting to prove that God does exist. You've already made the point that this is one of your primary motivations in the choice of your science fair project. Isn't that right?"

Shelly stared back in angry silence.

"I agree that it will add something to this project to make an objective analysis of this subject's cultural impact, because the Miller–Urey findings deeply stirred the faith–science dialogue. Additionally," Mr. Nicholson continued, "you will need to follow up on NASA's recent findings concerning Earth's early atmosphere. Their findings show that oxygen-rich compounds dominated our earth's earliest atmosphere. It was much more like our current atmosphere than what Miller and Urey assumed."

"Just a second," Melanie said, typing furiously on her laptop. "Here it is—'Earth's Early Atmosphere: An Update from Astrobiology at NASA'. It claims that previous experiments about the origins of life on Earth picked the wrong atmosphere."

"That means our project is pointless!" Shelly wailed.

"Not at all. This is the point I'm trying to make," Mr. Nicholson said firmly. "The Urey–Miller work was valid science. It's a very worthwhile subject for your science fair project. And the cultural impact is also a fascinating part of that story. But it's vital that you maintain an objective scientific perspective. As you can see, subsequent discoveries can radically change how society interprets the findings."

"Come on, Shelly," Melanie said. "This will be fun. I can already see us surprising people with this information. Mr.

Nicholson, would you please go ahead and ask about a day at SDSU?"

Shelly gave no response, her frustration written clearly on her face.

"Will do." Mr. Nicholson made a note on a legal pad on his desk.

"Jean, let's hear about your project," Mr. Nicholson said, turning to Jean and Ellen.

"We call our project 'The Useful Ecology of Yeast'," Jean Wilkerson said. "Ellen and I are going to show all the great things that yeast does."

"Jean got the idea when she was helping her mother bake bread," Ellen Longfeather added.

"You know they make beer with that stuff, right?" Shelly said with a snarl. "Are your teetotaling parents going to let you do a project like that?"

"It's also part of the process that creates communion wine," Jean responded coolly.

"Shelly, please . . ." Mr. Nicholson said, intervening. "Jean and Ellen, go ahead."

As Jean and Ellen reviewed the uses of yeast, I looked around the science room. Eleven students had made the early Saturday morning gathering. As the meeting progressed, sets of two or three students explained the projects they had chosen for the upcoming science fair. Sarah was the last to report. Her project on the life cycle of the muskrat was the only one without a partner.

When everyone was packing up to leave, Mr. Nicholson

came over to me and said, "Joshua, how wonderful that you were able to come this morning. Have you given any thought to what you might do for a science fair project? You won't have much time to prepare it."

"Uh . . ."

"Joshua's been helping me with my project," Sarah said hesitantly. "Maybe he could partner with me on 'The Life Cycle of Muskrats'."

"Yes!" I said. "We already planned to go out looking for . . . what did you call it?"

I saw a quick flash of joyful relief cross her face. "Ecological evidence for my . . . our display."

"Splendid," Mr. Nicholson said with a grin. "Sarah, you always do well at the science fair, but the judges look for collaboration in these projects, so this will help you. Joshua, this is the perfect way for you to get started. Sarah can show you the ropes."

"Thanks," I said after Mr. Nicholson walked away. "I didn't have any idea what to do for a science fair project."

"I should have warned you about that," Sarah said. "But I'm glad it worked out this way. Mr. Nicholson's right: I need a partner for my project."

"Well, my arctic chariot is at your service."

Sarah laughed.

Just then Jean came up to our table. "Hey, Sarah, are you ready for the game tonight?" A wry smile appeared as her gaze settled on me.

"Yeah, I'm ready enough. How about you? Lemmon

has that 6'1" center. Are you going to be able to handle her?"

"I did in the championship game at the New Year's tournament. At least I sort of neutralized her a bit. It helped that you scored 18 points. The main thing is that we won."

"You did great, Jean. And you kept us together under pressure. You're a good captain. I'm sure we'll do fine tonight too."

Jean held her hand up for a high five. As Sarah slapped her response, Jean said, "Nice to see you here, Josh. Sarah mentioned that you have been helping with her trapping."

"Yeah." I was starting to like Jean.

"I think you owe it to her. Your basketball is improving. After how you played last night, I wonder how long it will be before Coach makes you a starter. I think Marshal is going to be spending a lot more time on the bench."

"Uh . . . yeah. Sarah's helped me a lot," I said.

Jean seemed to enjoy my discomfort as she looked meaningfully at Sarah. "Well, keep up the good work. Heaven knows the boys' team needs all the help they can get. With a little luck, you guys might even make it out of the league cellar." She laughed so loudly that other eyes in the room turned our direction.

***

As Jean walked away, Sarah dawdled, packing up her

notes. I waited, determined to walk out with her. The classroom was empty except for Mr. Nicholson, who was sitting at his desk.

"Good luck tonight, Sarah," Mr. Nicholson said, looking up with a smile. Then he added, "We miss you on the JV, Josh, but Coach needs you on the varsity. It's been great to watch your improvement this season."

"Thanks, Mr. Nicholson." I smiled my appreciation at Sarah as we walked out the door. I was feeling good until I saw Melanie Crawford and Shelly Waters waiting just inside the main entrance.

"Hey, Dirk, it looks like you've found a new love slave," Melanie said with a smirk. "I couldn't be happier. Now maybe you'll stop trying to seduce my boyfriend." Shelly's nervous titter accompanied Melanie's obnoxious laugh.

"Nobody needs to seduce Marshal James," Sarah said. I saw the rosy shift in Sarah's complexion as she squared up in front of Melanie. I now knew that change signaled a dangerous combination of embarrassment and anger. Melanie wilted before Sarah's intimidating physique. Then she rallied as the meaning of Sarah's comment sank in.

"With a reputation like yours, you could start a business. Poor Josh here would have to stand in line."

I expected Sarah to turn incandescent, but she laughed instead. "Yeah, Crawford, it's a reputation you created. You should write novels and put your fiction to good use. It's a good thing I don't pay any attention to social media or I'd have to do something about it."

This time Melanie did wilt. Instead of responding she turned to me. "Don't get too arrogant about all your play-time, Cooper. Marshal is the best basketball player on that sorry excuse for a team. The school owes him that starting spot." She turned and marched out, drawing Shelly behind her.

"I don't get her," I said as we watched the pair battle the cold wind on the way to Melanie's car.

"The Crawfords are the richest folks in Wheaton," Sarah said, anger lingering in her voice. "They live in the fanciest house and drive the fanciest cars. Melanie's dad is a big shot in the ethanol business and he travels a lot. I think her mom works in the school lunchroom because she's bored and wants to keep tabs on Melanie. They certainly don't need the money. Melanie has always acted like a brat."

"Not Melanie, I meant Shelly. How can she stand to be friends with someone so mean?" I said as we made our way toward the two ancient pickups.

"Oh." Sarah looked thoughtful for a minute. "They've been best friends since grade school. When Shelly's mom was dying of cancer, Melanie supported Shelly the whole time. It's the only time I've ever seen her do things that were not purely selfish. The Crawfords even sponsored a big community fund-raiser to help the Waters with medical expenses."

"Shelly's mom died?"

"Yeah, it was terrible. She was sick for years before she died." Sarah stood with her hand on the Dodge's door handle.

"Was her mom an atheist too?"

"No, her mom was a staunch member of the Community Church. One day Shelly just claimed to be an atheist and started making a point of it, especially with Jean." Sarah opened the door of her truck.

I waved goodbye and climbed into the Beast's ice-cold cab.

Chapter 22

Valentine's Day

Late on a Monday afternoon during the second week in February, I sat at the kitchen table. I was watching the gently falling snow, which in South Dakota was worth observing because flakes usually lived a violent life on their way to an inconvenient drift.

I had just gotten home from school and on the table was an open Amazon box that I'd found on the porch. Sure enough, it was the Conibear No. 110 muskrat trap I'd ordered last week. The utility porch door wrenched open and I heard Mom stomping off her boots. It was too late to hide the evidence.

Mom, red-cheeked from the cold, entered the kitchen in stocking feet and was headed straight for the coffee pot when she noticed me. "Oh, hi, Josh. I wasn't expecting you home yet. But wait . . . this is an early morning practice week, isn't it?" She took down a large mug from the cabinet and filled it to the brim with steaming hot coffee.

"Yeah, it gets to be a long day when you have a 90-minute practice before school. But I'm getting used to it."

I pushed the Amazon package to the side as my Mom sat down across the table.

"Dad and I are so happy with the way you've adapted here. We were worried about how our decision to move would affect you, but so far it looks like the risk is paying off."

I nodded. Mom used to spend every waking moment in a dress suit, and now she looked natural in jeans and a plaid shirt. Was that hay in her hair?

Mom blew on her coffee and then took an experimental sip. "What's Coach saying about you getting a starting spot this week?"

"He said that I had earned the chance to start and he wanted me to know it. But he values the loyalty of seniors who've paid their dues. So, Marshal will continue to start for the rest of the season. He said I would get a lot of game time and that I was his pick for starting next year. It makes sense and I'm fine with it."

"That's quite a compliment. I'm proud of you, both for doing so well in basketball and for being so mature about team dynamics."

"There are only a couple of weeks left anyway. It's not like we are having a blockbuster season. I doubt we'll get beyond the division tournament." I leaned both elbows on the table in a way I hoped would obscure Mom's view of the package.

"What do you have there?" Mom reached across the table pulling the box toward her. Opening the lid, Mom lifted the spring steel contraption from the package and turned it over inquisitively. "What's this?"

I sighed. "It's a muskrat trap."

"A muskrat trap? Did you order this?"

"It's for Sarah."

"Sarah? Doesn't Sarah already have a bunch of muskrat traps?"

"Yeah, but this one is kind of a . . . valentine." Time stood still as I watched the startled look on Mom's face melt into a smile, and then she laughed.

"Oh!" Mom said when she gained control. "That certainly is novel."

"I didn't know what to do. Frilly cards, chocolate, and flowers seem wrong for Sarah."

"I suppose you're right. But how did you come up with a muskrat trap?" Mom asked, still chuckling.

"Uh, well, during the last month as we've been working on the science fair project, we've spent a lot of time together running her trap line and gathering stuff for our display. She's a different person when we're out there. She seems truly happy, kidding me about my city ways, and she laughs at my dumb jokes. I don't know." I paused. "I just really like her. I wanted to get her something that honors who she is. All I could think of was that trap. Is that stupid?"

Mom looked at me for a long moment before answering. "No, it's not stupid. It's a little unorthodox, but I think

I understand now." She handed the trap back to me. "The presentation could be improved. Maybe some ribbons, a card, and a nice gift bag would make it a bit more . . . romantic? I'd be glad to help."

"Uh, I guess."

"Josh," Mom said and then paused. "How do you feel about Sarah?"

"I'm not sure what to say, Mom. I owe all my success in basketball to her, so I'm grateful."

Mom nodded.

"You seem to like Sarah pretty well," I said.

"I do."

I continued, "She's been a real friend. We've taken flack for it, but it doesn't bother me. And nothing phases Sarah."

"That's true." Mom looked thoughtfully at me over the brim of her coffee cup.

"I've enjoyed working on this science fair project so much. The truth is I couldn't care less about muskrats. I just like being with Sarah. Our friendship is fantastic."

"But it's becoming more than friendship for you?" Mom asked.

"I think so."

"You want Sarah to become your girlfriend?"

I looked carefully at Mom, and seeing that she was sincere, I said, "Is that crazy, Mom?"

"Well, this sort of thing is never quite sane, but I think you're completely normal." Mom paused to think for a minute, and then she continued. "It makes me happy that you are attracted to a strong woman like Sarah. That reminds me of your father's good qualities. But I want you to guard your heart, Son. There's a darkness in the Dirk family. Even though I agree that Sarah is worth the effort, please be careful."

***

Thursday evening, Valentine's Day, I stood at the back window in my bedroom. Through binoculars borrowed from Gramps I saw two vehicles under the yard light in the Dirks' driveway. Why had Paul Dirk chosen today, of all days, to be home in the middle of the week? I couldn't deliver my gift to Sarah with her dad standing there.

I was about to go back to my homework when I caught a flash of movement near the sedan. Then its lights came on. What luck! Paul was probably heading into Joey's Bar and Grill. I watched impatiently as the sedan waddled down the heavily rutted driveway.

I grabbed my backpack containing Sarah's valentine, which looked much better after Mom had her way with it. Soon I was racing my snowmobile over the well-packed trail toward Sarah's house, and then I was standing at the back door knocking.

At first there was no response. I checked over my shoulder. Sarah's Dodge was sitting there under the yard light. I wondered if Sarah had gone to town with her Dad. But she hated to be with him when he was drinking. I knocked again.

This time the porch light came on, and I heard light

footsteps coming across the back porch. The back door opened to reveal Paul Dirk, dressed in stocking feet, dirty jeans, and an SDSU Jackrabbits T-shirt.

"Hey, Joshua! How the hell are you?" Paul said in slurred tones.

I took an involuntary step back. "Oh! Hi, Mr. Dirk."

"What's this Mr. Dirk crap? Didn't I tell you to call me Paul?"

"Yes, Mr. . . . Paul."

"That's better. Now what can I do for you?"

"Uh."

"I'll bet you're here to see Sarah."

"Yeah, is she home?"

"No, she just left. She went into town to fill up my car for me. She said it was my valentine. Did you know it was Valentine's Day?"

"Uh."

"It's too bad Sarah is underage. She could've picked me up some more beer. You can always use more beer." Paul barked a loud laugh. "Hey, come on in. No reason to stand out there in the cold." Paul stepped back from the door and gestured for me to enter.

I slipped out of my boots on the porch and put my backpack down and covered it with my coat. Then I followed Paul into the kitchen.

"Want a beer?" Paul said, reaching into the refrigerator.

"No thanks," I said quickly.

"I'm watching the Jackrabbits game," Paul said, waving

toward the TV sounds coming from the living room. "They're in Omaha tonight, but its half-time and I hate commercials."

"Yeah, me too."

"Have a seat." Paul pointed to a chair. "Are you sure I can't get you something? I think Sarah has some Diet Coke in here somewhere. Nasty stuff, but she seems to like it."

"No thanks. I'm fine," I said, as I perched on a kitchen chair.

"Suit yourself," Paul said as he collapsed into a chair across the table. "Sarah should be home pretty soon. Meantime I've got a chance to get to know you a little better."

"Uh. Okay."

"Sarah has been talking a lot about you lately. She never talks about boys."

"Ah, well, it could be because we're working on a science fair project together," I said, trying not to read too much into Paul's comment.

"I suppose. She's always done her science fair projects solo."

"I think she took pity on me because I started late and didn't have a project. And she's been helping me with my basketball skills. She's just being kind to a neighbor."

"Well, maybe," Paul drawled, scratching his stubbly chin. "But she chased the last boy who tried to play basketball with her out of the barn with a stick." Then he chuckled. "Don't mention that I told you. She gets kind of prickly over the incident."

"Okay." I wondered what that was all about.

"Well, I suppose the neighbor thing is at the root of it."

Paul took a long pull at his beer bottle. "Sarah sure likes your mom. Of course everyone loves your mom. She was popular back in high school."

"You're kidding."

"Nope." Paul ran his fingers through his unkempt hair, leaving a couple of rooster tails. "She was a senior when I was a sophomore. All us guys had crushes on her, but then she headed off for college in the Twin Cities. We never saw much of her after that."

"Mom never talks about high school," I said. "But she seems happy that I'm going to Wheaton."

"Yeah, it's a good school for a small town. It's even gotten better since Principal Longfeather came." Then Paul visibly drew into himself for a minute. He took another long pull on his bottle.

"What routes are you driving now?" I asked, attempting to steer the conversation away from Sarah and me. But Paul's stricken look plainly showed my blunder.

"Damn!" Paul chugged the remainder of his beer. As he stood up angrily and dug in the fridge for another, he said, "I won't be making any more runs for a while. They got me on suspension. Damn cop's breathalyzer must have been on the fritz. No way I was over the limit. I only had a beer with lunch. Frigging regulations."

Paul leaned on the open refrigerator door. He swayed and then looked at me. After a bit, he said, "Sorry, kid. There's no reason to burden you with that. It sounds like the game's starting again. You want to watch it or wait here for Sarah?"

"I'll wait here."

"Okay."

I heard the springs in the old couch creak as Paul flopped down in front of his television. In a moment the volume rose to where the commentary and crowd noises were quite clear.

I listened to the game for about fifteen minutes, wondering if I should slip out and go home. Then I heard the back door open, followed by the crack of the screen door closing. Sarah rushed into the room looking wild-eyed. She froze, stared briefly at me, sitting alone at the kitchen table, and then grimaced. She held up her hand for silence and stepped to the archway into the living room.

"Hi, Dad. I'm back. Your car is full of gas. Happy Valentine's Day!"

Paul's response was unintelligible.

"I asked Josh to come over so I can teach him a new move."

Some more vague words floated from the living room over the game commentary.

Sarah turned on her heel and marched through the kitchen toward the back door. "Come on!" she said in clipped tones.

The screen door slammed again as I rushed to jam my feet into my boots. Grabbing my coat and backpack, I went out the open back door, pulling it shut behind me. I could see Sarah's figure moving ahead of me under the halogen beams of the yard light. I was halfway across the yard when I saw her flip on the light in the barn. She was pacing the barn floor when I entered half a minute later.

"What are you doing here?" Sarah's eyes flashed but her tone was even.

"I thought I was here to learn a new move."

Sarah stopped pacing and looked at me carefully. "I had to tell Dad something. He's started to tease me about how much we're together." She walked over to where a basketball lay against the wall. Picking it up, she dribbled twice and then swished the shot. Even wearing her heavy winter coat, I could see how graceful she was.

Sarah retrieved the ball and then turned to me, basketball under her arm. "So, why are you here?" she said. Her voice was only curious this time.

I crossed the floor and sat down on a bale of hay. Opening my backpack, I carefully brought out the bright red gift bag tied with the pink ribbon my mother had helped me prepare.

"I brought you a valentine."

"Oh."

Sarah stared like a deer in the headlights. As I walked toward her holding out the gift, she looked ready to bolt. Then like the sun emerging from the clouds, Sarah's smile lit her face. She took the gift bag and opened it. She reached in, past the pink tissue paper, and pulled out the No. 110 muskrat trap, complete with the braided ribbon and dangling spangles Mom had supplied.

She looked stunned and then puzzled as she stared at the carefully decorated trap. Finally she looked up at me directly into my eyes. After a moment she began to giggle and then her giggles turned into fits of laughter. Collapsing, she sat on the floor, cradling the valentine in her lap.

It was a full minute before she could talk. Brushing from her eyes both hair and tears, she looked up and said, "You thought my dad had gone to town when the Mercury drove away, so that's why you came over now."

I nodded.

After the next fit of laughter subsided, Sarah said. "Poor guy, I bet you were surprised when my dad answered the door."

"You have no idea."

Sarah chuckled some more, obviously fighting to control her mirth as she stood up again. "I wish I had known you were going to do this. I would have gotten you something."

"You've already given me so much. I can't even start to thank you. I know it's a little odd for a valentine, but I thought . . . "

"You got it right!" she said firmly, cutting me off. "It's the only valentine I've gotten since grade school. But if I'd gotten thousands, this would still be the best, because, well, you understand."

She stepped toward me and put her arms around my shoulders, giving me a warm if somewhat well-padded hug. Then I heard a sharp metallic clang as the muskrat trap fell on the floor. Sarah leaned back from the embrace and took my head in both hands. She pulled my head toward her and kissed me. It was brief, but firm, and I knew she meant it.

But before I had time to respond, she pulled away and bent to recover the No. 110 valentine.

"Happy Valentine's Day, Josh. Thank you for my gift. I know just where I'm going to use it," Sarah said as she gathered up the gift bag and tissue paper. Her voice was soft and pleasant.

"You're welcome." Euphoria swelled inside me. Then I noticed that she was moving toward the door.

"Don't forget to be at school early tomorrow. I'm going to need your help loading our display into the van for the science fair."

"Sure!" I said enthusiastically to the empty doorway. As I stood there gaping, I heard the bang of the screen door on the back porch. Sarah was gone. I stood in the center of the barn for a moment trying to gather my wits. Then I shrugged. Turning, I picked up my backpack, flipped off the barn lights, and carefully closed the door.

Chapter 23

Assyrian Emissaries

"Joshua, Joshua, wake up!" Nathan shook me hard.

I opened my eyes to the dim light of Nathan's lamp. "What?"

"Get up! The Assyrians are here. Uncle Eliakim and Joah, the head scribe, are being sent out to meet their emissaries. We're supposed to carry things for them.

"Uh." I sat up and rubbed my eyes.

"Hurry! Uncle Eliakim is waiting," Nathan said as he chucked an outer robe at me, hitting me in the face. Sandals hit me in the chest.

I gripped my brother by the shoulders and stared into his eyes. "Nathan, I'm Future Joshua."

"No!" Nathan wailed. "It can't be!" He held the lamp so he could look me in the eyes. "Really?"

I nodded solemnly.

Nathan collapsed heavily on the bed beside me.

"The Assyrians are here?" I asked.

"Yes. Yes! And we're needed." Nathan jumped up again. "Joshua, you're just going to have to go along with this and do what I tell you. This situation is an emergency! Do you understand?"

"Yes, I get it."

Nathan picked up the robe and sandals from where they had fallen to the floor and pushed them back into my hands. "Here. Put these on and follow me. I'll fill you in as best as I can on the way."

***

Soon we were racing through winding ways toward the old city. "Just don't say anything, and do what I do. I'll try to find a way to let you know if something is wrong," Nathan said.

"Okay. Can you tell me anything about what's happening?" I said breathlessly.

"The largest part of the Assyrian forces is marching further south. They will bypass us and head for Egypt. But Dad's spies have been reporting the approach of a massive wing of the Assyrian army for a week now. What's coming toward us is more than enough to overwhelm Jerusalem."

"That could be a problem."

"It's the worst it could be!"

"Why the worst?" I asked.

"We hoped that the Egyptians would help us against the Assyrians. Now even if they defeat their part of the

Assyrian army, the Egyptians will never get here in time to save us."

"Nathan? Joshua?" said a familiar contralto voice.

I bumped into Nathan, who stopped suddenly, looking around. "Sarah?"

"Up here." Sarah was descending a steep stair coming down from the Broad Wall.

When she came into the circle of light produced by Nathan's lamp I had to remind myself that this was not my Sarah. It helped that her clothes were different. She was wearing a heavily padded vest that covered her cloak to her knees. On her head, she wore a peculiarly shaped leather helmet. She was carrying a wooden bow, and a quiver filled with arrows hung from her belt beside an immense dagger.

Flanked by four other bow maidens, Sarah asked, "Where are you rushing now?"

"Uncle Eliakim called for us. He wants us to help Master Joah record a negotiation with the Assyrians," Nathan answered.

"There's not much to negotiate. We've been watching the Assyrian forces from the wall. They started arriving just as we began guard duty in the third hour. They must've force-marched. Your father's spies predicted they wouldn't arrive until tomorrow."

"How many do you think there are?"

"Thousands and thousands of them. They're still marching down the Kidron Valley. It's hard to tell because all we can see is their torches. It looks like their encampment will not only cover both the Kidron and Hinnom Valleys, but will spread up onto the hills beyond. Naturally they are staying out of range," Sarah said, lifting her bow. There was a murmur of agreement from the other archers.

"That doesn't sound good," Nathan said.

"It's not. We're in trouble." I'd never heard Sarah sound so discouraged.

"We've got to hurry, Sarah. I'm worried that we're already too late," Nathan said.

"I've got to get going too," Sarah said. "Your mother needs my help storing food for the siege."

"Tell Mother what we're doing. She was asleep when we left."

"Alright," Sarah said as she broke into a trot.

"We've got to go!" Nathan heaved on my arm. As we passed through an archway into the City of David, some of the buildings we rushed pass looked remotely familiar. After we passed a set of buildings that I was sure were tombs for King David's descendants, Nathan turned onto a well-worn street. We descended the steep road flanked by an extension of the city wall and came to a fortified gate.

"This is the Water Gate," Nathan said. "There is Uncle Eliakim."

The man Nathan indicated was tall, with a long, salt-and-pepper beard. He wore a brilliantly white, full-length robe with a broad multicolored sash. On his head was a tall squared-off turban with a drape running down his back. He carried the ornate staff of his high office.

"Nathan, Joshua, over here!" Eliakim called. As we came

up to him, he said. "Joshua, take that basket with Joah's supplies. Nathan, carry Joah's writing desk and lead him carefully. He's having a little trouble seeing in this light."

I looked at the older man's long white beard and clouded eyes. As he stepped up to put his hand on Nathan's shoulder, he said, "Too many hours studying by candlelight, my son." His friendly voice quavered slightly. "I'm going to have you do the writing, Nathan. Just put down what I whisper in your ear."

"Yes, Master Joah," Nathan said gravely.

"Oh, here, at last, is Shebna." Eliakim pointed up the street toward a short man, dressed in similar attire, approaching rapidly. Two servants carried his baskets. "Come, let's get going. We have the king's business to do."

I looked up at the high flanking walls where hundreds of spearmen and archers stood, reinforcing the gate's defense. I also saw the brightly colored robes of businessmen and city officials. Word was out about Eliakim's mission. As we passed through the gate onto the steep pitch of the Kidron Valley, I saw that this was going to be wild, and I had no idea what was happening.

As the sun broke over the hill in front of us, it glinted brightly off a pool of water enclosed in rock walls. I could hear the water trickling through a stone-walled conduit that fed into the rough irrigation system. But it was not the water that drew my attention. Standing above the pool on the far bank was a majestic military display.

Two large four-horse chariots stood off about 150 feet, held in place by drivers. A contingent of spearmen and archers were closer at hand, each wearing brightly colored clothing and shining armor. Two officers in splendid attire approached the pool on horseback. But just across the water was a figure that dominated the tableau.

Already at the edge of the pool, sitting on a massive horse draped in a bright green blanket fringed with gold tassels, was a giant man. He wore supple leather two-tone boots and a green kilt that matched his horse's blanket down to the tassels. Polished brass plates covered his vest, which he wore over a red linen shirt. At his side hung a massive broad-sword in a gleaming red sheath, and on his head, topped with a blood-red crest, was a golden helmet that glinted in the rising sun. His tanned face featured a tightly curled black beard, cut square, reaching the middle of his chest.

"I am Rabshakeh, emissary of the Emperor of Assyria, general of his mighty host! Where is this king of Jerusalem who seeks to defy the will of the Assyrian Empire?" Rabshakeh's loud voice echoed off the walls above them.

Eliakim answered him. "I am Eliakim, Royal Steward of Jerusalem. King Hezekiah has sent me to answer your summons. I will relay your message to the king."

Rabshakeh growled as he turned his horse back to intercept the approaching riders. I could not hear what they said. Nathan had the portable writing desk in place with pen and ink out. As Joah whispered in his ear, he was already scratching away at his parchment.

Behind Rabshakeh, rank upon rank of soldiers were emerging from a swirling cloud of dust and filing down into the Kidron Valley. On the heights opposite Jerusalem, army units swarmed the hills, setting up camp.

Rabshakeh came back flanked by the other two officers on horseback. "Tell King Hezekiah that the mighty Emperor Sennacherib wants to know what great power gives him the audacity to rebel against Assyria." Rabshakeh's voice rang out against Jerusalem's walls. "Does he think that Egypt will come to Jerusalem's aid? Ha! Egypt is a broken reed that injures the hand of anyone who leans on it. The mighty Sennacherib has already gone to deal with Egypt."

Eliakim said, "I will tell him, General. But we do not depend on Egypt for our defense."

Rabshakeh looked annoyed. "You're lying! Are you a betting man, Eliakim? I'll give you two thousand horses: you find riders for them and attack just one of my captains. You won't be able to overcome him with even that much force. How can you think that the Egyptians with all their chariots and horsemen could do any better? You Israelites are fools!"

"We do not depend on the Egyptians," Eliakim said in a calm, even voice.

Taking a deep breath and lifting his face toward the walls of Jerusalem, Rabshakeh bellowed, "I suppose you are going to tell me that you trust what you call the Lord Your God." He laughed derisively. "How is that going to work? Didn't Hezekiah tear down all his altars? Didn't he confine worship to the temple in Jerusalem alone? I think your God is angry with Hezekiah for that blasphemy. I think it was your Lord, the God of Israel, who told me to come and destroy Jerusalem and this heretic of a king."

"I doubt that, but go on," Eliakim said. "Perhaps you would make more sense if we spoke in your native Aramaic language, General Rabshakeh. We speak it fluently. Then you won't burden the people on the walls with your silly words."

The general's face darkened in anger. "You are an idiot, Eliakim, to taunt me! Do you think that the mighty Sennacherib sent me to warn you alone? No! I come to warn all of you. Like you, Eliakim, the coming siege dooms the people on the walls to eat their shit and drink their piss in the days ahead!"

Turning his horse toward the walls of Jerusalem, he sat up, raising his voice even louder. "Everyone, hear the words of the Emperor of Assyria, the Mighty Sennacherib. Thus says the Greatest King: Do not let Hezekiah deceive you. He has no power to save you. He is pretending to trust the Lord God just to fool you into remaining loyal. No god can deliver you, just like no god saved any of the nations Sennacherib destroyed. No god saved the countries of Hamath, Arpad, Sepharvaim, Hena, or Ivah. Sennacherib even destroyed the Samarian people, who worship this same God that Hezekiah pretends to trust. You will be destroyed as well!"

As Rabshakeh paused for dramatic effect, he looked with triumphant glee at Eliakim, who returned a level stare. Turning back to the city walls, the general continued his bellowing. "Don't listen to your stupid king. Make peace with me. Come into the valley and give yourselves up. I will help both you and your families, and you will have your own homes and farms in Assyria. It will be a safe new land for you. It will be a land of grain and wine, a land of bread and vineyards, a land of olive trees and honey. It is a place where you can live. Come and live there. Don't die the terrible death you will suffer here in Jerusalem under the foolishness of your king. Don't listen to him. The God of Hezekiah can't save you as he claims. If you trust in Hezekiah, you will die horribly!"

Rabshakeh looked expectantly as the last of his words echoed off the stones of Jerusalem. The only sounds were the jingle of tack and the gentle moan of the wind. But the silence stretched from seconds to minutes. No one moved: no one on the walls, no one in Eliakim's or Rabshakeh's parties. Even the last of the Assyrians marching into the valley had passed into distant silence.

The sound of tearing cloth broke the quiet. Joshua turned to see that Eliakim had ripped the front of his robe, exposing his bare chest nearly to his navel. In quick succession, Shebna and then Joah did the same. Then Eliakim turned and led us back up the steep path to the Water Gate. As I picked up his basket to follow, I stole a glance at the Assyrian General, who was staring at us in astonished disbelief.

Nathan had packed up Joah's equipment rapidly and then led Master Joah through the Watergate just ahead of me. Behind us came Shebna with his two servants. As we slowed our pace to ascend the steep street between the high walls, the wooden door shut behind us with an ominous thud.

Sennacherib had trapped Jerusalem and us with it. The siege had begun.

***

Nathan and I sat in a secluded corner of the courtyard.

"How's it going with Sarah?" I asked.

"I am more certain than ever about a betrothal," Nathan said. "I truly love her."

"How do you know?"

"We kissed." Nathan's demeanor made it a boast.

I felt a pang of jealousy. "How did you mange that?"

"We were sitting right here, talking just like we are now. Then I was looking into her eyes, leaning toward her. She leaned too and it just happened."

"But she still insists on waiting?"

"Yes."

I rubbed my face, trying to sort out my weird emotions. "Have you told your Joshua yet?"

"No." Nathan looked down for a long moment. "I'm worried about it. He loves her too. Mostly like a sister, but it might be more."

"Then why did you tell me?" I asked.

"Because I needed to tell someone and you're safe. You don't know Sarah, so you can't have feelings for her.

"Oh." I didn't know what else to say.

Eli emerged with a platter of meat that he began to cook on the brazier.

"Come on. Let's see if we can help. I'm hungry," Nathan said as he stood.

Every muscle in my body ached as I levered myself to my feet. We had spent the day filling all available vessels with water. Even though Nathan argued that the new water tunnel would provide all the water Jerusalem needed for the siege, Mother wanted to make sure. So we had carried water for hours.

Just as the smell of roasting meat was about to drive me crazy, Mother turned toward the arch leading into the entry-way. "I think I hear Father."

We all heard the outside door close. As Benjamin came through the archway into the courtyard, she rushed into his arms. "Oh, Benjamin! What will become of us?"

Father took Mother into his arms and held her for a long moment. "Ah, Rachel, we can't know the future. We must simply trust the Lord God."

"But what if he has marked us for destruction as he did with the northern tribes in Samaria?" Mother's words were muffled against Father's chest.

"It makes no difference. Whether God delivers us from the Assyrians or delivers us to them, we must trust him. But I have great hope that God will save us. Hezekiah has been a good king. He restored true worship to Israel, and now we are striving to be the kind of nation that the Lord God desires. Only time will tell."

When Mother turned away from Father I could see that she was crying. She came over to hug Nathan and then me. She said,

"I think dinner is ready. Let's enjoy this meal. Meat is going to be scare soon, and after that, any food will be hard to get."

Sarah left an embrace with her father and hugged Mother on the way to the table.

We reclined on the pillows around the low table on which Eli set a large platter of roasted meat and vegetables. Mother lit the candles at the table and said the evening meal prayer. But before anyone reached for food, she said, "Father, would you say a prayer for us and for our city at this terrible time?"

"Certainly." Father lifted his hands with palms toward the sky. As he stared into the many hues of the sunset, he said, "O Lord, how many are our foes! A multitude has risen against us. Many people are saying, 'There is no salvation for us in God.' Hear us, Lord God."

"Let our words come before you." I looked around, startled as the rest of the family responded in unison.

"But you, O Lord, are a shield to your people," Father continued. "You are our glory. You are the lifter of our heads. When we cry aloud to the Lord, he answers us from his holy hill. Hear us, Lord God."

This time I was ready and joined in saying, "Let our words come before you."

"We will lie down and sleep." The tone of Father's voice was confident. "We will wake again, for the Lord sustains us. We will not be afraid of many thousands of people who have set themselves against us all around. Arise, O Lord! Save us, O our God! For you strike all our enemies on the cheek. You break the teeth of the wicked. Hear us, Lord God!

"Let our words come before you."

"Salvation belongs to the Lord. Let your blessing be on your people! Amen," Father concluded.

"Amen," we responded.

Chapter 24

State Tournament

"Joshua, time to get up!"

"Nathan, is it time for the second watch already?" I groaned.

"Nathan?" Mom said as she turned on the light in my room. "What is the second watch?"

I sat up on the edge of my bed. "Sorry, Mom. I was having a weird dream."

"Are you still having dreams about Nathan?"

"Sometimes."

"Hmm. Maybe we should talk to the school counselor."

"A dream now and then won't hurt me." I wondered if I would be in real danger if I got caught in Jerusalem when the Assyrians sacked the place.

"I guess not, but you'll tell me if they start to bother you?"

"Yes, Mom. What time is it?" I looked around for my phone.

"It's 7:30, and you have to be at the school to catch the bus by 9:00."

"Yes!" I pumped my arm. "No school today."

"That's one of the advantages of a small school. The whole town is packing up and moving to Huron for the weekend," Mom said.

"When Nathan went to the state basketball tournament in Oregon, nobody even noticed. I had to wait through a whole day of classes before I could ride with you and Dad," I said, stretching and yawning. "In Wheaton, they've canceled school, even for the middle school and elementary."

"Pretty cool, huh?"

"Yeah, really, Mom," I said, grinning.

"I'll tell Gramps you'll be down for breakfast soon," Mom said. "I think he's whipping up a batch of his famous pancakes."

I waited until I heard Mom's steps reach the bottom of the stairs, and then I reached for my phone.

"Save me a seat on the bus," I messaged to Sarah.

Almost no time passed before the response dinged. "No one sits with me anyway."

"I do!" I texted.

A smiley face emoji was Sarah's only response.

I set the new land-speed record for showering and dressing, and then I descended the stairs to the smell of pancakes, bacon, and eggs.

"Morning, Josh," Gramps sang out as I flopped down at the table. The greeting was accompanied by the thump of a large platter landing on the table. We said grace quickly on the way to Gramp's kitchen art, and soon I was up to my elbows in syrup over everything.

Dad came into the kitchen, followed by Mom. "Fresh coffee in the pot," Gramps said between bites of pancake.

Mom reached high into a cupboard to bring down two travel mugs and Dad brought the coffee pot to fill them.

"Eat those last two pancakes or they'll go to waste, Josh," Mom said, standing up to clear the table as we finished breakfast.

"Better his waist than mine," Dad said with a chuckle.

"Okay, I'll take one for the team." I forked the remaining pancakes onto my plate and reached for the syrup. "It's a dirty job, but someone has to do it."

Gramps laughed.

Later, as I washed sticky hands in the back porch sink, Dad came through carrying a coffee thermos and the pair of travel mugs. Donning his coat, Dad said, "Hurry along, Josh. We need to get going. We're going to drop you at school, and then on the way to Huron we're going to talk to a rancher about buying some more cattle. We don't want to be late to the game."

"I'll be right there, Dad." As I dried my hands, I watched Dad cross the yard to the big white Ford pickup Mom was warming up. The snow piles had shrunk in the warmer weather during the first week of March.

Gramps held the door for me as I pulled on my coat and we headed for the Ford. "Hope that blizzard holds off. We need a day or two to get things ready," Gramps said as he scanned the low-hanging clouds.

"It's not supposed to come in until next Wednesday, right?" I said, following Gramps into the rear seat of the F250's cab.

"Yeah, that's the forecast, but the weather can change fast. It always makes me nervous this time of year."

***

I watched Mom's big white truck pull out of the school parking lot and accelerate down the highway out of town. I turned back toward the school, carefully negotiating the alternately slick and crunchy surface. Then I paused to take in the white tableau of a humble school building and two parked buses emitting plumes of steamy exhaust against the background of a cornfield filled with dune-like drifts. Startled, I realized this was starting to feel like home.

"Hey, Cooper, you decided to pry yourself out of bed and come, huh?" The good-natured jibe from Sean Johnson came with a rush of warm air as the bus driver levered open the doors for me to enter.

"Yeah, Johnson. Not even the thought of having to ride to Huron with you could hold me back."

Sean laughed and held up his hand for a high five.

"He got you there, Sean," said Eddie Martinez, who was sitting next to Sean. He also held up his hand for a slap.

I pulled off my gloves and unzipped my coat as I worked

my way down the aisle. Sarah sat alone in a seat about half-way back on the right side. I stopped by her place and pulled off my coat and handed it to her. Just before I sat down, I caught icy stares from the back of the bus where Melanie and Marshal huddled together with Allen and Shelly.

"Hi," I said as I plopped down next to Sarah.

"Hi," Sarah responded with a funny little smile. "Is the Posse staring at us?" The Posse was Sarah's new nickname for Melanie and Marshal's clique.

"Yup." I grinned back.

"Let 'em."

I reached and touched the back of Sarah's hand. Her smile broadened as she locked fingers with me.

As the bus pulled out of the parking lot, I asked, "Are you feeling ready for today?"

"Yeah. White River shouldn't be too bad. They have one powerful player, but they're only seventh seed. Still, at state it's anyone's game."

"When's the game?"

"We're in the first game of session two. It starts at 6:00 this evening."

"6:00 p.m.?" I was surprised. "Why did we have to leave at 9:00 this morning?

"Coach wants us to watch the session-one games which start at noon. Ethan is playing Waverly–South Shore. If we get to the finals, it'll probably be against Ethan. They're undefeated."

"Wheaton would be undefeated except for that week you all had the flu."

"That was bad," Sarah said, pushing her long hair back over her ear with her free hand. Her expression was impish when she said, "So, are you all upset about having to spend the whole day with me?"

"No . . . uh, not at all." I laughed.

"Right answer." Sarah grinned.

We spent the rest of the two and a half hour bus trip pleasantly, with both relaxed conversation and long periods of comfortable silence. Lunch was the first order of business when we arrived in Huron and I wondered when getting to eat at McDonald's became such a treat. Maybe I was becoming a country kid.

***

"And at point guard for the Wheaton Rockets, Sarah Dirk!" the announcer's voice blared through the Huron Arena's sound system.

The crowd roared its welcome.

Sarah ran past the scorekeeper's table, bumping fists with each of the three officials for the game. Then she ran to the middle of the floor for a quick handshake with an opposing player from Corsica–Stickney. Next, she ran to the middle of the Rockets half court to slap hands with the Rockets who weren't starting the game. Finally, she went back to center court to stand beside the Jaguar's point guard to welcome the rest of the game's starting line-ups.

It was the same route she'd run yesterday in Wheaton's first game against White River.

"Well, she's got that routine down pretty well," Eddie said, raising his voice to be heard above the crowd.

I smiled back. "Yeah, she looks great for the semi-final game tonight!"

"You sound like a proud boyfriend," Sean smirked broadly, sitting on my other side.

"Yeah, well, Sarah was great," I said and I couldn't help the wide grin. "Eleven points and ten assists: that accounts for two-thirds of the fifty-nine points in our first state tournament win over White River last night."

"I didn't say anything against Sarah," Sean said, laughing. "You're her one-person fan club."

"Somebody should be standing up for her," Eddie said, "I think that bullying against you guys needs to stop."

"Correction – two-person fan club!" Sean said, still chuckling.

"Sean." Eddie leaned with mock menace toward Sean.

"Okay, okay: three-person fan club. Go, Sarah!" Sean shouted, cupping his hands around his mouth.

We caught the ugly look from five rows down when Marshal and Allen turned to stare at us.

"And there's Melanie Crawford's fan club," I said, returning Marshal's stare.

"Too bad for her! She's back on the bench since they brought Ellen up from JV for the tournaments," Sean said.

"Do I detect a potential Ellen Longfeather fan club?" Eddie said, grinning.

Sean's response was drowned in the roar of the crowd as the announcer finished introducing the teams. Then we stood for the national anthem and the game began.

"This is going to be a tough game," Eddie said as the buzzer rang out at the end of the first quarter.

"Sarah said that Corsica–Stickney would be difficult. They've won just as many games as we have this season," I said.

Sean pointed to a tall girl in a dark gray jersey trimmed in red with "JAGUARS" printed in bold letters. "Their center is top notch. She might have Jean outclassed. What does she have, four or six points so far?"

"Six," Eddie said confidently.

"We're probably going to have to put another guard on her inside," I said, shifting my position on the bleacher.

"Ellen and Jean work well underneath the basket," Sean said, standing to stretch. He sat back down as the ball came inbounds for the start of the second quarter. "That's why they brought Ellen up to varsity — that and her phenomenal growth spurt."

At half time we went out to the concession stand. Sean said, "We can't seem to get more than a three-point advantage."

Marshal and Allen were standing in line ahead of us. "Coach needs to get Longfeather out of there and put Melanie back in. She's a little shorter, but she knows what she is doing," Marshal said loudly.

Sean bristled.

Eddie put a hand on Sean's arm. "He doesn't know what he's talking about, Sean."

I said, "Hey guys, let's go to the restroom. The stink here may have cleared out by the time we get back." Then under my breath I said, "Marshal's an idiot."

But it was too late because Marshal caught sight of us. "You've got to do a better job boinking Dirk, Cooper. She's off her game."

"Whatever, Marshal." I held my temper as I led Eddie and Sean down the hall.

By the time we got back to our seats with our drinks and popcorn, the second half had already started. The score continued to seesaw back and forth well into the fourth quarter. We were down by one.

"Go, Sarah!" I jumped up. Sarah had just dropped a perfect set shot in from the head of the key. "That three pointer put us ahead by two."

Coach Arlington called out from the bench, "Full court press! Get into a full court press!"

The Wheaton girls spread out all across the court, each covering her assigned opponent as the Jaguars prepared to bring the ball inbounds. The coverage was so tight that the Corsica–Stickney player trying to throw the ball in decided to loft it down the sideline to her teammate on the other end of the court. Ellen stepped up and intercepted the ball. Then a quick pass to Jean in center court was followed by a snap to Sarah, who raced to the basket. The whistles blew stridently as an official signaled a foul on a girl who had tried to stop Sarah's drive. Another official turned to the scoring table and indicated that Sarah's layup counted for two points. Sarah sank her free throw for a five-point lead.

Corsica–Stickney called time out. When they came back on the floor they had determined looks on their faces. Evidently Coach Arlington had called off the full court press, because the Wheaton girls waited behind the half line as the Jaguar guards brought the ball up the court. There was a long series of passes as the Jaguars tried to find an open shot. Finally, with time running out on the shot clock, Ellen's opponent went up for a fifteen-foot jump shot. Ellen leaped with her arms held high to block the shot. It bounced scoreless off the rim but as she came down Ellen drifted into the shooter. Referees' whistles filled the arena.

It was Ellen's fourth foul. One more and she was out of the game. The buzzer blared as Melanie crouched at the scorekeeper's bench. She trotted confidently onto the court to relieve Ellen.

"Now we've got a real chance," Marshal called out over his shoulder. "Just watch Melanie show Ellen how it's done."

I felt Sean tense beside me, but Eddie slapped Sean's chest saying, "Let it go. Like Cooper said, he's an idiot."

The Jaguar that Ellen had fouled sunk both her free throws, reducing the Rocket lead to three. Then, contrary to Marshal's prediction, Melanie did not show Ellen how it was done. In quick succession Melanie fumbled the ball out of bounds, failed to cover her opponent for a layup, and then telegraphed her pass in bounds. The pass was stolen, resulting in two more points for the Jaguars. When she fouled her opponent on a successful twelve-foot jump shot, the free throw put Corsica–Stickney up by four. Melanie turned beet red and cursed within ear shot of the referee. The resulting technical foul elevated the Jaguars' lead to five and left them in possession of the ball.

Coach Arlington called time out and Melanie resumed her seat on the bench while Ellen checked in at the scoring table.

Over the next three minutes of play the Rockets carefully whittled the Jaguars' lead to two even though Ellen was cautiously protecting against her last foul.

"We've gotta work it inside to Jean. Her guard is getting tired," I said.

"Yeah! How about that for calling it," Eddie said, as Sarah made a quick bounce pass to Jean inside. But when she tried to make the shot, her guard clobbered her with a misplaced block. Jean had two attempts from the foul line. She missed the first one but convincingly swished the second to cut the Jaguar lead to one point.

The whistle blew loudly. "That's the Jaguars' last time out," Sean said.

"Think that'll make a difference?" I asked.

"There are only thirty-four seconds on the clock," Eddie said. "The Jaguars have the ball, but they won't be able to stop play again if we get control of the ball."

When the game resumed, Eddie continued his

commentary. "Looks like they're planning to hang onto the ball for the last shot just before the buzzer."

"Why aren't we fouling them to stop the clock?" I asked.

"The officials would call an intentional foul, and they'd get two foul shots and control of the ball afterword. We have to be careful and aggressively go for the ball," Eddie explained. "Like that! Way to go, Jean."

Jean deflected the pass and Ellen scooped up the ball before the other team could get a hold of it.

Sean shouted "Ten seconds, Ellen. Get it to Sarah!"

Ellen's pass was rushed but it was close enough that Sarah could jump and snag it. When she came back to the floor, three Jaguar girls appeared between her and the basket pinning her in place. The looks on their faces showed that they knew full well how dangerous she was. Sarah crouched like she was going up for the final shot. Her guards closed in and then through a tangle of limbs, Sarah passed the ball to Jean who was sliding quietly down the court into the key. Her lay-up was picture perfect, erasing the Jaguar's one-point lead and giving Wheaton a one-point advantage.

The final buzzer was barely audible as the crowd exploded in cheers. The Wheaton girls had won!

"I was sure that Sarah was going to take that last shot," I said breathlessly.

"Yeah," Eddie said, literally bouncing on the balls of his feet. "So were the Jaguars! They triple-teamed her."

"One of them should have been on Jean. How did she get

down the court that fast?" Sean was still slapping me on the back.

"I still don't see how Sarah got that pass through. They were all over her," Eddie said, bouncing some more.

"That was one of the first things she taught me," I said. "Now, I know why. A two-point layup can win the game just as well as a three-point Hail Mary shot. It looks like we just made it into tomorrow night's championship."

Chapter 25

Championship

"Dad said he was going to make it to the championship game tonight," Sarah said as we sat in a booth at the Huron McDonald's eating lunch. Her tone was casual, but I could tell this was important.

"When do you think he'll get here?"

"Not sure." Sarah had a funny look on her face. "He texted me to say he was on the road about an hour ago, but it can take him a while to travel anywhere."

I decided I'd better not ask what that meant. "It's nice that he's going to make it."

Sarah gave me another funny look.

"Well, if it isn't the two love birds," Marshal James announced loudly. "So, Cooper, you think you can keep monopolizing the best source for action in Wheaton?" He pushed a finger though a looped thumb and forefinger to emphasize his meaning.

Behind Marshal, Melanie and Alan laughed raucously. Shelly, who was trailing a step behind, looking goggle-eyed at Marshal.

Sarah froze.

"That's about enough, James," I said. I slid out of the booth and stood up, facing him. "What's your problem?"

"The problem is that you have a slut for a girlfriend," Melanie said, stepping up beside Marshal. "Maybe that's the way you big city boys like it, but here in Wheaton, we have morals."

I knew I shouldn't rise to the bait, but this was too much. "In Portland, you'd have been suspended for how you use social media, Melanie."

Marshal stepped directly in front of me and lowered his voice. "Watch it, Cooper. You don't get to say things like that about my girlfriend and get away with it."

The irony of his words hit me as hard as I punched him right in the center of his face. He went down flat on his back. "Well then, you stop talking shit about Sarah!"

Marshal started to scramble back to his feet but then froze. I felt Sarah standing at my side. I glanced to see her fists clenched and her face a thundercloud. Marshal went pale and then he lay back down. Melanie crouched beside him. She started digging in her bag when his face began a crimson fountain.

"Look what you did to him!" Melanie wailed.

I started to respond, but Sarah touched my arm and restrained me with a quick shake of her head. "Come on," she said grabbing our coats from the booth and leading me to the exit.

I looked over my shoulder to see the Posse huddled over Marshal's prone figure. I tried to feel bad about what I'd done, but I couldn't.

"I probably shouldn't have done that," I said, giving her a sidelong glance as we went along.

Sarah said nothing, but she put her arm around my waist and hugged me. I put my arm around her shoulder and pulled her close.

"Do you think they'll stop now?" I wondered. Sarah's face remained expressionless. I couldn't decide whether the single tear that appeared in her right eye was sadness or anger.

"I don't know," she said. "It's always been something that just had to be endured, like the weather."

"He seemed more afraid of you than me."

"Yeah." Sarah's laugh was bitter. "I'll have to tell you about that sometime." She let go of me and stepped aside to check the time on her phone. "We've got to get back now. I have a team meeting in twenty minutes. I think coach is worried about facing the undefeated Ethan Rustlers tonight. Can you help me keep watch for my dad this afternoon?"

"Sure," I said. "My folks will save a seat for him."

"That'd be great." Sarah turned to walk on, then she stopped and reached to take my hand. "Thanks, Josh."

I looked at her, still trying to read her face. "You're welcome, but I don't know what for."

"For standing up for me." She laughed, her normal expression returning.

"Yeah, I almost got myself pounded." I shrugged.

"Not that, silly." She said reaching to touch my cheek. "It just really felt good to have someone take my side."

I just smiled as we walked on through the icy March wind.

***

About four and a half hours later, I was still standing at Huron Arena entrance watching the parking lot. The wind had picked up and the clouds were crowding out the sun's last attempt to shine for the day.

"Have you seen him yet?" Gramps came up behind me and laid his hand on my shoulder.

"No, not yet, Gramps."

"When did Sarah think he'd come?"

"She thought he'd be here a couple of hours ago. She waited with me as long as she could, but the coach wanted the team to eat supper together. I promised I would stay and watch for him."

"What are your plans for supper, then?" Gramps asked.

"I don't have any."

"Why don't you go get something to eat," Gramps said. "I can watch for Paul."

"No. I promised Sarah I would stay here until her dad comes."

"Can I bring you some food?"

"That would be great, Gramps," I said. I was starting to get hungry.

"What do you want?"

"I'd eat a couple of those hot dogs from the concession stand. Oh, and how about a bag of chips and a coke?"

"Coming right up," Gramps said over his shoulder as he headed back into the Arena.

"Thanks, Gramps," I called after him.

After another hour, Mom came to look for me. Putting an arm around my waist, she said, "Still no sign of him?"

"No," I said, "but I got a text from Sarah saying she'd talked to him by phone. He was just a few miles outside Huron and would be here soon."

"That sounds promising."

"How can it take someone six hours to drive from Wheaton to Huron? It only took us two and a half hours on the bus."

"Well, Josh, I'm not sure. However, knowing Paul, he probably made some stops along the way."

"There's nothing between here and home," I said.

"Paul probably knows the location of every bar in eastern South Dakota. I'm sure he'd know where to stop if he wanted to."

"Oh."

"The game is about to start. Ethan and Wheaton have finished their warm-ups and are about ready to be introduced. Are you still going to wait out here?" Mom asked.

"Yeah. I promised Sarah."

"Okay. You know where we're sitting. We have two seats saved. You can join us as soon as Paul comes." Mom gave me a quick hug and walked down the broad hallway toward the roar of the crowd.

***

Forty-five minutes later Dad walked up. "Looks like it is starting to snow."

I stared glumly out of the big glass windows at the entryway. "Yeah, Dad. It started coming down about twenty minutes ago."

"Gramps doesn't think we should be concerned yet. He says the main storm is a few hours away," Dad said. "But, I think we're going drive home tonight rather than staying another night in Huron."

"We never used to drive in the snow at night in Portland."

"Things are different here in the Midwest, Josh. The designers planned the roads to handle snow, and as long as the highways stay open, the road crews work through the night. Also, I think your mom wants an excuse to put that big Ford in four-wheel drive. I'm sure we'll be okay. Any sign of him?"

"Nope. Not yet," I said, feeling exasperated.

"You're missing a good game, you know."

"I've caught a lot of it on the monitors," I said, nodding toward one of the big flat-screen televisions mounted high on the wall. "They're doing pretty well, aren't they?"

"They're doing just great. Up by seven at the end of the first half. Sarah is on fire and she has the rest of the team right with her."

"She wants to win this championship and she's worked hard for it all year — the whole team has. I just wish her dad was here to see it."

"Is that Paul's car?" Dad said, pointing.

I stepped up to the window and shaded the glass with my hand to block the overhead glare. "It could be."

A car drove lazily along the row of parked vehicles toward the arena entrance. As it came into the brightly-lit entryway, we could see Paul's rusted out Mercury sedan crawling along slowly. It swerved toward the parked cars and then back the other way, finally pulling onto the sidewalk and stopping about twenty-five feet from the door. We went outside to see what was happening. As we rounded the car, the driver's side door creaked open. Paul Dirk awkwardly tried to stand up, slipped, and fell to the ground.

"Hey, guys! It's a little slick out here." Paul was slurring his words so badly that it took me a minute to figure out what he said.

"Can we help you up?" Dad said, starting to bend over Paul, who had gotten to his hands and knees.

"No, No. I can do this. Done it thousands of times." Paul braced himself against the side of the car and levered himself to his feet, where he swayed unsteadily. "We better get into the game. The second half is probably about to start."

"That's right," I said. "Where were you? We expected you for the start of the game, Mr. Dirk."

"What am I going to have to do to get you to call me Paul, Son?" He leaned against the car for balance.

I clinched my jaw. "Okay, Paul, where were you?"

"Oh, I'm a wily coyote, Josh." Paul grinned broadly and attempted to tap the side of his nose. The action sent him off-kilter and he nearly fell again. He regained his balance. "I went to Big D's sports bar to watch the first half of the game. It's after half now so I'll get into the game for free. How about that for good planning?"

"Did you have something to drink over there?" Dad asked.

"Well, of course. You don't go watching an establishment's TV without buying some booze to patronize them." Paul laughed and winked.

"Probably would have cost you less if you just came straight to the game."

"Now, Ben, what's the fun in that?"

"Well, Paul, there's a young lady who really wants her dad at her big game. It would be more fun for her if you were here, rather than at Big D's."

Paul straightened up and looked intently at Dad. Then he smiled. "Yeah, I suppose you're right. Let's get going before we miss it altogether."

"Give me your keys," Dad said, holding out his hand. "I'll put your car in a parking place while Josh helps you get to your seat."

"It'll probably be okay right there," Paul said, but when

Dad continued to hold out his hand, he dug in his pocket and surrendered his keys.

The falling snow and the cold wind seemed to help Paul steady himself. He followed me back into the Arena. After a trip to the bathroom, I guided Paul into a seat beside Gramps.

"Hey, Paul." Gramps shook Paul's hand. "Glad to see you made it safely. Our girl is having quite a game."

Paul stared toward the court. His eyes did not seem to be following the play. By his look, I wondered if he were going to cry.

Gramps studied him carefully. "Are you okay, Paul?"

Paul turned away from me to look at Gramps, but I heard him say, "I almost missed Sarah's big game. I've missed most of her games this season. I don't know what's wrong with me. I feel like I'm under siege or something. I'm worried it'll finish me. And that won't be good, will it?"

"I think you know what's wrong, Paul." Gramps had to raise his voice to be heard through the noise of the crowd. "Your real enemy is the bottle."

Paul sat in numbed silence.

"Your Dad beat it, Paul. He had twenty-two years of sobriety when he died."

Paul remained quiet for a long time, and then he turned back to watch the game. "Take the shot, Sarah!" he called out. "Did you see that? They fouled her. They fouled her! You got that right, Ref."

I let out a breath I hadn't realized I was holding. I watched as Sarah walked to the foul line. "Way to go, Sarah," I shouted as she sunk the first foul shot and then the second.

"She's pretty good, isn't she?"

I realized Paul was talking to me. "Yeah. She's terrific."

Paul slapped my knee. "She's gotten even better since she started working with you. I think you're good for her, Josh." Paul laughed and turned back to the game.

I felt confused by his complement. I suddenly realized how angry I was becoming over Paul's frustrating behavior.

When I refocused on the game, the teams were huddled at their benches for the quarter break. I leaned forward to look down the row at my parents. Dad had his arm around Mom and she was offering him some of her popcorn. Their smiles were relaxed and loving.

Gramps' face was alive with excitement. "Go, Rockets!" he called out as the team broke their huddle and took their places on the floor. I knew that watching Wheaton teams play was Gramps' favorite thing to do. Having them play in the championship game of the state tournament was pure ecstasy.

Then I glanced at Paul. His face was slack and he was fighting to keep his eyes open. He looked haggard, like he'd been through a war. Maybe that comment about being under siege wasn't so far off.

"Where's Sarah?" Paul asked.

"She's on the bench," Gramps said. "Looks like Coach Arlington is resting some of the starters. Melanie is in for Ellen."

"Why's the coach doing that?" Paul said. "Doesn't she know this game can get away from her in a hurry?"

"I suppose, but this is the senior girls' last chance to play high school basketball. I think she wants to get them a little game time so they'll all have played in the state championship game."

Five minutes later the crowd of Ethan fans on the other side of the stadium exploded in a roar as the Rustlers closed the gap to six points. The Rockets called a time out.

"I guess that's enough game time for the second team," Paul slurred. He cupped his hands around his mouth and yelled, "Put Sarah back in!"

Coach Arlington must have agreed because the starting team was checking back in at the scorekeeper's bench.

"That's more like it." Paul settled back in his seat with a satisfied look on his face.

I watched anxiously as the clock ticked off the game time. We scored two more points: up by eight.

"I don't think Ethan is going to give up that easily," Gramps said after a roar from the other side of the stadium confirmed that the score was back to six points apart.

I looked at Paul out of the corner of my eye. He leaning forward, elbows on his knees, looking like he was falling asleep. I wondered if I should do something to wake him up.

Sarah scored a three-pointer. The explosion of sound around us startled Paul into sitting bolt upright in his seat. "What?" he spluttered. "Oh, we're up by nine."

"Only two minutes to go," Gramps said as the opposing team brought the ball up the court again.

A collective groan from the Ethan fans marked a missed shot by their point guard and Ellen's quick scramble to come up with the rebound.

"Slow the game down," Paul yelled through cupped hands.

"Looks like they are," I said. "Dribble and pass. We practiced that stalling routine enough. Too bad the boys' team never got much of a chance to use it."

There was a shrill blast from the referee's whistle. An outburst of shouting all around us had everyone in our vicinity on their feet. "That was an intentional foul!" Paul roared.

Jean was lying on the floor with a big Ethan player standing over her. The ref charged the Ethan center with a foul.

Jean stepped up to the foul line but bounced the first shot off the rim. She swished the second to put us up by ten: the best spread of the game.

"Looks like that's taken the fight out of them," Gramps said as the Rockets brought the ball back in bounds after the free throws.

I watched the clock run smoothly toward the game's final second. When the buzzer sounded, a burst of cheering erupted all around us. "We won! We won the state basketball championship!" I shouted.

"I told you they could do it, didn't I?" Gramps exclaimed.

We both turned to look at Paul, who was standing silently between us. There was a look of intense concentration on his face as he swayed in place. He fell into his seat. The color drained from his face. Gramps scrambled on the floor for something, coming up with an empty popcorn bag that he pushed toward Paul. With Gramps' help, Paul managed to get the bag into place as he started retching violently into it.

I wondered what to do. The air reeked with the smell of vomit. It was all I could do to avoid throwing up myself.

"Josh, why don't you go down and join your classmates. We can take care of this here," Gramps said.

Mom produced a pack of wet wipes from her purse.

"Okay, Gramps." I made my way down, wedging through masses of wildly celebrating Rockets fans, looking for my friends. I caught a glimpse of Sean Johnson's head above the crowd and headed his direction. The basketball players had just finished their formal line of handshakes with the opposing players. Then each team moved toward their side of the court to line up for the awards ceremony.

"Can you believe we won?" Sean said, clapping me on the back.

"Sarah was unbelievable," Eddie said. "She got us going with those early buckets. Ethan never quite got back in it after that."

We turned and watched as official-looking people wheeled a table with trophies and medals out to the center court. The announcer introduced a group of representatives of the South Dakota High School Association, their corporate partners, and an officer from the South Dakota National Guard. Then, one by one, the team members, student managers, and coaches came out onto the floor. The officials handed them medals and trophies – first the Ethan Rustlers as the runners-up, and then the Wheaton Rockets as the state champions.

A photographer lined up the Wheaton basketball team for a picture with their medals and their trophy.

"Are they done?" Sean said. "Can we go congratulate them?"

"Wait." I pointed as the tournament organizers wheeled another table out onto the floor. "What's that for?"

The announcer was quick with the explanation. "We'd now like to direct your attention to center court as we present the All-Tournament Team awards."

"I forgot about this. They're going to pick the best players to form an honorary team representing the whole tournament," Sean said.

"Sarah should be on it," Eddie said, holding up his hand for a high five from me.

After listing players that represented all the other teams in the tournament, the announcer finally said, "Jean Wilkerson and Sarah Dirk from the Wheaton Rockets."

After the award ceremonies were over, we made our way onto the congested arena floor. We joined the party of Wheaton students rejoicing with our victorious basketball team.

Sarah was near the center of the group, receiving congratulations from all sides. When she saw me, she came over and threw her arms around me. She kissed me soundly in front of the entire arena. At first it caught me off guard, but almost immediately I responded in kind. We held each other long enough to start drawing applause and wolf whistles from nearby spectators.

"We won. We won the state tournament!" Sarah exalted as she stepped back.

"That is so cool, Sarah. You were great."

"Did Dad come?" Her tone was suddenly more serious.

"Yeah, he made it. He is sitting with my family up there." I waved in the general direction.

Sarah hugged me again. "Thanks for waiting for him," she whispered in my ear. "Was he drunk?"

Pulling back, I nodded.

Sarah's face saddened, but not as much as I expected. She sighed. "I'm glad he made it safely. That's what counts."

"Yeah, you're right," I said as Sarah broke away to follow her team into the locker room.

Chapter 26

Sennacharib's Letter

"Are you okay riding home with us, Son?" Dad said, turning to look at me. I was stretched out on the back seat of Mom's Ford 250.

"Yeah," I answered. "With the blizzard coming we need to get home and get things ready. I know you need my help."

"Thanks, Josh" Mom said, focusing through the thick white streaks of snow that were flashing past the windshield. "You wanted to ride home on the bus with Sarah, right?"

"Yeah, but now Sarah is riding home with her dad and Gramps," I said wistfully. "How did Gramps get Paul to let him drive them home?"

"He had the keys," Dad said, laughing. "I still had them from parking Paul's car, so I gave them to Gramps when we cooked up this plan. Paul couldn't do anything about it. Besides, despite his protest, I think he's glad Gramps is driving."

"Right. I'm glad too, especially for Sarah's sake." I stared out the back window. I could barely make out the headlights of the old Mercury behind us, but I was glad it was there. Sarah, Paul, and Gramps were following us back to Wheaton. I balled my coat up to make a pillow. The warm air from the rear heater felt good. It had been a long night and it was going to get even longer once we were home.

***

I bumped my head as I fell. I thought I must have slid off the truck's seat, but cold stone pressed against my face. I opened my eyes to the dim flickering of a torch bracketed to the wall. Taking hold of the wooden bench just above, I pulled myself up. On the far end, a familiar figure was hunched over, asleep.

"Nathan. Nathan," I said. My words croaked because my throat was dry.

My brother stirred but gave no response.

I shook his shoulder. "Wake up. Where are we?"

"Argh." Nathan's head snapped up. Then he yawned and stretched. "What?"

"Where are we?"

"You know where we are, Joshua. Quit fooling around. Tonight is too serious for that."

I looked intently at the shadows flickering on my brother's face. "It's me, Nathan—Future Joshua."

"Oh . . . it's you," Nathan said in surprise. "You always pick the most awkward times to show up."

"I don't pick the times. This just happens to me. You know that."

Nathan returned my look and sighed. "I suppose. Anyway, I'm glad you woke me up. We're not on guard duty, but we shouldn't be sleeping."

"What're we doing?" I asked again.

"Uncle Eliakim called for us to wait here in the palace messenger's duty room. It's the second watch of the night. I must have fallen asleep waiting."

"Your Joshua must have fallen asleep too," I said. "That must be how I got here. Somebody's coming."

Footsteps grew louder, coming down a hallway. A soldier poked his head into the room. "Okay, you two. Eliakim wants you in the throne room," he said, and then disappeared.

Nathan stood and said, "Come on. I know the way."

The long hall had several torches in sconces lighting the way. We came to a double door flanked by armed guards. One opened the door and waved us through.

***

I didn't know what to expect when we entered the royal audience hall. What I saw was both less and more than I anticipated. The room was relatively small. It was about three times the size of a large living room, with walls about ten feet high. Rich dark wood paneled the room on all sides. Gold reflectors on the lamp stands made the place so bright that I had to squint until my eyes adjusted.

"Ah, boys," Eliakim called out as we entered the room. "Come over here." There were only two other people in the room – Uncle Eliakim and a distinguished man with a neatly trimmed beard and long silver hair bound by a gold circlet. King Hezekiah sat on an oversized chair made of the same dark wood as the paneling. Gold ornamentation augmented the lustrous gleam of the throne as it stood on its dais. The King wore odd clothes made of ugly brown cloth, roughly sewn. It looked like he was wearing a burlap bag. I imitated Nathan's bow before the king and then stepped back behind Eliakim with my brother.

"I'll take Benjamin's two boys as torchbearers and go right away, Your Highness," Eliakim said. Just then I noticed that Eliakim was wearing sackcloth as well.

"Make sure he reads it carefully, Eli. This is a serious offense. Sennacherib is more than capable of destroying Jerusalem, but now he mocks the Lord God. Not even the king of Assyria has the authority to do that." King Hezekiah handed a large parchment scroll to Eliakim.

"Yes, Sire. I'll make sure he reads it. What do you want me to say to him?"

"Tell him that I've gone to the temple and spread this document before the Lord. I prayed with all my heart that the Lord of hosts rebukes this arrogant Assyrian for his blasphemy. I asked God to make his name known in all the earth by saving us from destruction. I want to know if God has heard my prayer."

Eliakim bowed in acknowledgment.

I noticed the dark circles around King Hezekiah's eyes. He had a haggard look despite his regal appearance.

Eliakim gazed at the king for a moment and then said, "The Lord said to my Lord, 'Sit in the place of honor at my right hand until I humble your enemies, making them a footstool under your feet.'"

Hezekiah sat very still and then said, "King David's psalms are full of wisdom. I've always tried to do what he'd do. I need the kind of faith he had when he faced Goliath. Thank you, Eliakim. Now go and find out what Isaiah says."

Eliakim bowed, signaled us to follow, and left the room.

***

A guardsman handed us torches on our way out of the palace. The streets were unusually dark. Nathan said it was because Jerusalem was conserving its lamp oil. The light of the moon glinting off the upper parts of the temple helped some. As we passed the temple grounds, we came to a gate in the wall that was being guarded by a large contingent of soldiers. This gate, called the Fish Gate, led onto the highlands beyond the Temple Mount. The commander recognized Eliakim and quickly passed us through.

"This is the only gate still in use," Nathan whispered. "We

can defend these heights unless the Assyrians make an intentional effort to take them. So far they haven't."

After about a quarter mile, we came to a large house and grounds surrounded by a wall. It was an apartment building similar to the one where Nathan lived. Door guards dressed in palace uniforms meant important people lived here.

"We're here on behalf of the king," Eliakim said to the officer on duty.

"He said to expect you," the soldier replied. "Go on up. He's waiting for you."

"It's kind of unnerving to serve a seer, isn't it?" Eliakim asked the officer.

"Yes, at first, but you get used to it, sir."

We followed Eliakim through the front arch, up the stairs to the right, and down a hallway with several doors on each side. Finally we came to the end of the hall. Eliakim knocked at a slightly larger door.

"Come in, Eliakim, and bring Benjamin's sons with you." The booming response was only slightly muffled by the door.

Nathan looked at me and shrugged as we followed Eliakim into the well-lit room. A small bed with rumpled blankets sat against a sidewall. A narrow table stood against the opposite sidewall holding a few dishes, obviously the remains of a supper long forgotten. In the center of the room was a giant table covered in scrolls, inkwells, pens, and fresh parchment. But the room was dominated by the immense presence seated at the head of the large table. Isaiah was a bear of a man. His curly gray locks hung to his shoulders, framing his deeply creased tan face. A huge, wiry salt-and-pepper beard rested on his chest.

"I've come by order of the king to beseech help from the great holy one, Isaiah," Eliakim said with a bow.

"Please cut out that formal nonsense, Eli. We don't have time for it," Isaiah said with a snorting laugh. "Hezekiah is worried about the Assyrians, I take it. And he should be. We all should be."

"I came to bring you this. The king wants you to read it." Eliakim handed the scroll to Isaiah.

Isaiah opened the scroll and started reading. We stood quietly and waited as he rolled the paper from spool to spool, studying every inch of it. The room was quiet except for an occasional growl from Isaiah. Finally he closed the scroll and slammed it down on the table.

"Camel dung! Who does this Assyrian pretender think he is? A destroyer of gods? He has blasphemed the Lord God. There will be no mercy for him." Isaiah's eyes flashed and his face grew red with anger.

"King Hezekiah spent all day in the temple with it spread out before the Lord, praying for our deliverance," Eliakim said.

"A good use of his time. At least we have a king who's willing to pray to the one true God." Isaiah scratched his beard. "Why did Hezekiah send the scroll to me, Eli?"

"He wanted to know how the Lord would answer his prayer."

"Ha! He's a man of prayer, but an impatient one," Isaiah

barked, laughing. "Well, I do know God's answer to this one. The Lord God says, 'Neither Sennacherib nor his forces will ever come into Jerusalem. They won't even shoot an arrow at it, nor assemble with shields to assault it, nor build a siege mound against it. I, the Lord God of Israel, will defend Jerusalem for my own sake and the sake of my servant David.'"

In the odd silence that followed Isaiah's pronouncement the words seemed to echo off the walls.

"Tell that to King Hezekiah." Isaiah handed the scroll back to Eliakim. "And tell him to put his faith in the Lord to defend his people."

Eliakim bowed low. "Yes, Isaiah. I will tell him that and deliver the Lord's word to him."

I did my best to imitate Nathan's bow before we left Isaiah's room. I was having trouble believing this experience. I doubted God's existence, but I knew Bible history from Sunday school. Dream or not, I'd just seen the prophet Isaiah. He was one of the greatest prophets of all time, and from what I'd observed, I could believe it.

***

The walk back to the Fish Gate was somber. Eliakim seemed to be pondering Isaiah's words. I mimicked Nathan's silence despite the questions that bubbled up inside me.

The king was still sitting on the throne in the audience hall when we returned. He seemed bleary-eyed with exhaustion but straightened as Eliakim approached the dais.

I hoped he'd gotten a little sleep while we were away. He looked so tired.

"Did you get a chance to talk to him?" the king asked before Eliakim had finished his bow.

"Yes, Sire. Here is his answer." Eliakim cleared his throat and held his hand out as if he were delivering a package. "The Lord God says, 'Neither Sennacherib nor his forces will ever come into Jerusalem. They won't even shoot an arrow at it, nor assemble with shields to assault it, nor build a siege mound against it. I, the Lord God of Israel, will defend Jerusalem for my own sake and the sake of my servant David.'"

King Hezekiah brightened visibly and sat up straighter on the throne. "Truly, Eliakim, that's what he said?"

"Yes, Your Majesty. And Isaiah said, 'Put your faith in the Lord to defend his people.'"

"That's wonderful news." The king looked delighted, but as he relaxed he also sagged with fatigue. Gathering himself again, he said, "Eliakim, I want to talk more with you, but you can let your servants go."

"Yes, My Lord King," Eliakim said. He turned and nodded to us. He was already turning back to talk to Hezekiah as we left the room.

Nathan guided me through the richly decorated hallways to the palace's main exit. As we went through the ornate wooden doors, Nathan said, "It's almost the end of the second watch. Let's see if we can find Sarah at her post on the walls."

"All right."

As we crossed the barren rocky ridge that connected the

Temple Mount to the City of David, Nathan said, "Look over the city walls. You can see the Assyrians camped on the heights on the other side of the Kidron Valley from here. There must be thousands of them."

Nathan saluted the officer at the Valley Gate, putting his fist to his chest. I did the same as we entered the City of David. The watch was changing so there were a lot of soldiers on the streets. After making our way through the ancient city, we climbed a narrow wooden staircase to the top of the broad wall. Sarah sat at the guard post, attaching feathers to arrows.

"Hello, Nathan, Joshua. Just a minute and I'll put this away so we can go home together. The new watch is already on duty. I was going to finish this last batch of arrows, but I can do that tomorrow." She gathered her tools and materials into a basket and carried them toward a small shack built on the city side of the wall.

Nathan wandered toward the outside edge of the wall, where he sat down on a boulder set near the brim to provide cover for archers. Looking down to where the Kidron and Hinnom Valleys joined, he said, "I can't believe how massive the Assyrian forces are. Their watchfires fill the valleys and spill up onto the hills. How can Isaiah be sure that God will save us?"

I followed him to the edge and gazed down on the field of lights that spread out over the terrain. Certainly the situation seemed hopeless. Isaiah said to have faith, but there's no way you could look at that and believe Jerusalem would survive. Suddenly a vision of Portland at night, seen from the top of the Water Tower, superimposed itself over the scene below. The ground far below called up to me.

"Joshua!" Nathan reached out and grabbed my arm, pulling me back. "Be careful! They still haven't finished the outer rim of the wall. Are you okay?"

"Uh, yeah. I think so," I said. "It makes me dizzy to look down at all those campfires."

"Why are you two out in the middle of the night?" Sarah said, coming up behind us.

"Uncle Eliakim wanted us to help him with an errand for the king," Nathan said.

"We went to see the Prophet Isaiah," I said, recovering quickly. I still felt amazed.

Sarah laughed.

"What?" I said.

"You looked so excited about it."

I shrugged. "I mean, uh . . . why did you laugh?"

"Well," Sarah said quietly, "Isaiah has a reputation for being cantankerous."

"He doesn't like anyone to bother him. Not even the king," Nathan added with a significant look at me. "You know that, Joshua."

"Yeah," I said. "I'm just tired, I guess. Not thinking straight."

"I heard he yells and throws things," Sarah said with another chuckle. "Did he do anything like that?"

"No," I said. "He was polite."

"Even if he'd thrown things at us, he hears God's word.

That's what makes a holy man, not manners," Nathan said with conviction.

"So if he tells us that the Assyrian emperor will never conquer Jerusalem, will it come true?" I asked.

"Is that what he said?" Sarah exclaimed excitedly.

"Yes," Nathan answered. "It's hard to believe with that out there." He pointed to the flickering lights in the valley.

"When Isaiah says that he has a word from the Lord," Sarah said, "he has never been wrong."

"Never?" I asked.

"Never," Nathan said.

"Come on, Nathan. This news is wonderful," Sarah said. "Let's get home so we can tell my dad and your parents."

"I just hate to get people's hopes up," Nathan said.

"But it is a hope," Sarah said, persevering. "It's the only hope we've got. We should hang onto it with all our might, shouldn't we?"

Nathan shrugged.

I looked down over the edge again. Despair seemed so easy and hope was so hard. But Isaiah's promise was still ringing in my ears. Like a belligerent fly, it could not be ignored.

Nathan stood and, reaching, he took hold of Sarah's hand and led the way toward the stairs. I froze, watching them. How could I be jealous? It was ridiculous. This was a dream, but it felt so real. After a moment I hurried to catch up, lost in thought.

Chapter 27

Blizzard

My bed jerked and I almost rolled out. I'd only just gone to sleep in the little bedchamber in Jerusalem. Then Dad opened the passenger-side door on the Ford and the bitter winter wind whistled in. A flurry of fat, wet snowflakes landed on my face. Suddenly I was fully conscious.

"Josh, go get your overalls on. You and Dad need to start getting the cows into the feedlot," Mom said, her voice raised over the wind. "I'm going to give Gramps a ride back from the Dirks'. We'll be out to help soon."

"Let's go, Son," Dad said. "The weather is getting bad fast."

I rolled out of the pickup, still not quite alert. The shock of the icy air and the heavy snowflakes slapping me in the face were waking me up fast. "Man, it's cold!" I said.

Dad helped me into my coat and gave me a little shove

toward the house. Turning back, he said, "Better get going, Rachel. We won't be able to drive in this much longer."

I was stomping off my shoes when Dad entered the utility porch. He reached for his rusty brown overalls and tossed my snowmobile suit to me. "Put this on over your clothes, Josh. We don't have time to do the whole long underwear thing. Besides, Gramps says that drifting snow will be more of a problem than the cold. We've got to get those cattle to where we can feed them during the storm."

"The snow's already starting to get pretty deep, Dad," I said, peeking out the window. "Are you sure Bonnie and Clyde will be able to handle this?"

"Mom said not to use the horses. We'll be using the snowmobiles."

"All right!"

"But you have to keep the speed down. The visibility is starting to get bad. We're just going to herd the cows out of the pasture into the feedlot behind the barn. They'll have shelter there, and we can feed them from the cattle shed."

"Okay, Dad," I said as I followed him out the door.

About thirty minutes later I was idling my snowmobile through the blinding snow, moving three straggling cattle through the gate into the feedlot. Dad's headlamp played back and forth across the herd.

Pulling up beside me, Dad called out above the rising wind, "I think that's all of them, Josh. I counted thirty-seven. Go ahead and close the gate."

When we got back to the machine shed, Gramps and Mom were stringing a rope from the barn to the main door on the shed.

"This is a guide rope," Gramps explained. "See how the wind is picking up? When it gets going strong, we'll barely be able to see our hands in front of our faces. This rope is how we'll get out here if we need to."

"Okay. I get it," I said.

"We've already strung a rope between the house and the barn," Mom said. "Follow the rope back to the barn. You need to take care of the horses. Give them a little extra grain to help with the cold."

As I stepped outside, the force of the wind nearly took me off my feet. The house and barn disappeared behind a screen of white. I worked my way along the icy rope, clinging desperately to the only sense of direction I had. The roar of the wind was so loud that I couldn't hear my own thoughts. I was completely blind. The white chaos drilled into me, taking away all my senses except the growing cold that was claiming my body inch by inch. Suddenly, tripping over a sinister snowdrift, I fell and lost hold of the rope. Panic flooded into me. I flailed about, careful not to step away from where I'd fallen. Where was it? Then I touched something. Relief flooded in when I found it. I followed the rope with my hope returning and walking even more carefully in blind faith, until I bumped against the solid reality of the barn door. My sheer joy at the pleasant warmth of the barn was matched by the horses' whickering. Bonnie and Clyde looked as happy to see me as I was to see them.

When I finished with the horses, I waited by the barn door listening to the storm, hoping for a lull. When one came I quickly followed the rope back toward where the house was supposed to be. I saw the dormers of my room briefly above a rolling wave of snow and then nothing when it crashed over me. If anything, the ferocity of the storm increased before I reached the side of the house. It took me a minute to figure out how to get through the back door and then I was stomping off my boots and beating the snow off my clothes before hanging them up to dry. When I came into the kitchen, Mom was just putting a teapot on the stove.

"Where are Dad and Gramps?" I asked.

"They went to string a rope from the barn to the cattle shed and check on the herd," Mom answered. "It's a good thing we moved that hay out to the shed last fall. We won't have to haul it from the barn during the storm."

"I thought Gramps was crazy for making us wedge those bales up into that little space under the roof, but I guess he knew what he was doing."

"Gramps," Mom said, laughing, "usually does know what he's up to. He's a crazy old coot, but he's crazy like a fox."

I laughed.

A blast of cold air and a few errant flakes of snow made their way into the kitchen from the utility porch. "How about some eggs and bacon, Rachel?" Gramps called out. "I know it's late, but we've been working and I'm hungry."

"See what I mean?" Mom said to me. "Okay, Dad." She raised her voice, addressing the open archway to the back porch. "I'll get out the frying pan and we can cook up a storm to match the one outside. But you're doing the dishes."

***

I woke in pitch dark. I was sure I was back in Jerusalem, but then I heard Sarah's ring tone on my phone. I picked it up, staring blearily at it, and noticed it was 3:45 a.m. The storm was still rattling the windows and the snow was blocking the yard light that usually lit my room at night. I answered the phone. "Hi. What's up?"

"Joshua!" Sarah sounded frantic. "Joshua, there's a fire. I can't put it out."

"What happened?"

"My dad was up cooking in the night and a fire started in the kitchen. Dad got burned. I think he's hurt pretty bad. Oh, Joshua, what should I do?"

"Did you call 911?"

"The dispatcher said the storm's stopping emergency vehicles from getting here. They told me to use salt and baking soda on the fire in the stove. It's out. It's flared up twice and I beat it down, but I can still hear it sizzling inside the wall. And Dad's unconscious. Josh, please help me!"

The panic in Sarah's voice scared me more than anything.

"Okay, Sarah. I'm going to talk to my parents. I'll call you right back."

Running downstairs, I shouted, "Mom! Dad! Sarah's house is on fire. Gramps! We've got to help her."

"What's the matter?" Mom appeared in the hall at the foot of the stairs in her bathrobe. Dad was close behind her.

"Sarah called," I said, holding up my cell phone. "She said that her dad was cooking and a fire started on the stove. It burned Paul. Sarah managed to get the fire out on the stove, but somehow it's burning in the kitchen wall and she can't stop it."

"How badly is Paul hurt?" Gramps asked, coming up behind them from the kitchen.

"I'm not sure," I answered. "Sarah says he's unconscious."

"That doesn't sound good," Dad said, stepping over to lift the blinds and peer out the frost-covered window.

"We've got to help her, Dad," I said.

"But how will we get there?" Mom asked solemnly. "I'm not sure we could find our way out of the yard, let alone get over to the Dirks' place."

"But we've got to try, don't we? Mom! Dad! She could die if that fire really got going. And what about Paul?"

"Ben, what's the temperature outside? Can you see the thermometer on the window casing outside?" Gramps asked.

"Yeah, it's 15 degrees," Dad said, rubbing some frost off the window to get a better look.

"That's above zero, right?" Gramps asked.

Dad nodded.

"The cold is dangerous but not immediately life threatening. I think we could try it."

"But Dad," Mom said, "How are we going to find our way over there?"

"Josh, how good are you with that GPS thing on your phone?" Gramps asked.

"That might work," I said, suddenly feeling hopeful. "Sarah and I were playing with it while we were out trapping in the dark. I think I could get us from here to Sarah's house."

"What do you think?" Gramps asked the two other adults.

"I don't know, Dad. It seems so dangerous," Mom said hesitantly.

"Yeah, you're right. I can't deny it." Gramps rubbed his chin.

"But what if it was us needing help, Rachel? Wouldn't we want our neighbors to try?" Dad said gently.

"Oh, Ben," Mom sighed, wrapping her arms around him. "Of course we would."

"If someone is going, then we're all going," Dad said, looking into Mom's upturned face. "Are you with us, dear?"

Mom gave him a quick hug in answer and headed for the bedroom to get dressed.

"Give Sarah a call, Josh, and tell her we're coming," Dad said as he followed Mom.

In a matter of minutes we were all standing in the wan light of the machine shed, moving the snowmobiles toward the open overhead door.

"I'll go first with my sled," Gramps said. "Josh and his GPS can ride with me to keep me pointed the right way. You two follow on Josh's snowmobile."

"Go slow, Harlan," Dad said as he strapped an ax and three fire extinguishers to my snowmobile. "We probably won't be able to see your lights more than a dozen feet away. I'll try to stay right on your trail, but it'll disappear quickly in this wind."

"Pray we make it safely to help Paul and Sarah," Mom said as she sat down behind Dad. She was holding a big first aid kit on her lap.

Snowmobile engines started and we crept out into the storm. A strange lull hovered as we began. The headlights revealed drifts like white dunes in an alien landscape. Then the wind came blasting back, bringing the swirling snow like a tidal wave crashing over us.

I had to press the faceplate of my ski mask against my phone to watch the little blue marker crawl, with painful slowness, toward the GPS representation of the Dirk house. "A little to the left," I shouted into Gramps' ear.

Usually I could make it across the snow-covered pasture in about five minutes. We'd been traveling for twenty minutes. "It should be right here, Gramps," I shouted. Without thinking I prayed in panic, "Lord God, please don't let it be burned to the ground."

I was thrown against Gramps as the snowmobile came to an abrupt stop. There, about six feet away in the headlights, was the unmistakable corner of a building. Even looking through the blinding snow, I could make out the weather-worn siding of Sarah's house. I was exultant—it wasn't in flames.

Gramps seemed to know where we were. He turned the snowmobile right, crawling up over a gigantic drift at the corner of the house. The flash of my parents' headlights behind us was reassuring as we found our way to the front door. I had never come into Sarah's house this way, but Gramps waded across the front porch and cleared enough snow to wrench the screen door open and then barged into the house. I was right behind him.

The air was smoky but breathable. Sarah appeared in the hallway to the kitchen with her face covered with soot-streaked tears. She flew into my arms. "You made it. You made it!" After a quick hug, she grabbed my hand and dragged me back down the hall. The smoke got thicker as we went.

"Where's the fire?" Gramps called out as he followed close behind.

"It's in the kitchen and it keeps flaring up out of the wall behind the stove." Sarah's voice was shaky with panic.

As we came into the kitchen, I saw a tiny tongue of flame emerge from a blackened gap in the panels. Sarah grabbed a soggy bath towel and attacked it. The wall sizzled, but the flame winked out.

"Ben, help me move this stove out of the way," Gramps called as Mom and Dad entered the kitchen.

The smell of burnt fabric added to the smoke in the air. "Good thing we still had our gloves on. That stove is red hot," Dad said as they pushed the appliance out of the way.

"Hand me that ax, Ben," Gramps said after liberally spraying the area behind the stove with one of the fire extinguishers.

As the hole opened up blow by blow, little burning flakes dropped out onto the floor where Dad sprayed them with the fire extinguisher. Gramps swore under his breath, "Gosh darn it. They left the old sawdust insulation in there. No wonder the fire is running in the wall."

"Sarah," Mom said softly, putting her arm around the stricken girl. "Can you show me to your dad?" They headed toward the living room, with Mom fumbling at the latches of her first aid kit.

I turned to watch Gramps take another mighty swing at the wall. Water sprayed halfway across the kitchen.

"Must have hit a water line," Gramps said, stepping back to survey the situation.

"We've got to get the water shut off," Dad said.

"I've helped Elias around here enough to know where the main valve is in the basement," Gramps said. "But let's not be too hasty. That water running down inside the wall is a good thing, and the spray into the kitchen is helping with the smoke."

On cue, steam started pouring out of the wall. Gramps left to shut off the water. When it stopped, Dad picked up the ax and went back to work on the wall. They didn't quit until the blackened outside perimeter of the fire was revealed.

I handed Gramps the second fire extinguisher, which he promptly emptied onto the burnt area just for good measure. When he set it down, he said, "That should do it. I think we're safe now. Josh, why don't you check on the others? We'll keep an eye on this for a while longer."

I noticed a small snowdrift forming on the welcome mat by the front door. When I pushed the front door firmly closed, I got another glimpse of the raging storm outside. I wondered how in heaven's name we ever made it here safely.

Then I went on into the living room. Paul was lying on the sofa and Sarah and Mom were bent over him. "How is he, Mom?" I said, coming up behind the pair.

"I think he's going to be okay," Mom said, turning to look at me. "He has some nasty burns on his hands and a slight burn on his face. But there is nothing life threatening."

"I called 911 to let them know our situation," Sarah said. She stood up and took my hand in hers. "Thank you so much for coming. You saved us. All of you saved us."

"I'm just happy we got here in time. I'm glad your dad is okay. Why was he unconscious?"

Sarah let go of my hand and turned away for a minute. When she turned back, she had a determined look on her face. "He was drunk. He passed out. This whole thing happened because Dad was drunk." Her eyes welled up.

Mom stood up and put her arms around Sarah. "It's okay, dear. Things are going to be okay."

When Gramps and Dad walked into the room a few minutes later, Mom let go of Sarah.

"Is the fire out for sure?" she asked.

"Yes, we've got it," Dad said. He pulled Mom into his arms

and kissed her. "We did the right thing, Rachel. You were so brave."

Mom beamed at him.

"That kitchen's not going to be usable until it gets some serious repair," Gramps said. "How's Paul?"

"He's okay, but his burns are going to hurt," Mom said. She walked back over to the couch to check on Paul. He was still unconscious, but his chest rose and fell steadily.

"It's dreadful out there," Dad said, stooping to look out the window. "I don't think we should try going home unless we have to."

"No, I think we need to hunker down and ride out the storm right here," Gramps said.

"But what about the cattle, Gramps?" Mom said.

"They'll be okay, Rachel. We might lose a couple, but that's always a risk in a blizzard." Gramps paused to look around the room. "There are more important concerns at stake here than the cattle. I'm just glad we made it safely and in time."

Chapter 28

Intervention

The blizzard lasted another sixteen hours. With Sarah's help, Mom managed to pull together a meal from stuff they found in the pantry. Thank goodness the microwave still worked. Dad and Gramps melted some snow for coffee.

Paul dozed off and on, occasionally groaning with pain from his burns. Sarah hovered over him, making sure that he got regular doses of ibuprofen.

I tried to help where I could. I'd never seen Sarah this anxious.

After a while Mom said, "Josh, why don't you lie down and rest for a while. I'll help Sarah."

Mom's tone made this more than a suggestion. "Uh, okay, Mom," I said, realizing that I was exhausted. I stood for a moment, looking around the living room. Paul had the couch and Gramps was slumped in the only stuffed chair, snoring softly. Dad was stretched out on the floor asleep.

"You can go lie down on my bed," Sarah said as she pointed down a hallway.

Sarah's room expressed her personality well. It was not frilly, but feminine and immaculate. The gun cabinet standing in the corner next to the bed gave it that spice that I loved about her. I stretched out on top of her bedspread and was soon asleep.

Dad woke me about six hours later. "The storm's dying down. We need to dig out the snowmobiles and get them started."

By 9:00 p.m. Sunday evening the weather was almost completely calm.

"We'll go home and tend the cattle, Gramps," Mom said "You and Josh can stay here and wait for the plows to bring the fire department. The dispatcher said that they might make it before midnight.

"Did you tell them it was nothing to worry about?" Gramps asked in a surly voice.

"Of course, Gramps, but you know how the sheriff is. He wants to make sure that everything is thoroughly checked out and reported," Dad said, pulling on his stocking cap.

"Yeah, and that's why I didn't vote for him. Too much of a bureaucrat for my taste."

"Gramps," Mom said softly.

Paul chuckled and then moaned.

"All right. We'll wait," Gramps said grumpily. "I suppose we should get Paul checked out anyway."

"We'll bring some food and water when we come back in a couple of hours," Dad said. He opened the front door to usher Mom out.

The sound of two snowmobiles outside faded as they made their way back home. Paul was sitting in his favorite chair, but the TV was dark. "Sarah, can I have another dose of pain-killer? This really hurts." Paul waved his two bandaged hands in the air.

"No, Dad, you've got to wait another hour." Sarah was sitting on the couch holding my hand. She had washed her face, but blackened places still marked her clothes. Sarah was drooping with exhaustion. She had only slept in catnaps while taking care of her dad.

"Okay, Paul," Gramps said, dragging a wooden chair over and sitting about four feet from Paul. "We're going to talk."

Paul shifted in his chair and glanced over at the two youths on the sofa. He said, "Sarah, maybe you and Josh should go see if the plow is coming."

"No. They need to be here, Paul," Gramps said firmly. "I want Sarah to hear this." He cleared his throat. "Paul, your dad made me promise that I'd keep an eye on you when he lay there dying in that hospital bed. I've done that, and I've also tried not to be intrusive. But now your alcohol problem almost killed you and Sarah. I think it's time for me to speak up."

"I suppose," Paul said with a croak. "I kind of expected it."

"You know you're going to need some help to lick this, don't you?"

Paul stared straight ahead for a minute. His cheeks blossomed a ruddy red. I wondered if he was angry or embarrassed. Probably both, I guessed.

"Dad," Sarah said softly. "He's right. Please." Her voice caught as she fought back tears.

Paul shrugged and looked down at his feet. "I suppose. But Harlan, I can't afford any of those fancy treatment centers. What am I supposed to do?"

"Josh, loan me your phone for a minute." Gramps stood up, reaching for the phone. I handed it to him. He walked swiftly out of the room and back toward the kitchen.

Sarah and I sat in embarrassed silence. We could hear Gramps talking to somebody, but couldn't understand what he was saying. I watched Paul out of the corner of my eye. Sarah's father sat stone-faced, looking straight ahead, occasionally wincing with pain. Sarah's hand was soft but unmoving in mine. She was staring quietly at the floor in front of us. I could feel how tense she was.

It took a while, but finally Gramps came back into the living room. "Paul," he said, "I called your boss, George Rasmussen."

"You what?" Paul started to rise from the chair. "Ow!" he yelped, suddenly clenched in pain. He sat back down.

"Don't worry. George and I are old friends. He was a good friend of your father's too."

"Yeah, I know. That's how I got the job. Is George going to fire me?"

"He said he was considering it. You were driving drunk, Paul. That's cause for termination in the trucking business. I think it's been his friendship with your dad that's kept him from pulling the trigger."

"I know." Paul slumped miserably in his chair.

"When I told him what happened, and that I thought I might be able to get you to treatment, he had another idea." Gramps paused, taking a long look at Paul.

"So what's this other idea?" Paul finally said.

"He said that the company insurance would handle the expense of your treatment. Even on suspension, your coverage is still in force. He'll keep it that way until you finish."

"I suppose that's something. But I need to work. I've got to find a job or we'll starve," Paul argued.

"I told George you'd think that," Gramps said. "I got him to agree that you could have your job for a trial period if you complete treatment. You can't work now anyway, Paul. Your hands need time to mend. You can do your healing in treatment."

"But what about Sarah? Somebody needs to take care of her," Paul objected.

"Come on, Paul. Sarah has been taking care of herself since she was thirteen and you started driving a truck."

"That's true, Dad," Sarah put in softly.

"But you can't stay in this house. There's no running water and the kitchen isn't usable," Paul said.

Gramps looked steadily at him and said, "Rachel, Ben, and

I have agreed that we can make room for Sarah at our place. She can stay there while you're in treatment. We'll help her get the repairs done on the house so it's ready when you're finished."

"But what if there's no place to go? Treatment centers are hard to get into, you know."

"I took care of that. There's a bed all set up for you at a center in Sioux Falls. Ben and I will drive you there right after the emergency folks get done checking you out."

"It looks like you've thought of everything," Paul said in clipped tones.

"Yeah. I helped your dad with some of his Alcoholics Anonymous work. He taught me how to get someone to treatment. I can't think of anyone he would want me to help more than you."

"What if I say no?" Paul said, a stubborn expression spreading across his face.

"I suppose you could do that, Paul." An edge of anger crept into Gramps' voice. "But it'd be the stupidest thing you've ever done."

Paul stared back for a long moment and then visibly slumped. "I've done more than my share of stupid things," Paul said softly. "Okay. I'll go."

My hand was starting to hurt because Sarah was gripping it so tightly. I only realized it when she suddenly let go to rush across the room and hug her father. "Thank you, Dad. I've been so worried."

Paul hugged her back, saying, "It'll be okay, pumpkin. It'll be okay."

Chapter 29

Deliverance

I WAS ASLEEP BUT I COULD FEEL MYSELF FALLING. On the way down I grabbed for the bedpost to keep from hitting the floor too hard. The bedpost wobbled, clattering when it hit the ground as I landed on one knee. Opening my eyes to the predawn sky stretched above I knew I was outside. It was cool, but not winter-in-South-Dakota cold—I was in Jerusalem.

Slowly my eyes adjusted, and I could make out my surroundings. What I'd thought was my bedpost was a spear. The broad, sharp blade glinted as I shifted it out from underneath my leg. I was lucky it had not cut me in the fall. Had I been asleep on my feet?

I could see just enough to make out my surroundings. I was sitting on a broad area paved with flat stones. I knew of only one place in Jerusalem like this, and I'd helped build it — the city's new wall.

That realization brought everything into perspective. Jerusalem was behind me, locked in the darkness of siege. Ahead of me, past the edge of the wall, thousands of Assyrians prepared to attack and destroy my family's home. Half rising I peered over the brim of the wall into the valley where something peculiar was happening. I could see the embers of the enemy's watch fires glowing, but there was very little light in them. It was like the Assyrians were just letting them burn out.

A familiar figure lay on the pavement a few feet away. Nathan's spear and shield lay beside him. I crawled to my brother's side and shook his shoulder. "Nathan! Nathan! Wake up!"

He moaned and then turned away from me, still sound asleep.

"Nathan, wake up!" I shook him harder, but with no success. Finally I gave up.

I started to move toward the outer edge of the wall so I could get a better look into the valley. My eyes had adjusted so I could see a little better. Prone forms were scattered all about. Nobody was moving anywhere on the wall. It was clear that everyone was asleep, or worse. As I crept past the guard hut, I stumbled over a figure that I recognized as Sarah.

I caught my breath at how beautiful she was. In the darkness my heart filled in what my eyes could not see. She stirred slightly. I waited and watched, not wanting to disturb her. I was trying to remember that this was not my Sarah.

Finally I knelt beside her and gently shook her shoulder. At first nothing happened, and then she moaned, stirring slightly.

"Sarah. Sarah, wake up!"

With a quick movement she vanished from under my hand and I was staring down twelve inches of a nasty, sharp blade. Sarah crouched in front of me, ready to use her dagger in a very lethal way.

"Who are you?" she said in a low, threatening voice.

"Sarah, it's me. Joshua," I said, holding my hands up.

She brushed the hair out of her eyes and rubbed her face, squinting at me in the low light.

"Joshua. It is you. Why aren't you at your post?"

"Uh."

"Wait, was I asleep?"

"Yes, would you mind putting down your dagger?"

"Oh," she said, straightening. She sheathed her weapon.

Relaxing, I said, "Everyone seems to be asleep."

"Really?" She turned around, looking in all directions at the prone forms barely visible in the pale light. "You're right. They are either sleeping or dead. But there's no blood. They must be sleeping."

She gazed at me in a way that was so achingly endearing that I caught my breath. I took a step toward her before I stopped myself.

"Are you all right, Joshua? I didn't mean to frighten you. I was caught off guard."

"It's okay, Sarah. I'm fine."

After a long moment Sarah said, "Joshua, who is guarding the wall?"

"I'm not sure if anyone is."

"Why are all the defenders asleep?" There was a bright note of concern in Sarah's voice.

"I don't know."

"Could this be some sort of attack by the Assyrians?" Sarah asked.

"Attack? What do you mean?" A new voice spoke from behind us.

"Nathan? You're awake?" I said.

"Joshua? Why are you two the only ones on guard? Where is everybody?"

I gestured all around us. "They're all asleep. You were asleep a few minutes ago. I couldn't wake you."

"Joshua," Nathan suddenly sounded severe, "what's going on here?"

"I don't know, Nathan. I was just telling that to your beloved here." I gestured toward Sarah who had moved a couple of steps away to examine someone lying on the ground.

"But I never told . . . wait . . . really?"

"Yep," I said. Then, lowering my voice, I whispered, "I'm Future Joshua."

Nathan sighed and shook his head. "You do pick the strangest times . . ."

I started to protest.

Nathan held up his hand and continued in a low voice, "I know. I know. You have no control over it."

"No control over what?" Sarah said as she rejoined us.

"Over this odd situation," Nathan said without missing a beat. Then he looked around again. "Everyone's asleep."

"Do you think it's something the Assyrians did?" I asked.

"Father would have heard through his spies if the Assyrians could do something like this. Besides, remember what Isaiah said, 'Neither Sennacherib nor his forces will ever come into Jerusalem.'"

"It looks like we are completely open to attack," Sarah said as she turned toward the outer brim of the wall.

I turned to follow her gaze. The stars were invisible near the horizon as the pale light of the coming dawn pushed its way into the atmosphere. The outline of the high country across the Hinnom Valley stood out in sharp relief against the brightening sky.

"What's that?" Nathan asked.

"What's what?" I responded.

"There's some kind of movement down there," Nathan said.

I stared down into the valley. Even as the sun started to crest the horizon it was still almost entirely dark below us. But as I watched, I caught one furtive movement out of the corner of my eye and then another. I wondered if that was what Nathan was seeing. I strained to focus while the light slowly intensified. I watched as the odd flits and flaps of movement spread out below us with the dawning sunlight beginning to pour into the valley.

"Doesn't it seem odd that all the fires have burned out?" Nathan pointed at the wisps of rising smoke that shimmered in the light high above the Kidron Valley.

"That is strange," Sarah said. "They should be stoking up

fires to prepare the morning meal. But that's the last smoke from dying fires."

Sarah took a couple of steps closer to the lip of the wall to peer further into the valley, which was still wrapped in shadow.

"Maybe they're letting the fires go out while they assemble to assault the walls at dawn," I said, hoping I was wrong.

"That's not their way," Nathan said. "They spend months building a huge earthen ramp against the wall and then they march into a city and destroy it. They haven't even started building a ramp. Besides, we'd hear them if they were assembling below us."

"What's that sound?" Sarah gestured along the wall toward the City of David.

It was slight at first, but the sound of metal clanging and leather rasping was soon heard all around us as the sleeping defenders of the city woke and stood up. The murmur of voices rose as bright beams from the rising sun broke above the Mount of Olives and cast the top of the wall into stark contrasts of gleaming light and dark shadow.

I shaded my eyes with my hands as I desperately tried to get a clear view of the valley below me. "Can you see anything, Nathan?"

"Whatever is down there is moving all over the place."

It was true — the flits and flaps had turned into a general undulation that made the valley look like waves on the sea.

"It's birds," Sarah said. "The valley is covered with birds."

"What? That can't be," Nathan said.

"No! She's right, Nathan!" I said, still shading my eyes. "The valley is covered with birds. I saw some fly up into the light as they circled. They're mostly crows and ravens, but I think there are other kinds of birds down there."

The trumpeting blast of a shofar sounded further down the wall behind us. Then it was answered by another, deeper-sounding shofar on the other side of the City of David. More joined until an entire chorus of them, sounding almost continuously, insisted that the city awaken from its ominous sleep.

As the sun came up another tick, an errant shaft of light stabbed down toward the valley, illuminating the upper edge of the valley floor directly across the Kidron.

"That's a chariot," Nathan said, pointing to the jumble of wheels and harnesses cast into sharp relief by the intense beam. "It looks like it was trying to flee from the valley, but it's not moving now." After a moment he added, "The horses are lying down in the traces. I think they're dead."

"It looks like Jerusalem is awake at last," Sarah said, glancing along the wall one way and then the other.

"That's your unit commander, Sarah," Nathan said. "He may want to gather your archery squad." But the tall, grizzled soldier only paused long enough to string his bow swiftly, in one practiced motion. Then, picking up a quiver of arrows, he started strolling along the outer edge of the wall, peering into the valley below him.

Following the commander's example, Nathan, Sarah, and I moved to the wall's rim to gain a better look into the valley as it slowly filled with golden dawn. All around us people rubbed their eyes, stretched, and attempted to throw off the effects of the city's unnatural sleep.

As the murmuring rose about them, Nathan said, "Nothing at all is moving down there. Something is littering the ground under those swirling birds."

"Corpses!" Sarah said in a shocked tone.

Another blast of a shofar pushed through the growing rumble of the crowd. "Look! I think that's Uncle Eliakim and the king's guard coming out of the Fountain Gate." Nathan pointed toward a procession of soldiers with spears. A figure in white robes led them slowly into the valley from the base of the wall. "They're heading straight for the Assyrian command tent."

"I can't quite make out what they are doing," Sarah said.

"Maybe they're searching for something," I said.

"Here comes Uncle Eliakim," Nathan said. "What's he carrying?"

"It looks like a banner with streamers on a long pole," Sarah said as we followed her along the wall to get a better look.

"That's the Assyrian standard, the one they used to lead their entire army into the valley." Nathan pointed excitedly.

Eliakim waved the standard, then threw it on the ground.

A roar of exultation exploded from the walls and then the city behind us echoed the joyful commotion.

Sara turned and ran toward us. I involuntarily took an expectant step towards her, but she flew into Nathan's arms. My pang of jealousy was swallowed up in the joy of realizing they were safe now. Nathan and his Sarah would share a life together in Jerusalem.

The roar of the multitude went on for a long time. With it rose the excitement and relief of people rescued from the threat of imminent death. When we could hear each other again, Nathan quoted the words Isaiah had spoken, "For God will defend this city to save it, for his own sake and the sake of his servant David."

I looked out over the edge of the wall to the valley floor far below. As I peered through the brightly slanting beams of light piercing the swirling flights of carrion birds, I suddenly felt a flash of joyful hope so intense it hurt. The ground no longer called me down, but instead it rose to meet me, forming a path into tomorrow.

Chapter 30

Water Tower

Sitting on the catwalk, I dangled my feet over the edge of the metal grating. I was leaning my head against the safety railing that encircled the top of the Wheaton water tower. As I looked down through the morning sunlight, it felt odd. It was just ground . . . a hundred feet away, that was all. It no longer called to me. Beyond it lay a little midwestern town of no particular significance other than becoming my new home.

"It's been a tradition for years that couples climb the water tower together," Sarah said, sitting next to me. "I guess I never imagined it was a tradition I'd keep."

"Why not?"

"Because I didn't plan on becoming a couple."

"Really?"

"Not while I was in high school. I thought you had to go

to some place like Kuwait to find someone, the way Dad did." Sarah smoothed down an errant lock of my hair.

"I like it," I said with conviction.

"You like what?"

"I like the tradition. I've been wanting to climb up here since I first came to town." I looked down again. It was still just ground down there. "But I can't believe that you'd have any difficulty becoming a couple." I looked up at her. "You're so beautiful, talented, and smart. Any guy would want a relationship with you."

The shadows deepened as a cloud floated across the sun. Sarah looked toward the ground and paused for a long moment. She sat down beside me. "I want to tell you something."

"Oh."

"Yeah. It's something I've wanted to tell you for a long time."

I adjusted my position, turning to look at her.

"It's about Marshal." Still looking down, Sarah paused before continuing.

Brushing an errant lock of hair out of her face, I waited.

"It's about why there is such bad blood between us."

"Before he started going with Melanie, Marshal came over to my house. He said he wanted to play some basketball."

I nodded.

"It was kind of like the day I met you. I should know that a boy doesn't just drive into your driveway and want to only play basketball."

"Really?"

"You don't know how close I came to kicking you off the property. If it hadn't been for your grandfather's truck, I probably would've."

"Yeah, you probably should have," I said and couldn't help grinning.

"I'm glad I didn't." Sarah smiled back. After another pause she went on. "Marshal and I played basketball for a while. Then—I've never told anyone about this before—he grabbed me and kissed me. I was so surprised I didn't react at first. But when he pushed me down to the floor and started pulling at my clothes, I kneed him hard, right where it counts."

"Oh, Sarah," I said softly.

"I was mad, outraged. When Marshal rolled off me, I jumped up and started kicking him. When he tried to get up, I punched him right in the face. I hit him again and again. I don't know how many times, but he left a trail of blood as he ran out the door. My knuckles were skinned and sore for a week."

I reached out and took Sarah's hand gently and lifted it to look at it. When I looked at her face again, moisture in the corner of her eyes was the only indication she was fighting tears.

She continued. "After Marshal and Melanie got together, about a month after he attacked me, Melanie started in on me. At first it was just a couple of twitter posts from an account called HotToTrot saying that there was juicy news about Sarah Dirk. Then some photoshopped Instagrams circulated from the same account name."

"What did you do?"

"Nothing. I figured it would blow over. Then a story started going around about how I had lured Marshal to the barn to get him in the sack. Ugh. With what Allen and the other guys starting saying . . . well, people believed them. They probably thought I got what I deserved."

"That's terrible, Sarah. I had no idea."

"It's a good thing you didn't. You might never have had anything to do with me. According to everyone except Jean, I was open for business for boys all over the county." At last, she couldn't hold it back and started weeping.

I reached out and hugged her. We sat like that for a long while.

"I don't understand how Marshal and Melanie could be so cruel," I said.

"If it hadn't been for Jean I'd never have gotten through it. Even so, I couldn't tell her the whole story. I was too embarrassed."

I pushed a strand of hair out of Sarah's face and smiled at her. "I'm glad you have a friend."

"And you," Sarah said quickly. "You've been a great friend and more." She kissed me.

We sat in silence for a while. Then Sarah laughed.

"What?" I said, turning to look at her.

"I think my problems with Marshal's lies might finally be over."

"Yeah. I've noticed people treat you differently now that you're an all-state basketball star."

"I suppose, but that wasn't what I was talking about. Melanie sent out one of her little darts against me last week. All I heard was people gossiping about how pathetic she is. Everyone knows it's her, and they know it's nothing but lies."

We sat looking at each other for moment. Then Sarah said, "I'm still glad you punched Marshal in the nose."

"Sounds like I was kinder to him that you were."

Sarah hit me in the shoulder and gave a little choking laugh. "That's not funny."

I smiled at her.

"Well maybe it is. Anyway, things have changed and I'm glad."

"Me too," I said.

A warm breeze blew gently, bringing with it the smell of spring.

"Josh," Sarah said in a different tone of voice.

"Yeah."

"Do you remember the first time you helped me run my trap line on your snowmobile?"

"Yes." I'd hoped she'd forgotten.

"You told me about how sad you got about your brother and your parents."

I was quiet for a long time, looking down at the silent ground.

Sarah waited.

Finally I said, "Yes, I know I told you about that."

"Are you still sad . . . that way?"

I took several moments to think before I said, "I'm still sad. But I don't feel the same about my sadness."

Sarah reached and took my hand, saying nothing.

"I don't think I'll ever stop feeling sad about Nathan's death. He meant too much to me. Not being with him, not being able to talk to him, not seeing what he does with his life is really, really awful. But that sadness is a part of my life now as much as Nathan was. I don't actually want it to go away."

"I think I understand."

"But I need help to be able to carry the sadness. You help. You help a lot."

Sarah smiled.

"My parents help. They've really put things back together."

"Yeah, they're fantastic," Sarah said softly. She curled herself around my arm and put her head on my shoulder. We sat together that way for a while.

Bright, slanting beams of light pierced the springtime haze over recently plowed fields as the clouds moved away from the face of the sun. I remembered a flash of joyful hope so intense it hurt. The sound of the cicada's swelled in the light. It was like I could hear the universe sing the creation song of Cosmic Background Radiation.

"I feel like life comes with a promise," I said. "Not a promise that everything will be perfect. But a promise that we'll be able to deal with it."

Sarah sat up again, looking at me and smiling. Gripping my hand, she lifted and kissed it. "Thank you. That's what I needed to know."

We looked out over the view from the water tower. It was a wonderful little town in a rich productive land holding the promise of life. "I guess this is God's country."

"What?" Sarah said in a dreamy voice.

"Nothing. Just something my Dad says." And I smiled at her.

"Oh, that's nice." She smiled back and then put her head on my shoulder.

Sarah's hand felt good in mine and I wondered if Nathan would have liked Sarah. Then, with a start, I realized that he did for sure.